D1173438

A Familiar Shore

by

Jennifer Fromke

Write Integrity Press
Canton, Georgia

A Familiar Shore

ISBN-13: 978-1-938092-02-2

ISBN-10: 1938092023

Scriptures taken from the Holy Bible, New International Version®, NIV®. Copyright © 1973, 1978, 1984, 2011 by Biblica, Inc.™ Used by permission of Zondervan. All rights reserved worldwide. www.zondervan.com.

This book is a work of fiction. Names, characters, places, and incidents are either products of the author's imagination or used fictitiously. Any similarity to actual people and/or events is purely coincidental.

Published by Write Integrity Press, 130 Prominence Point Pkwy. #130-330, Canton, GA 30114. www.WriteIntegrity.com

Printed in the United States of America

for Jon

Chapter One

In a daze, Meg barreled down the highway toward her father. An unfamiliar urgency in his voice drew her to the coast like true north pulls a compass. Her gut fluttered as she drove a rented Rav4 into Southport, North Carolina and parked across from Provisions, her favorite coastal dive on the eastern seaboard.

Stepping out of the car, she took a deep breath and pulled on the cuffs of her jacket as she slowly exhaled. *Don't rush in. Be controlled.* Her jeweled sandals provided little protection as she picked her way through the maze of potholes masquerading as a parking lot for the shack-like restaurant.

Provisions perched on the edge of the Cape Fear River. As Meg neared the building, a mixture of fried seafood and boat fuel assaulted her nose. A smile crossed her face and memories crossed her mind each time she breathed the incongruent scents.

The lunch crowd spilled out the front door in a line displaying great anticipation and remarkable patience. Meg pressed past the people waiting to order and shoved her way onto the porch. Rolled up canvas "walls" hung from the eaves around the perimeter.

Popsie waved to her from their favorite table, in the corner farthest from the kitchen and closest to the water. Though Meg usually visited whenever he docked *Gilda* near Charlotte, she burned up the asphalt today for a potential client Popsie wanted her to meet. But he sat alone at a table for two.

As she reached the table, she removed her jacket and threw it over her shoulder. "I'm not going to need this nice suit, am I?"

"It wasn't wasted. You look like a million bucks." Popsie smiled at her with a familiar sparkle in his eye.

"Does it make me look desperate?"

He waved his hands in front of him, as if he were wiping a blackboard clean. "No. No."

She kissed him on the cheek and glanced around at the cut-offs, tank tops, and Hawaiian shirts worn by every other person in the restaurant. "You wouldn't tell me so anyway, would you?"

Popsie chuckled until it turned into a cough. "Have a seat. I ordered us some conch fritters and sweet tea."

Meg sank into the plastic chair and looked out over the water. Docks began where the restaurant ended. Boat slips hung like ladder rungs off the main dock. Lunchtime brought with it the fishy aroma of the day's fresh catch, as boats returned to their berths.

Meg folded her arms across her chest. "He didn't show?"

"Let's just say he decided to remain anonymous for the time being."

"I'm glad I get to see you and I'm going to enjoy the conch fritters, but I just drove three hours to meet him. On the phone you sounded like this couldn't wait."

"He sent some papers for you."

She raised her eyebrows. Maybe the trip could be salvaged after all. "I figured you goaded him into hiring me as a charity case and he pulled out at the last minute."

"You, my dear, are not a charity case. And I'll tell you right now, you're as good as hired."

The fritters arrived at the table, occupying all of Meg's attention for a few moments. One bite of the deep-fried goodness transported her straight back to childhood. It tasted like fried ocean—and home. She frowned at the thought of her crazy youth, and her skewed view of family life. Growing up on a boat, home was everywhere, and nowhere.

Her eyes traveled to Popsie's face, another piece of fritter melting on her tongue. The sweetest man on earth, to be sure. What ever possessed him to adopt her as a six-year old? Thank God, he did.

"So, he'll hire me sight unseen? What's wrong with him? Does he want me to do something illegal?"

Popsie reached for his briefcase on the floor. "He's an old friend of mine, so be nice. The job's not illegal, but it's a doozy."

Meg wiped her hands with three paper napkins. "You need to eat some of these too, you know." She licked her lips and shoved the basket toward him. "OK, I'm ready for the 'doozy.' Lay it on me."

Pushing the fritters aside, Popsie pulled out a large gold envelope. "He's rewriting his will."

She sat up in her chair. "Does he have a big family?"

"That's an excellent question. Turns out he has a bunch of kids he hasn't spoken to for twenty years, but now he wants to include them in his estate plans." He slid the envelope across the table toward her.

"Seriously?" She took the envelope, but didn't look at it. "Twenty years? That's terrible! Why'd he do that?"

Popsie winced. "Maybe they did it. Why do you assume it was his fault?"

"Hmm. Probably because my parents did that to me and I still feel gypped." She saw Popsie look down and knew she had crossed the line. "I didn't mean it like that. You know that I cherish you more than anyone in this world. You know that, right?" She fought the urge to conk herself in the head. Instead, she picked at a hangnail under the table. How could she let her mouth run out of control like that?

Popsie stared at his hands. "I know. I guess I hoped I was enough for you all these years. I'm just an old man, but I did the best I could."

"I'm sorry. You've been great—and you're not old." Even though he wore his full head of white hair a little long and always windswept, it framed his leathery face in the perfect way. "You are unequaled. And you have been enough. I would be alone in the world if not for you. I just don't understand anyone who would turn his back on family." She picked at a rough spot on the table with her fingernail. "Family is a gift."

Popsie pursed his lips. He massaged his hands, but kept quiet.

Meg sipped tea from a giant plastic cup. "OK, so let's get back to business. What exactly does he want me to do?"

He pointed to the envelope. "Read the letter on top. That's what he sent to each of the kids—there's five . . . er . . . four of them."

Meg extracted the papers from the envelope. She looked at him after reading the first paragraph, but he nodded for her to continue.

20 May 2010

Dear (Child's name),

It's been a long while. No excuses. I want you to know all is forgiven on my end. I'm sending a peace offering of sorts in hopes you might forgive things on your end as well.

I am updating my estate plans and my lawyer will travel to meet with the family. I assume everyone will be at the lake house Memorial Day weekend to open up the place, so I'm sending her there. Megan Marks is her name and she needs to privately interview each of you. She will write the will with no input from me.

I do not trust myself to make these decisions. I assume you have changed to some degree in the last twenty years, and rather than making a judgment based on what I knew of you back then, I'd like it to be based on who you are today. Meg does not know any of you, she doesn't know our history and I feel she will provide an objective point of view, which should benefit those of you who are most deserving.

I have given her a list of the assets to be distributed to my family, asking her to pay special attention to those who deserve to benefit the most and who will honor my memory with the greatest respect.

My directives to her are these:

1. Meet and interview each of my children and as many extended family members as possible.
2. Divide the list of assets among my family members as she sees fit.
Everything on the list must be given to a

*member of my family (which may include spouses
and children), but not every family member must
receive something from the list. It need not be
equal and it is entirely up to her.*
   3. *The will must be ready for my signature by June
   7th. This point is non-negotiable.*

*Please treat Meg with the utmost respect and be honest
with her—about everything.*

I never stopped loving any of you.

Sincerely,
Dad
Duke Vanderzee
Encl: Affidavit

Meg checked the restaurant for hidden cameras. Her voice
started low, but rose to a muffled shriek. "Is he insane? He
didn't even ask me before he sent this out. And he wants me to
write his will with NO input at all from him? Who would let a
complete stranger do that? Does he hate his family that much to
put them at the whim of . . . me?"

Popsie pointed to the stack of papers in front of her. "He
figured you'd be a little surprised. Look at the next sheet of
paper under the letter."

She pulled out an affidavit signed by three separate doctors,
a notary, and a judge. Meg read the entire sheet, which affirmed

the sanity of Duke Vanderzee, as of yesterday's date. Perfect. It could actually be legal.

Meg looked up. "Why? Why me? Why this way?"

"Think about it. There could be all kinds of reasons."

She reread the documents. "One thing he's right about. I definitely don't know him or his family. Is that why he didn't want to meet me?"

"Could be. It's as good an explanation as any."

"OK, look at all the reasons I shouldn't do this right now. First of all, he wants it done by June 7th. That's two weeks."

Popsie nodded and smiled at her.

"Plus, I . . . well . . . this is bizarre. I'm not sure how I'd feel if my biological dad did this. I'd be ticked that he didn't talk to me for so long and then all of a sudden he sends a letter and a lawyer. Some *reconciliation*."

"I believe there is one more item in the envelope. Why don't you take a peek at that?" Popsie's mouth twitched like it always did when he was amused but trying hard not to show it.

Sure enough, when Meg looked she saw a small envelope at the bottom. Inside, she found an airline ticket and a pile of cash. "What?" She read the short note accompanying the money and looked up at Popsie. Her jaw fell open again. "Is this guy for real? He wants to pay me $100,000 for my services."

Popsie laughed. "That sounds fair." He gazed out toward

the boats docked in front of the restaurant. "Well, I guess I've done my duty—you have the proposition. He'd like to know by tomorrow whether you accept it or not. Maybe you want to talk to Cody about it before you decide anything, huh?"

Staring across the river, she said in a small, distracted voice, "Yeah, I probably should." She paused, then hit the table with both hands. "Ooh! I almost forgot. Guess what?" She held her left hand out toward him, her heart pounding as she waited for his reaction.

A reluctant smile crawled across Popsie's face. He took her hand and inspected the new ring. "Congratulations. Cody, I presume?"

She batted his upper arm with a wimpy open hand. "Popsie. Of course. He called you last week, didn't he?"

Grabbing her hands, he sandwiched them between both of his on the table. "Yes, he had enough good sense to ask for your hand."

The weight and warmth of his hands pressed through to her heart. Popsie, overprotective, over-concerned, but overly generous as well. "Think about it. I'm going to be part of a huge family! I'll have sisters—three of them. And a little brother, aunts, uncles, and two sets of grandparents. I can't believe it. We're thinking August for the wedding."

Still holding her hands, he lifted them in the air between

them. His eyes searched her face. "Are you happy, Meg?"

She slid her hands until they covered his and rested them on the table. "Yes. Unequivocally, irrevocably, super happy."

His deep blue eyes shimmered, but did not spill over.

She got up to hug him. "Thanks for being happy for me."

His face drew into a tight-lipped smile.

Meg stood at the prow of the eighty-six foot long, 1975 Burger—the ultimate motoryacht from "back in the day." She inhaled the warm, fragrant sea air with deep breaths and closed eyes. Living on Gilda placed them in a state of "retro luxury" like old Hollywood glamour. Nice, but not ridiculous. Might've been ridiculous at one time, but not now. Popsie often said, "We live a bohemian lifestyle but we require a proper Southern upbringing." She aimed for 'bohemian' but feared she ended up closer to 'proper.'

She examined her fingernails as she leaned her elbows on the bow-rail, water swooshing below. Chipped three of them today. Life on the water didn't mix with the urban yuppie lawyer thing. She basked in the salty evening, happy to be on the move, headed toward another harbor . . . and Cody. She weighed her decision. Who did Vanderzee think he was? Her stomach turned at the way he assumed she would do his bidding if he threw enough money at her. She hoped Popsie wouldn't be too disappointed if she turned down the job.

A wide stripe of light reflected off the smooth water. Moonlight mixed with ocean to illuminate the evening, almost as light as day. When they reached open water, her head cleared, like always. Popsie understood why she loved—why she needed—to look toward the horizon with nothing between her and forever. A warm feeling crawled up inside her every time they cruised out in the open, avoiding the relative protection, comfort, and predictability of the Intracoastal Waterway. The sound of slow, shuffling steps interrupted her thoughts, so she turned.

Popsie raised a hand in greeting. "I thought I might find you up here. Captain Steve said we'll have to head in soon. Care to sit with me for awhile?" He gestured toward the padded bench seat stretched across the bow.

"Sure. I was just catching up with old friends."

He smiled and grabbed her hand.

For an only child growing up on a boat, imaginary ocean friends didn't seem crazy. "I miss this."

"I miss you when you're in Charlotte. But you find more clients every month. Pretty soon, you'll forget about little old me and this bucket of nails."

"Yeah, right. This old bucket of nails is home. And you will always be on my mind, so no worries there." She tucked her arm through his and hugged with both hands. Moonlight glinted off her new diamond, carrying her thoughts toward marrying Cody, and leaving Popsie. But she chased away the lingering nostalgia as they sat. "Is something on your mind?"

He swallowed. His lips moved, stopped, and pressed into a thin line. "I wish I could put this off until after your wedding, but it's not going to wait." He placed his age-spotted and wrinkled hand on top of her smooth one. "Your ol' Pop is sick."

"What kind of sick?" She managed to eke out the question before the weight of his words pressed into her heart.

He took a deep breath and sighed. He searched her face with great tenderness in his eyes. "Cancer."

The word reverberated in her brain, ricocheting off emotions and memories. It battered the recesses of her heart until everything inside hurt. The taste of metal filled her mouth and she couldn't speak.

He nodded at her ring. "I didn't want to spoil your moment, your good news, but I don't have much longer to live."

The solid bench beneath Meg dissolved and for a moment a strange floating sensation distracted her. When she looked up, the sky seemed to spin away. Her head pounded and the air—or her brain—shimmered. She shuddered as she tried to grasp what he said. Popsie. Dying. The thought ripped a gaping hole in her soul. "Are you sure?"

Popsie nodded. "Yes. They told me it's a matter of weeks, give or take."

Swallowing tears and gulping for air, her words tumbled out loud and panicked. "But how? When did you find out about this? How can it be only weeks? Why is it so—fast?"

Placing his arm around her shoulders, he leaned her back against the cushions and gazed up at the stars. "A couple months ago, my stomach started bothering me every time I ate. I ignored it until I couldn't stand to eat anymore. Last week, the doctor in Charleston ran some tests and they figured it out. Pancreatic cancer. It moves fast and since I waited so long, I used up most of my time not knowing. I guess that's better anyway. But I hate that your birthday is coming up, and now your wedding."

She tilted her head, leaning into his shoulder. Strong, reliable Popsie. When she arrived yesterday, she refused to acknowledge his drawn look and obvious weight loss, but thinking back, she had noticed. He escaped health problems for so many years. At eighty-three, this news should not surprise. But it caught her unaware, like a bug, a millisecond before hitting the windshield.

She didn't notice when the tears started falling, but now they took over. Her body shook with sobs as she clung to Popsie. Her father, her hero, her whole family.

The familiar clunk in the back of her gut jarred her

thoughts. It conjured up the habitual worry never far from her mind. *What if Popsie dies before I grow up?* As a twenty-seven-year-old woman, it sounded ridiculous, but she recognized the constant undercurrent she battled daily, racing against time. Now defeat loomed before her eyes like a wave that must break when it nears the shore. She sensed her personal stability wavering. Powerless to stop the mudslide of her emotions, she grasped for something that might bring a glimmer of hope into the situation.

Meg snuffled. She pushed away from Popsie, wiped her face and took a deep breath. "What can we do? What about chemo or radiation? Or surgery?"

"I opted out of treatment."

Meg gasped.

He cut her off before she could blurt a response. He clasped her hand and squeezed it tight. "In my case, they told me treatment would make me miserable and maybe only give me a couple extra weeks. Quality over quantity."

She rolled her eyes at the familiar words. "But this is your life."

Smiling, he placed his other hand on hers. "Yes, it is. And that's my mantra. Which means I live it all the way up to the end, no compromise."

"But . . ." Tears welled up in Meg's eyes again, but she

urged them back. She could no more ask him to act against his convictions than she could act against her own. She loved him for all that he exuded: confidence, peace and capability. And now he'd be gone in a matter of weeks. "How are you not in a hospital bed right now? You don't even look sick. Well, you've lost some weight. Are you in pain?"

"Some days are worse than others."

Meg stood and paced in front of Popsie. "I'm cancelling everything. I'm moving back for the duration."

He waggled a finger in her direction. "Oh no, you're not, Missy. I see where this is going. You are not staying here on a death-watch. I'm going to sail into the sunset on my own terms."

Meg walked over to face him. "If I have to let you go, I'm going to stock up on 'Popsie Time' while I can. My clients can wait. Cody will wait. He'll understand."

"What about that proposition from Mr. Vanderzee? I think you should do it."

"No way! I'm not leaving you." She continued to pace, mentally running through all the logistics she would need to handle.

Popsie looked down at his hands. He stared out over the water and when he finally spoke, his voice came out low and firm. "Meg. I need you to do this for me."

She halted.

His hands ran up and down his thighs. "I wasn't completely up front with you earlier. I owe Vanderzee a huge favor. I connected you two as payback for something he did a long time ago." He studied his shoes for a moment and then looked up at Meg, clearing his throat. "I know it doesn't make sense right now, but you doing this job for him is the only way I can set things right before I'm gone." He winced and his hand flew to his side.

Standing still, arms crossed, she took a breath to speak but he held up a hand in protest.

"I'm sorry to put this kind of pressure on you, but I want a clean slate when I go."

Meg shook her head. He said he needed her to do this. Popsie didn't need things. But how could he send her away? She couldn't afford to miss his last weeks for this lousy "old buddy" of his.

Her hands fell to her sides as she faced him. A thought struck. Her voice came out small. "Are you saying you don't want me here with you?"

"We spent a beautiful lifetime together on this boat. All that's left for me is the worst couple weeks. You don't need to see that." He paused, looking out over the water they both loved. "Will you do this one thing for me?"

Meg turned and walked back to the bow-rail, staring at the

moon as it rose higher into the sky. Popsie made a place for her when she didn't belong anywhere. He loved her and showed her the world; he taught her to fly and gave her wind and space to soar. This stupid job represented her last opportunity to show him she was grateful. And he needed her.

But what if she missed . . . the end? He needed her to be with him at the end. She needed to be with him. She imagined all the little things she could do for him, fluffing up pillows, dispensing pills, reading their favorite swashbuckling novels aloud. But the one thing he asked would fling her far from his side.

Meg automatically shifted her weight as the bow turned toward shore. She focused on the swirling confusion of white water where waves splashed against the hull. What if she did take the job? While very unusual, the task appeared straightforward. Meet the family, write the will, fly home next week. And the payoff would allow her to turn hopes and plans into reality for Orphan Advocacy. Those kids could start getting help right away.

She turned around and found Popsie looking at her with . . . what was it? Sadness? Something else? Definitely something else. He wanted her to go.

She fought against disappointment, but clung to the sound of Popsie's voice needing her. "OK, I'll do it. But I'm not taking my time on this one. I'm coming home as soon as I finish, and then I'm staying with you 'til the end. Got it?"

His eyes twinkled like they always did when she bossed him.

Chapter Two

Repeated shutter clicks sliced into Meg's consciousness. She scrunched her face as she rolled over, nearly falling off the narrow bench seat. Catching her balance, she gripped the edge of the seat and pushed herself up, squinting in bright sunlight, which seemed to beam directly from the horizon into her eyes.

More clicks. "Mornin', Sunshine!"

As she rubbed the backs of her hands across her eyes, last night's insomnia clung to her bones, clutched at her mind. It had driven her up here, to the bridge, where starlight kept watch over her as she finally inched into a restless sleep beneath the bright red canvas bimini.

Stretching her arms over her head, Meg yawned herself fully awake, and the clicking stopped.

Cody's silky southern cadences oozed across her rough edges. "You're beautiful when you sleep."

She couldn't stop a chuckle. "As opposed to now, when I'm awake?"

Cody rushed to her side, camera slung over his shoulder. "No, no, no. I mean, you're always beautiful." He searched the morning sky, as if for inspiration." It's just that your sleeping beauty is a rare sight for my eyes."

The now familiar whirl inside spun up through her chest. His words sank deep into her soul, and she replayed them often. He knew who she was and what she needed to hear. "Nice recovery. And by August, you'll be able to watch me sleep any time you want."

He slid his arm around her shoulders, and they leaned back against the bench cushions, facing the sunrise. Last night's phone conversation hung in the air between them. Meg bit her lip as she ran her fingers up and down Cody's freckled arm. "So much for our romantic weekend. I hate that I'm spoiling it."

He took her hand, holding it up to catch a ray of Charleston sunrise in her diamond, like it sparkled on the water behind the boat. "We have ten thousand weekends ahead of us. A few days are nothing when you look at the big picture."

Cody's kiss on the back of her hand shot a wave of pure relief through Meg's tense muscles. "Do you know how amazing you are?"

"You, my bride, have blinded me to everything but your sweet face."

"OK, now we're laying it on a bit thick." She tickled his ribs.

Jumping away from her fingers, he laughed. "OK, you're right. But I couldn't resist this light on your sleeping face. I'm sorry I woke you with the camera."

Sinking back into the bench cushions, Meg stretched her arms out in front of her. "It's time for me to get up anyway. I'm glad you could get here so early. My flight leaves in a couple hours."

Cody shifted to face her. "So, he's sending you to Michigan?"

Nodding, she stood and sniffed the air, deciding from the mucky smell that it must be near low tide. Grabbing a cloth and spray bottle from a side compartment, she smirked at the irony of beautiful Charleston, rich in history, steeped in tradition, boasting hundreds of historically significant, stunning homes. This city—with all its pretense and grandeur—suffered the stench of the mud flats every low tide. She shook off her reverie. "I've never been that far north. I hope it's not freezing."

"Are you sure you want to take this on right now? I mean, it all sounds kinda vague. What do you even know about these people? Are they safe to be around?"

Charleston Harbor bustled into the morning, boat traffic already heavy. Near and distant engines coughed to life and various horns sounded across the water. She squirted glass cleaner on part of the windscreen surrounding the bridge, and wiped away the salt collected overnight. "I guess they're just a normal family. Four adult siblings, plus their families. I don't know how many there are total." She launched into her mental notebook: open file for each person.

Cody propped his elbows atop the bench back. "Do lawyers do this? I mean, are you supposed to write the will all by yourself?"

A lonely skiff on the river captured her attention. The pilot, a solitary bearded gentleman with stiff white hair, sat ramrod straight, steering with one hand on the outboard motor. He kept to the edge, dodging commercial and pleasure craft with ease, his eyes focused ahead on his destination, open water. "It's a pretty weird request. But Popsie said he needs me to do it. So I'm going."

"Yeah. So what do you know about this client?"

She finished wiping the port side and turned to look at him. "Popsie told me he's an old friend, probably from the Navy or something. I'm not worried. The only thing that bugs me is that he ignored his kids for twenty years. But if I can help them reconcile, maybe that's a good thing. Plus, he's paying a ridiculous amount of money."

Cody leaned forward, elbows resting on his knees, gaze cast downward. "Not to play the devil's advocate or anything, but why do you think he's paying so much?"

"I guess he wanted to make it worth my while. It does put me out a long weekend with you. But think about it, I've been fundraising for over a year, trying to get Orphan Advocacy off the ground. This will turn things around for us in a single weekend."

Cody shifted back in his seat. "So after you get paid for this job, where will things stand?"

Meg tossed her dirty rag into the seat beside Cody and grabbed a fresh one to finish her window cleaning. "We'll have enough to sign the building lease, and open the doors. I called the building manager last night and he thinks we're talking less than two months.

A low whistle escaped Cody's lips. "That's fast. Are you gonna be ready?"

"I can't even tell you how excited I am about this. The only major pieces I still need to put in place are a few endorsements and some long-term gifts. Much as I hate to say it, this job is a God-send."

Cody stood, hands stuffed into his back pockets. "Sounds like it's exactly what you needed. And Popsie knows the guy too, right? He wouldn't steer you wrong."

"Exactly."

Cody's arms closed around her shoulders. "I'm gonna miss you, though."

Turning into his firm chest, Meg closed her eyes. "Me too."

He steered her back toward their seat on the bench. "What will the crew have left to do if you steal all their work?"

"Habit. Can't help it. We didn't always have a full crew. It was just me for a lot of years. Plus, it helps me think."

She basked in his wide-open smile. His light touch sent tingles up her arm while her mind wandered into their future. What would his face look like when he saw her for the first time in her wedding gown? She hoped his expression would weaken her knees; she'd have to lean on Popsie—her thoughts hit a brick wall as last night's conversation crashed into her consciousness, upsetting the fragile emotional balance so recently attained.

Cody's expression changed from happy to compassionate, as her own face froze, sending cold spikes through the rest of her body.

His hands caressed her arms. "What? What'd I do?"

Meg crumbled against him. She closed her eyes to hide the cheerful sunlight reflecting off the surrounding white deck and chrome. Choking back tears and willing away the blackness that threatened to creep across her mind, Meg clung to Cody. "Popsie won't be there."

"Huh?"

"The wedding. In August. Popsie has . . . weeks. I just realized." Lonely tears dripped down her cheeks.

"Oh, Meg." Cody hugged her close.

Her red carry-on suitcase blocked the stairs leading from the galley up to the wheelhouse. Thankfully, she had plenty of clothes for this quick trip, since she planned to meet Cody in Charleston anyway. Meg sat at the table, orange juice in hand, foot tapping the floor. Her eyes flashed across the table to meet Cody's. "Should we tell him?"

He nodded.

Popsie's knife froze midair; peach jam dripped onto the toast in his other hand. "What?"

Meg laughed. "Don't worry. It's good news."

A woman dressed in khaki capris and a red polo with Gilda embroidered on the front approached the table. Sheila delivered a plate of eggs, her hand popping up to check the beauty-parlor blonde hair crowning her bubbly personality. "Oh goody. What's the good news?" She pointed at Popsie with a red-tipped nail. "Ease up on the jam there, big boy."

Meg's eyes flicked to Cody, and she couldn't stop a smile from taking over her face. "Popsie, we're moving the wedding to Miami and it's next week, so you can be there."

"Oh!" Sheila clapped her hands, but then suddenly froze with an expression on her face like she'd done something wrong. She wrinkled her brow, spun around and hovered over the sink, scrubbing the tar out of whatever ill-fated pot had been left to soak.

Meg looked to Popsie, baffled by the mate's reaction.

His face looked like he'd swallowed a lemon but didn't want anyone to know about it. The happy mood in the galley soured. He swallowed hard and stared at his plate. "I've messed things up enough already. Don't change anything for me." He bit into the gooey mess of a breakfast he held, eyes on the toast.

Sheila banged some dishes in the sink, a sure sign she was upset. She spoke over her shoulder. "Don't be such a grump, Mr. Marks. They're doing something nice for ya here." She turned toward Popsie and pointed. "Guy Marks, that is too much jam on your toast. You know what the doctor said."

Meg glimpsed the questioning look on Cody's face with equal question in her own mind. She shrugged and placed a hand on Popsie's shoulder. "I couldn't bear the thought of walking down the aisle alone, with no one to give me away. You're the only one I really want at the wedding anyway."

Cody nodded. "We've already decided to marry. We're not going to change our minds, so we figured, what's the difference when we tie the knot?"

Meg scooped some eggs onto her plate and grabbed a biscuit. "We've already worked it out. I'll be in Michigan in a couple hours, so Cody is going to handle most of the details."

She pulled a folded sheet of paper from her jacket pocket and handed it across the table to Cody. "Here's the list so far."

Cody opened the paper and lightning fast, whipped his gaze toward Meg. "You want me to take Anchor?"

She knew this would be the worst part, and tried not to cringe. "Honestly, I called three of my neighbors. No one can take him. It's my fault for forgetting to book the kennel for this weekend. But if I leave him with Popsie, he'll end up in Key West."

Now Cody's face took on a sour expression, one he did not appear to fight. His words came out forced. "You know he hates me."

Meg picked at her thumbnail. Anchor, her over-exuberant, golden-doodle puppy did seem uncomfortable around Cody. "He's getting better lately, though. And since we're going to be married in a week anyway, Anchor is practically yours now. This might be just the thing you two need. Bonding."

Cody's uncertainty hung in the air, but he nodded and spoke low. "Maybe so." Clouds seemed to clear from his face in the pause of conversation. He returned to the list. "Good thing I have this week off. There's a lot to do. I'm gonna call Mama in on this if it's okay with you. She'll be a huge help."

Biting her tongue, Meg struggled to hide all traces of a visible reaction. Every time Cody's mother came to mind, Meg remembered the scent of freshly baked goods. Patches of flour dust on every piece of clothing, the woman was a virtual bakery on stout legs, held down by laced—up "Little-House-on-the-Praire-style shoes. Her genuine smile always brought warmth to Meg's heart, but her sense of style only seemed to work well within the confines of their fifty-year-old farmhouse. And the thought of her mother-in-law—no matter how wonderful—planning her wedding, caused an enormous internal cringe. "You probably need a little help, huh?"

Cody held up the list and cocked his head.

Squashing every bright orange qualm flashing in her brain, Meg pasted on a tight smile. "Yeah. You know I love your mom."

"Great." An invisible weight seemed to lift off Cody's shoulders right before her eyes and the tension between them eased. Meg did love his mama. But every time she tried to call her "Mama," it felt too strange on her tongue. Usually she chickened out and sputtered a wimpy "Mrs. McKenny." She'd have to get used to calling her Mama. She'd have to get used to having someone in her life that acted like a Mama.

Breaking the obvious silence, Popsie brushed his hands together as he did every morning after breakfast to clean off his crumbs. He raised a plain white coffee mug filled with hot water and chugged what remained. He scooted toward Meg, hinting she needed to let him out of the booth-like seating around the table. As he shuffled toward the rear staterooms, he dismissed himself. "Sounds like you have lots to talk about. Come give me a hug before you leave."

Sheila finished wiping a dish, replaced it in a cupboard, and disappeared into the forward crew quarters.

Cody sipped his coffee, staring at her over the rim. "How did that go over?"

Meg ran her thumb along the ridged chrome edge of the table. It resembled the old 50s Formica-top tables. Popsie grew up in a much simpler time, and now she had ensured that his going would become more complex, adding a wedding to what little time he had left. "I have this feeling Popsie's not saying something. He seems less than happy."

"The man is dying. Can you blame him?"

"No. You're probably right." She watched Cody eye the list again. Chewing her lip, Meg struggled for words. "I know we're throwing it together fast because of me, but it's my only wedding. And you did say work is really slow this month. I guess I thought I'd shoot for the moon and see how much stuff from my 'dreamed about it since I was a little girl list' we could pull off in a week."

"You focus on this job in Michigan, and I'll see how much we can pull together." He squeezed her hand until it almost hurt.

"I promise our wedding will be wonderful. If we walk away married, it can't be anything but perfect. But I'm not going to promise it will be exactly what you always dreamed. Or even close. Are you sure this is how you want it?"

Eyes stinging, lips pressed together, Meg gave him several short nods. As soon as she could speak, her words tumbled over one another as she gulped her breaths. "I need Popsie to be there because he's all that I have, and I want him to know that I'm going to be okay without him because I'm all that he has too and I need . . . I want . . ." Her voice broke and she sniffled.

Cody raised her hand to his lips. He unfolded himself from the table and stood, his blond curls nearly grazing the ceiling. His low-country drawl sounded like a hug should. "Here's an idea. What if you come with me to Charlotte and fly out from there? You might could ease Anchor's transition to me a little bit."

Meg drew herself up to standing. The legal realities of her task crowded her mind as she calculated the possibility of finishing it quickly enough to weed out the less-than-hoped-for elements from this wedding before it was too late. And her time with Popsie was so limited. She could afford no delays. She glanced at her watch. "Better stick to the plan. I need to skedaddle."

She looked up into disappointed eyes, brushed a kiss across

Cody's cheek, and headed toward her stateroom for one last look-around.

"Meg?"

Cody's cracking voice tugged at her heart, turned her head. With shoulders slumped and hands stuffed into back pockets, he looked a little desperate, but in a sweet sort of way. "Since I'm donating my weekend too, can I at least get a couple minutes for goodbye?

As soon as she glanced at her watch, regret pinged inside her chest. She closed the distance between them and sank into his arms. Pulling away sooner than she should have, her mind was already on the dock and looking for the cab that should be waiting for her by now. She traced the line of his jaw with her forefinger, pressed it into the dimple on his chin. "I'll be back before you know it."

Cody's mouth struggled into a resigned smile. "Call me when you get there."

Chapter Three

Meg bustled into the waiting cab, dropped her head against the tall leather seat behind her and waited, eyes closed, to be whisked away. Cody was the epitome of the perfect guy with the perfect family. She savored the thought of Christmas this year. She could smell the fire in the dining room of the farmhouse and imagined sitting shoulder to shoulder with Cody's siblings and extended family. Christmas without Popsie would be difficult, the McKenny's would prevent it from being impossible.

She released a loud sigh as the car pulled away.

"Ain't it a bit early for such a heavy trouble on ya this mornin'?"

Her eyes popped open and she fastened her gaze on the cabbie, a dark man with a friendly tone. In her mind, next Christmas collided with Cody's disappointment, Popsie's plea, and visions of her hoped for, fairy-tale wedding. "I'm afraid so."

She stared out the window, her gaze blurred by a numbness of her own choosing. The disappointment in Cody's eyes was a direct result of Meg pursuing Popsie's dying wish. Or her readiness to begin. And get back. Popsie's eyes would have betrayed a similar look if she had chosen to stay with Cody for the weekend instead. How did this one thing come down to a choice between the two men she loved?

Meg pulled a loose thread from the cuff of her blouse, peeking through the sleeve of her crimson jacket. She replayed the moment when she told Cody she wanted to leave right away. Watching the hope flee from his face had dissolved her confidence in that decision. She could have stayed, driven to Charlotte with him, grabbed a later flight. But the briefcase leaning against her leg bulged with fresh yellow legal pads, and the letter to Mr. Vanderzee's children.

Emblazoned in her mind, that letter lit a fire inside Meg. Or was it Popsie's pleading eyes that made her say yes? It wasn't the money. At least, she hoped not. What did Cody think of her reasons for leaving like this? She didn't trust her jumbled mind to judge her own actions. But his eyes. Disappointed, yes. Did she also see a grain of doubt in them? Did he add up her choices and find himself too low on the step-ladder of Meg's priorities? Did he have a point?

Meg checked her watch again. Cody would still be on Gilda. She could change her plan. But the only child inside her reared its ugly head. She had a plan. She'd made a decision and as her fiancée, shouldn't he support her no matter what? Plus, now that he'd taken on so many wedding details, he needed to get going on that. Moving the wedding date up was his idea, so at least that shouldn't be a point of contention.

She let out another loud sigh.

The cabbie's eyes peeked at her in the rear-view mirror. "Everything okay, ma'am?"

"I just hate it when other people make me feel guilty for doing what I think is best." But Cody had not dished out this guilt. It might be all inside her head. But maybe not.

His open palm smacked the steering wheel with a light slap. "Don't you know it. I have people telling me which road t' take all day long. Who knows better'n a cabbie the right road?"

"See? That's what I think." The car made a sharp turn onto the highway and Meg slid across the cracked vinyl seat.

"OK, then." The driver nodded and turned up the radio.

Jazz fusion filled the car as she kicked off red patent ballet shoes and tucked her feet beneath her on the seat. Leaning the side of her head against the cool glass, she paid little attention to the sights beyond the window. Popsie flashed in her mind's eye. The debonair Guy Marks. Random images of him throbbed through her memory in time with the double bass on the radio. Sharp blue eyes sparkled against perpetually sun-tanned skin. His bare feet chased a younger version of her across the sand until they splashed in ocean waves. Competent, calloused hands wrapped bowlines around a cleat.

Her heart hurt at the thought of being in the world without him. Her hand moved to her chest, as if it could soothe this kind of pain. The compulsion to finish the Vanderzee job grew minute by minute. Now every moment she spent away from Popsie pushed her closer to the precipice of loss.

She couldn't go back to Cody right now—too much lay ahead. *Get it done and get back to Popsie.* Cody would understand. He had to.

Guy Marks scrutinized several boats cruising down the Intracoastal Waterway behind Gilda. A Hatteras pushed his luck, tried to pass a fifty-foot Egg Harbor and drew the attention of a cruising sheriff patrol boat. Guy shifted in his seat several times and looked at his watch. Meg must be almost there by now. He stared at the newspaper before his eyes, but failed to comprehend even a single word on the page. Folding the paper, he tossed it to the coffee table. He hoisted himself out of the chair and walked forward through the salon ignoring the new fixture installed that morning. It didn't even seem like his home anymore with that big white monstrosity dominating the room. He shambled into the pilothouse.

Gleaming chrome shone on the control panel from regular polishing. Captain Steve stood at the helm. Guy's gut wrenched every time another man's hands touched the controls of his boat.

Steve eyed him askance. "Wanna take the helm for awhile?"

Guy placed a hand on his shoulder. "I can't."

A heavy pause filled the space between them. Steve directed his gaze to the water ahead. "It wasn't that bad. I saw the damage."

"That's like saying the scar on your child's face isn't that noticeable. Doesn't matter if you can see it or not, knowing you let it happen just about breaks your heart." Guy shook his head back and forth.

Sunlight flashed as it reflected off the window of a yacht they passed on the starboard side. "You were docking. It was a tight slip."

"Did you ever wreck one?"

"You didn't wreck her. And no, I never did. But I ripped a sail on Stars and Stripes during beat-run practice once. Skipper canned me. That felt pretty bad. Couldn't touch a piece of rigging for a month."

"So you know." Guy stepped around Steve toward the computer navigation system mounted to the port side of the wheel. High gloss teak wood gleamed on the walls, the floor, and all the cabinetry surrounding the console. He caught sight of his reflection in the shiny sliding door leading out to the portside walkway. His baggy pants and shuffling steps looked like an old man's. At least he still wore his topsiders without socks.

Guy touched the mouse and the screen flashed to life, displaying the nautical chart, Gilda's current position, and the course as plotted by Captain Steve. "So, we're heading out at the next inlet?"

Steve failed in an attempt to hide a small smile. "I wanted to avoid a few trouble spots out there, sir. We've passed the worst of them now. Open sea in less than an hour."

Guy stroked shiny wood framing the window. He stared toward the East, but failed to register homes and docks lining the Intracoastal Waterway. "Good. Where do we dock tonight?"

"I'm making for Savannah, sir. We'll resupply there and continue south tomorrow. Barring unforeseen trouble, I believe we'll arrive in Key West by mid-week."

"What weather are we expecting?"

"Winds SSW 5-10, eighty degrees, partly cloudy. Should be smooth sailing."

"I didn't mean to check up on you."

"Yes you did. And it's fine, sir."

Guy turned to go. "You're a good man, Cap'n Steve."

"No sir. That's you."

Guy pressed his lips together and nodded once. An uneasy guilt stiffened his shoulders. He dragged his hand across the raised leather bench running across the rear of the pilothouse.

Shuffling out the door, he passed the ugly hospital bed in the salon of all places, and drifted through the back doors onto the aft deck.

Two minutes later, Sheila bustled to his side with a fresh mug of hot tea. "It's the Good Earth Tea. I think this is the best one on your tummy."

"Thank you, Sheila." Holding the mug six inches below his mouth, he pressed his lips together and stared at the water churned up by Gilda's props.

Sheila stood at his side, but he refused to look at her.

"It's not your tummy that's bothering you now, is it?"

Popsie took a tentative sip from the steaming mug. "Nope."

A loud huff escaped Sheila's mouth while her hand flew to her ample hip. "I knew it. Now stop stewing about it and tell me."

With a roll of the eyes, Popsie winced in pain more emotional than physical. "I had a talk with Cody this morning before he left."

Sheila wheeled around and plopped herself on the long leather bench lining two sides of the aft-deck area in an "L" shape. She faced him now and tried to capture his gaze, which fixed beyond the open windows. "What did you do?"

The answer came after a long pause. "I'm not sure."

"What? Mr. Marks, spill it."

"I was afraid." He cleared his throat. "I am afraid for him."

She shook her head like the pendulum on a grandfather clock. "He's a good boy. I thought you approved. Why would you do this? She can't stay single forever, you know." She looked right into his eyes. "She's going to be hoppin' mad, you know."

He nodded. Sipped his tea. Nodded again. "I voiced one concern to him. About Meg. It's up to him to see if I'm right or wrong."

Sheila stood shaking her head again. "I can't stand to listen to this. I hope you know what you're doing, because it almost sounds like you don't want her to be happy. I saw him walking away with a slump in his shoulders. I thought he just missed Meg. But you slumped those shoulders, didn't you?"

Guy worked his lower lip side to side against his upper lip. "Possibly." He sipped the tea again. "But I think it will come right in the end."

Sheila marched away stomping every step into the deck. She called back to him over her shoulder. "You better hope so. I know I do."

Spying a photo perched on the coffee table, Guy scuffled to retrieve it. A low rumble vibrated through the floor at the sweet sound of twin V-8 diesels propelling the boat toward cruising speed. He settled back into the director chair, facing astern. His fingers traveled over the familiar image of himself and Meg after their first long night together on Gilda. She sat upon his lap, her head snuggled under his chin. He could still feel his arms around her tiny six-year-old frame. Warm rays from the sunrise streaked across miles of empty ocean to warm their faces, with nothing in between to stop them.

A short, soft-looking woman padded onto the aft-deck. "Mr. Marks, how we feelin'?"

He examined her blue scrubs, looking for a nametag. "I'm fine. You don't need to hover over me, you know. The doctor said I need to have you here, but right now I don't feel like I need anything."

"Oh, that's fine. It's my job to make sure you have whatcha need, so I'm just checkin' in. Not sure if I introduced myself properly or not, but I'm Marcie Coggins." She reached her hand out to shake. "And I have to tell you, this is definitely the most amazin' home I've had the privilege to offer my services in. My stateroom's every bit as nice as the Taj Mahal, I'm sure."

He nodded. "Thank you."

She pointed to the picture frame in his hand. "Tell me about yer picture."

He tilted the photo toward her. It depicted the two of them asleep shortly after the sunrise moment so crisp in his memory. He gripped the edge of the frame and his imagination caught a whiff of baby shampoo.

He handed the frame to her. "That's my little girl. Of course, she's grown now. It was our first day together on this boat."

"She's adorable."

"Yes ma'am. She woke me up in the middle of the night. Scared me to death. I opened my eyes and this little imp stood beside the bed with eyes big as saucers." He smiled at the thought. "She held a little blanket up to her face and she said, 'Can't sleep.'" He chuckled with some effort. "Cute little bugger."

"So what didja do?"

"Poor thing was scared as a turtle all stuck up in her shell. So I picked her up and we left the harbor right away." He looked up at her curious face and gave her his sneakiest grin. "Crew didn't like that one so much."

"It was the middle 'a the night?"

"Three o'clock in the morning. We cruised out a good ways, dropped the anchor, and then waited on the bow bench up front for the sun to rise. I swear it rose just especially for the two of us that day."

"And then ya'll fell asleep."

"Yes ma'am."

Marcie placed the photo back in his lap. "What a sweet

memory. Will I get to meet this wonderful little girl?"

Guy hugged the photo to his chest. "Well there's the million dollar question." She would be angry with him, for sure. But would she stick it out long enough for the whole truth to come out? Did he dare to hope she would return? He doubted she would want to. He didn't deserve her. Thoughts of his late wife flashed through his mind before he could stop them. Rachel. Another woman he didn't deserve.

"Oh." A bulky silence hung in the air, until Marcie painted over it with her cheerfulness. "So, Captain Steve tells me we're headed to Key West."

Guy nodded with slow deliberation and forced a smile for Marcie. "They have beautiful sunsets there."

She patted his shoulder and turned to go. "I can't wait to see it. I think I'll go finish settling into my room. Holler if you need anything now, ok?"

Guy sipped lukewarm tea from his favorite stained white mug. He stood and walked toward the open windows framing the aft deck. The salty breeze lifted messy hair off his forehead as he watched the water churn in the wake, leaving a trail of foam behind them. He couldn't bear it if Meg didn't forgive him for this. Their tiny family had survived this long because of the inimitable bond between him and his girl. Would his former actions dissolve that bond? What if . . .?

Fire ripped through his gut. He grabbed his stomach and squeezed his eyes shut. Pain pulsed through his torso and he fell onto the cushioned bench in front of him. His white mug hit the carpet with a thud. Pulling his legs up toward his mid-section, he took deep, slow, breaths.

On the ground, safe and sound, Meg texted Cody as the small plane taxied to the gate. *Are you still with Popsie?*

```
N. Ppl comin @ 9 and he wntd to lve
asap. I took off to get out of way.
```

The sting of their awkward goodbye that morning hung over her head. But the wedding also weighed heavy on her mind. She decided to press him. *Whatcha gonna do today?*

```
Boss called. Wants me in Charlotte for
the pre-race stuff tomorrow.
```

Oh no. *Are you working the whole day?*

After an extra-long pause, worries scurried into her mind. When his answer finally arrived, it didn't serve to ease them.

```
Only shooting candids, behind scenes.
Marty's @ hospital. They need me.
```

Before she could send a reply, he followed up again.

Don't worry re: wedding stuff. We're on
it.

In other words, Mama's on it. Deep breath.

Meg peered out the window as the plane eased into the
gate. She counted on her fingers and rehearsed in her head the
most important items on the list. Happily married Mama must
know something about weddings. Her marriage seemed almost
perfect. Meg's fingers actually twitched, longing to pull the
Bride magazine from her briefcase; but other matters needed to
take precedence now. She texted a quick thanks, stuffed the
phone in her bag, and rose to collect her things. Game on.

Meg squinted her eyes against the brightness of the day as
she exited the terminal at Cherry Capital Airport in Traverse
City, Michigan. Crisp, clean air filled her lungs and gave her a
shot of confidence. She could hold her own across the table
from any lawyer in Charlotte. Small town family at the lake?
Piece of cake.

She rolled her bright red carry-on, which supported a
matching shoulder bag further into the cool sunshine of northern
Michigan in the springtime. Searching for the car and driver
arranged by Mr. Vanderzee, she scanned the area for someone
holding a sign.

Amidst slow-moving SUVs and a few parked sedans, a well-kept vintage Chevy Malibu drove past and skidded to a halt with a loud screech of the tires. She watched as both doors simultaneously opened and two young women who looked about twenty stepped from the car. Meg stared at their precise sameness. Head to toe, their appearance matched in every way. Hairstyle, eye makeup, clothing, even pink toenail polish. As they drew near, she noticed their dark ponytails bobbed in exactly the same rhythm, left-right, left-right. They wore matching black flip-flops, skinny jeans, hot pink wrap tops and matching heart-shaped lockets on gold chains. Thin and tall, they reminded her of fireworks.

Large identical smiles beamed at Meg as they drew near. She noticed only their top teeth had been straightened. "You must be her!" said the one on the right.

The one on the left said, "Are you Megan Marks?"

Shame rolled up from her gut until it bloomed into a full hot blush. Busted for staring. Her jaw fell open as she looked around, hoping for a mistake. Families in sweatshirts toting piles of luggage stood in stark contrast to the neat and professional uptown look Meg sported. She stood before them, an embodiment of the proverbial red thumb. But they didn't seem to care.

"Yes. Sorry." She forced her business smile. "I'm Meg Marks. Pleased to meet you." She extended her hand and both twins gave her a big hug, at the same time.

"Welcome to Michigan!" they said together.

Girl on the left said, "I'm Jane."

Girl on the right said, "I'm Janell."

Meg couldn't stop herself from saying, "Really?"

"Yes." They answered together, smiles bigger than ever.

Meg set her jaw so she wouldn't be caught with her mouth gaping open again. She allowed herself a small smirk. "So, Mr. Vanderzee sent you then?"

Girl on the right said, "Oh, that's Granddad. Yup. We've been assigned to you for all your transportation needs while you're here. Cruisin' in the Malibu!"

They grabbed her luggage before she could turn around and found herself tucked into the backseat next to a giant pile of pink sweatshirts. An empty McDonald's bag lay on the floor with at least six tubes of lip-gloss.

A whoop and a call echoed from the front seat. "Buckle up. Here we go." Meg lurched into the pile of sweatshirts, scattering them across the backseat, as they peeled away from the curb, wheels squealing.

Heart pounding, eyes trying to focus, Meg pulled herself upright and slapped her seatbelt on as fast as she could. Only a lap belt. She searched the blurry airport falling behind them, and hoped there would be a car rental company near the cottage. Mr. Vanderzee had referred to this transportation as a "ride." What other discrepancies would she find when they reached the "cottage?"

"So Meg, where did you fly in from again?" Janell looked over her shoulder.

"Charleston. But I usually work out of Charlotte, North Carolina."

Janell said, "Wow. That's far."

Meg's eyebrows popped up for a moment. "It's not too bad, only about a two-hour flight. Have you visited the Carolinas before?"

Jane tilted her head to the side and gripped the steering wheel tightly. "Oh no, we don't travel too much."

"We're saving up for the big one!" Janell's eyes opened wide and glazed over as she stared off into space. "It's our biggest dream yet."

Jane said, "Yeah. We've been saving up for almost four years now and it's probably only going to be like . . ."

"Like one or two more years and we'll have enough. We're going on . . ."

Together, they finished the sentence, "an Alaskan Cruise."

Their voices sounded dreamy like a very cheesy travel commercial on TV. Only the twins were serious.

"Wow." Meg bit her bottom lip to keep a straight face.

Janell's eyes refocused on Meg. "Yeah. We love the Eskimos, so we decided that would be the best way to get up there and hang out in their lands and everything. We do lots of research and stuff to keep ourselves in the mood."

"In the mood?" Meg felt her eyes opening wider.

Jane fiddled with the radio. "You know, in the mood for Alaska. We're going to be ready when the time comes—we're 'into it' now and we want to stay 'into it' until we save enough money to get there."

Janell waved her hand in Meg's direction. "So, tell us about Charlotte. Would we like it there?"

"Well, it's still emerging. I live in the uptown area, close to everything in the city. I like to drive down to the beach on weekends if I can."

"You can drive to the beach?" Jane looked over her shoulder towards Meg. The car veered to the right at the same time.

"Janie!" Janell reached over and helped her straighten the car.

Meg looked at her hands. They ached from gripping a pink sweatshirt with all of her strength. She released the shirt and tried to smooth the wrinkles. "I didn't mean to distract you." Hoping to choose the name of the girl who was NOT driving, she said, "Janell, maybe you could tell me a little bit about this area."

"Well, you'll see a ton of cherry trees on this drive. Did you know cherries have zero cholesterol in them?"

Jane kept her eyes on the road this time. "Yeah, and did you also know there are only twenty countries in the world that have the right growing conditions for cherries? Russia is one of them."

With her eyes focused on the inside of the car, Meg averted her gaze from traffic and Jane's driving skills. "That's interesting."

"Jane knows all the cherry facts and stuff. She'd be better for the telling." She looked at Jane. "Wanna switch?"

"Sure, after we get through this light."

Meg watched the light turn green. The Malibu turned right and accelerated to the speed limit. A moment later Meg felt the cruise control engage.

Jane unhooked her seatbelt. "Ready?"

"OK, go!" Janell unhooked her seatbelt and slid across the bench seat.

Jane gripped the steering wheel and pulled herself toward the windshield and off the seat. Janell slid underneath her and grabbed the steering wheel on the left side, peeking her head around her sister. "Got it!"

Jane bounced onto the seat to the right of Janell and slid over to the passenger side. Both seatbelts clicked simultaneously and Jane turned to face Meg and Janell.

Meg's jaw gaped open again. "Y'all!"

"What?" Both voices sounded genuinely curious.

Gripping the edge of her seat, knuckles white, Meg stared out the window. Rising panic bubbled just beneath her skin. "How long did you say this drive is going to be?

Chapter Four

The Malibu lurched to a stop in the middle of nowhere.

Jane opened the door in a hurry and grabbed Meg's hand before she could protest. "C'mon! You have to see this."

Janell skipped in front of the car to join them. "A cherry orchard in bloom is the best thing about spring up here."

They led her into a sweeping panorama of trees and blossoms stretching over hills in neat rows to the horizon. Cherry blossoms sprinkled down around them on every side. Meg tilted her face up, enraptured by thousands of floating petals on a cool breeze.

Janell spoke over her left shoulder. "You lucked out. The blooms are late this year."

"Yeah. They're usually gone by now." Jane skipped past them down the long row of trees.

Janell took off at a run. "Race ya!"

Jane broke into a sprint and they disappeared over a hill, leaving Meg alone in the quiet orchard. A gentle wind tickled the trees, sending swaths of blossoms swirling to the ground, and scenting the air with sweet fragrant puffs. Marveling, Meg sealed the memory in her mind as the first natural scent she loved that smelled nothing like the sea. Where Popsie lived. He would never smell this orchard.

Blinking back tears, she looked down at her shoes in the grass. The strangest things brought near the reality of Popsie's looming death. A boat on a trailer, an older gentleman walking beside the road, the color blue. It didn't take much to trigger a visceral reaction from Meg, disrupting life for a few minutes. As soon as she could, she crammed the thoughts into the back of her mind and though the grief hurtling toward her remained constant, she somehow managed to reduce the blaring roar to a background hum.

She turned and meandered back the way she came. Craggy tree branches reached out to her and offered the passing comfort of life bursting free from stubborn, cranky wood. Hands behind her back, the sun shone warm on her shoulders as she strolled through this unfamiliar world. While beautiful, it accentuated the loneliness she dreaded but knew far too well.

Finally, she reached the place she had entered the orchard. The twins advanced toward her, arm in arm, smiles dazzling. The girl on the left wiped her brow and panted from running a wide circuit through the orchard. "What'd ya think?"

Her sister put her arm around Meg and pointed at her. "She loved it. Look at her face."

Desperate to remember the peace beneath the falling petals,

and loath to admit her melancholy to these happy girls, she merely smiled as they climbed into the car. As the Malibu screeched onto the two-lane highway, she stole a backward glance over her shoulder.

Meg fumbled with the metal key in her struggle to open her door at the "Call of the Loon Bed & Breakfast." She burst through the door, dropped her bags, and threw herself onto the bed.

Unnerved by the less-than-careful driving, stunned by the beauty of the orchards along the road, and exhausted from travel, Meg succumbed to fatigue. Twin voices ricocheted in her mind as she recalled the constant conversation propelled by endless cherry trivia and a genuine zest for life. They probably struggled to avoid the family "side-show" label, but Meg caught glimmers of their intellect and relished their warm welcome, however dangerous the ride.

Lying on her back, Meg examined the knots and swirls embedded in the bird's-eye maple panels covering the ceiling. The muscles in her back relaxed for the first time since she stepped off Gilda. Popsie and crew would be traveling south today. Regret loaded worry onto her already full plate. How did Popsie convince her to leave him? Her instincts told her to run home. Only her desire to honor Popsie's wishes kept her focused. She would finish this task, and fast.

A knock at the door ended her momentary repose. She popped up before she could think, heart pounding. Wiping her face with bare hands, she stood to face whatever stranger stood behind the door. Would it be one of the Vanderzees? She groaned at the butterflies attacking her stomach.

A muffled cry broke her swirling thoughts. "It's us! Can we come in?"

She closed her eyes, let out a sigh, and noted her heart rate heading back in the direction of normal. "Sure. C'mon in."

The twins burst through the door and the room brimmed over with their enthusiasm. "Hi, Meg. Guess what?"

"What?" Meg tried not to look exasperated. Starved for time alone, she needed to process and plan. Ten minutes had barely taken the edge off an already eventful day.

One twin–Jane?–jumped onto the bed and lay on her belly with knees bent and feet crossed behind her. "Uncle Kenneth's leaving—you have to go see him right now!"

The other twin wrung her hands and bounced up on her toes. "Can you come now? We need to get you up to the marina in Charlevoix right away!"

Meg's heart thumped into panic mode again. Her hands flew to her head. Someone else's bad planning turned into another emergency. "I knew something like this would happen."

She dropped her hands. "We have to leave right this minute? Really? And where are we supposed to go?"

Janell looked about to explode, still bouncing up and down. "Uncle Kenneth has to take his boat up to Mackinaw City. He was gonna leave tomorrow, but there's supposed to be bad weather."

Jane cut in. "Yeah. Maybe a storm out over Lake Michigan. If you want to interview him, we have to catch him before he leaves the marina, 'cuz he'll be gone the whole weekend."

"You're sure this is my only chance?"

Twin heads bobbed in unison.

Meg tore into her bag, searching for a suitable outfit. "I need five minutes to freshen up."

Jane rolled onto her back. "OK. Make sure you wear some kinda soft shoes or something. He's a little bit crazy about that dumb boat. You can't get on with heels."

Janell nodded, eyes big, face serious. "We've tried."

Meg swapped her linen suit for khaki's and a polo shirt. She could embrace a predicament like this—a man who loved his boat. She slipped her bare feet into topsiders. "Girls, I think I've got this one in the bag. Let's do it."

The drive to Charlevoix passed quickly. Trees lined the wide road, bumpy from asphalt patches. Driveways disappeared into the woods on either side, leaving very few homes visible. Longing for a latte to perk up her senses, Meg figured she would have to settle for pinching herself in this remote landscape.

She unbuckled and scooted up to lean against the front seat. "Is there a way for me to tell you guys apart? I hate that I have to guess when I call you by name."

"You can't tell us apart?" They spoke in unison.

That had to be a joke. "No. Y'all look exactly the same."

"No way," said one twin.

"Nah-uh," said the other twin. "I like the way you say 'y'all.' It's so cute."

Meg looked at one and then the other. "Seriously. How do I know who is who?"

The driving twin searched out her face in the rearview mirror. "I'm Jane. I have a freckle on the very tip of my nose. Janell's eyes are bigger and more round than mine."

Janell turned on the seat to look at Meg. "She also has a scar on the inside of her forearm. We call it the swoosh." She turned to Jane. "Show!"

Jane held up her left forearm and there was a light brown scar in the shape of a Nike swoosh.

Meg sat back in the seat. "Thank you. Jane has the freckle

and swoosh. Janell has big eyes. I can remember that. I think."

As soon as they entered the city proper, pink, purple and white flowers lined the curb on both sides of the street for several miles. Old homes with deep porches and brightly brimming flower boxes gave way to antique shops, real estate offices and an ancient Whippy Dip. The entire town screamed, "Visit me!"

Meg tried to absorb the tiny resort town all at once. "Where do we meet Kenneth?"

"Here." Both voices chimed.

The city marina anchored downtown Charlevoix. A wide rolling green, hardscaped with rock walls, fountains, and a band shell, connected the center of town to the water, half a block deep and two blocks wide. At the far side of the green, a maze of docks jutted into a small round lake, barely half-a-mile across. Architecturally unique homes lined the shore all the way around, most sporting elaborate boathouses.

Meg's hungry eyes scanned the scene before her. "This lake is tiny and those boats are huge. How can there be so many boats? Where is the outlet?"

The twins laughed together. Their laughter sounded like harmonized music—complementary but not identical. Jane tossed her ponytail around. "There's a channel that connects this lake to Lake Michigan. You must have missed the bridge we crossed, looking at my swoosh."

Janell pointed across the tiny lake. "On the other side of Round Lake, there's an opening into Lake Charlevoix, just over there. This harbor connects the two lakes."

After they parked, Meg stepped out and heard the familiar sound of sailboat rigging clanging against masts, a diesel motor revving, and the gentle lap of water against seawall. A fresh, clean scent replaced the old salty air for which she usually longed. Meg surprised herself by saying, "What a beautiful place."

Jane pointed toward a Bertram Sportfish in the middle of the second row of docks. "Do you see the third one on the right? That's Cutthroat. Uncle Kenneth's still here."

Meg leaned back into the car to grab her briefcase but found nothing there. A panicky, "forgot to study for today's test" kind of apprehension flashed in her chest. Ill-equipped and unrehearsed, Meg turned to face the opening round of her task.

Empty-handed, Meg neared the water and tried to remember the questions she planned for this moment. If today was her only chance to talk with Kenneth Vanderzee—she wanted to give him a fair shake.

As soon as she stepped onto the floating dock, tension in her back dissipated. Who would name his boat Cutthroat? She automatically jumped into the game she and Popsie always played when they saw an interesting boat name. First step: describe the owner based solely on how he named his boat. Step two: meet the owner and vote which guess landed closest to the mark.

Before she guessed about Kenneth Vanderzee, Meg spied him on his hands and knees, scrubbing the deck. The buzz cut, Marines t-shirt, and bulky biceps all pointed to an ex-military type. Sunlight glinted off shiny gray hairs salting an otherwise black head of hair. Despite his medium build and her vantage point from the dock above him, he intimidated her.

Meg stopped at the stern of *Cutthroat*. The odor of cleaning supplies hung like a cloud around the boat. She raised her voice over the scraping of a scrub brush. "Mr. Vanderzee? I'm Megan Marks. I believe you're expecting me."

Kenneth Vanderzee stood up and threw his brush into a sudsy bucket of water. "So you're the lawyer I've been waiting on, huh?"

"Yes, sir." She gestured toward the boat. "May I?"

He grabbed an elaborate tackle box, moved it aside and held out a hand to her as she approached the starboard side from a narrow dock. "Sure. Watch your step now."

She lightly gripped his hand and stepped aboard with grace and an ease known only by those used to being on the water. "Thank you."

"Nice shoes. Do you boat?"

"Yes, I do." She flashed him a jesting smile and looked around the aft deck as if she approved. State-of-the-art navigation, radar, and communications; impeccable upkeep, and enough fishing gear to keep ten guys busy for a week. "From the looks of things, you are addicted to fishing."

His face lit up and he cocked his head to the side. "I may have misjudged you. I was expecting a stuffy lawyer. You're not stuffy at all." He pulled a lure out of his box and handed it to her.

She laid it in her palm. About five inches long, the lure was painted like a green and yellow striped fish with bright pink at one end. Three double-pronged hooks hung from the bottom. "Muskie, huh?"

The look on his face told her she passed the test. He took the lure back, replaced it in the box, and gestured for her to sit in a deck chair. "I only have about twenty minutes before I need to bust outta here, so let's get down to business."

Meg settled into the chair. As she searched for the best way to start, Ken interrupted her thoughts.

"I don't know what Pop is giving away, but I'll take the boat—whatever it is. He always had a boat. That's all I want."

Startled by his candor, and appalled at his lack of emotion, Meg struggled to respond. "I . . . I'm not at liberty to reveal the assets of my client at this time."

Ken sat back in his chair with his arms folded across his chest. "I know there's a boat. We all live near the water. He taught us to love it. I wanted to get to you before the others and tell you I want the boat—or one of them if there's more than one."

Meg clenched her jaw so tight she felt pain shoot down her neck. When he finished speaking, she forced herself to release it so she could speak. "Mr. Vanderzee, your father wanted me to get to know each of you and base my decisions about his assets on that. I think maybe we should start over."

Ken looked at his watch. "OK, what do you want to know?"

Meg looked him in the eye. "Tell me a little bit about yourself. And then describe your father."

His cheeks puffed out and then he released his breath. "I'm a marine. Served in Desert Storm. Two tours. No PTSD. Now I rebuild engines in my own shop." He tilted his head back and closed his eyes. He spit each word from his mouth, pausing in between. "My father. Partial. Cowardly. Guilty. Gone." As he said the last word, he opened his eyes and shifted his gaze over her left shoulder.

"Guilty?"

"Forget I said anything. It's been a long time. I guess he

finally remembered us in his old age. Seems completely disingenuous. What's that about?"

"Honestly, I know less than you do. I haven't even met your father in person."

Ken's eyebrows arched high over his wide-open eyes. "Old man must be crazy."

Meg instinctively reached for the briefcase that was not there. She tried to cover by scratching an imaginary mosquito bite on her knee. "Quite the contrary. I have an affidavit signed by three physicians stating that he truly is of sound mind."

Ken leaned forward, resting his elbows on his knees. "Assuming that's all true. What's he done about the taxes? Is everything going into a trust so we can avoid probate? Are you helping him to shelter the *assets*? If you don't set this up right, you know the government will take everything anyway. The will doesn't even matter if it's not done right."

Meg faked a cough, covering her mouth with her hand to hide her true reaction. He thought he could teach her about taxes before she even decided to include him in the will? Meg thrust rash words into a mental garbage can before she spoke. "I can assure you we will do everything possible to ensure the inheritance is handled in a way which will provide the greatest benefit for everyone concerned."

Ken sat up. Speaking with zeal, his hands flew around in

wild gestures. "They want to take everything away from us so they can buy more votes for themselves. Every government is corrupt at some level. I hate government. Every new president marches in and ends up taking more of my money and more of my freedom. If I can cheat the government out of a dime, I'm going to do it—even if it costs me a dollar."

Meg stared at Kenneth, speechless. What provoked this outburst?

His face flushed an angry shade of red. "Our country was started because of governments who reached too far. The founding fathers set up our country to get away from governments like we have now. But taxation DESPITE representation is what we're stuck with."

Meg felt her eyes bugging out. Had she been in control of even one moment of this conversation? She started to speak, but he cut her off. Again.

Ken threw his hands into his lap. "I've gotten myself all worked up. I'm sorry. I've been working on some campaign planning for my Libertarian friends this week. It always gets me thinking about how this country started and how far we've been flung off track. You didn't come here for all that."

He could say that again. Meg needed to jump into the conversation. "It's fine. I was hoping I could ask you one last question before you go."

"Shoot."

"Tell me who you believe is most deserving of an inheritance from your father. And who is least deserving?"

"Least deserving—Ruby. No question." He paused to think for a moment; fist at his chin, index finger pointing to the corner of his eye. "Most deserving would probably be Joey. But he's dead."

Meg crinkled her brow. "Who's Joey?"

"My big brother. He died a long time ago."

This brash, artless man heaved the words at her. Meg couldn't stop her eyebrows from shooting up, nor her eyes from stretching wide open. Her words stumbled out. "I'm very sorry about your brother."

He nodded, glanced at his watch and stood. "I'm sorry little lady, but my time is up. I've got to get this bucket of fishing gear up to Mackinaw City today."

"Of course." Meg stood and looked around one last time. She crossed her arms. "Why Mackinaw City?"

Ken gestured toward the dock and offered her a hand. "It's a stopping point, that's all. Tomorrow I move her to Rogers City. My fishing buddies'll meet me and we'll take on supplies there for the North Channel trip—a dream vacation if you like to fish."

Meg stepped off the boat and turned to say goodbye. He

Jennifer Fromke | 69

already headed toward the cabin door. "Thank you Mr.
Vanderzee. I appreciate your time."

"Yup." Without looking back, he waved as he disappeared
into the cabin, leaving her alone on the dock with more
questions than answers.

Chapter Five

Thoroughly dismissed, Meg wandered in the general
direction of the car through East Park, adjacent to the marina.
Reeling from the interview run amok, she marveled at her
complete loss of control and lack of assertion throughout the
conversation. A bitter taste filled her mouth when the words
"man-handled" passed through her mind. Though she never
experienced anything like it on a physical level, she wondered if
this qualified as the same thing on a mental level.

She swiveled around and surveyed Round Lake once again.
Fascinating homes hemmed the lake in, and she wondered what
crazy family members might be lurking behind the manicured
lawns and extensive boat houses. Cutthroat eased out of her slip
and motored wake-less past the docks on her way to Lake
Michigan. At least Uncle Ken told the truth when he kicked her
off the boat. Apparently he did plan to leave.

She asked him two questions. How could she make a
decision about his inheritance based on only two questions?
Shadows appeared shorter than they should be, but the sun
infused a yellowy tone into the late afternoon light. Priding
herself on her uncanny ability to know the time without a watch,

Meg could not guess it here without the ocean or even a shred of personal confidence to buoy her. In fact, she imagined herself floating around like a buoy cut loose from its anchor.

From the corner of her eye, she spied her identical guides. They loped toward her wearing enormous smiles, one of them carrying a large white paper bag. The side of the building behind them advertised in giant letters, "Murdick's Famous Fudge," The sweet, warm aroma of chocolate engaged her nose and infused her spirits with a tiny speck of hope. As they approached, she said, "What's in the bag? Is it . . ?"

"Fudge!" All three laughed.

Jane said, "It's tradition. Murdick's Fudge is unparalleled."

Janell's ponytail bobbed non-stop. "Plus, they make homemade caramels—our favorite. Friday afternoon somebody always makes a fudge run. We'll go through the whole bag by Monday, no problem."

Jane hooked her arm through Meg's and pointed them in the direction of the car. "Usually we're so sick of sugar on Monday, we don't want any fudge the whole rest of the summer."

Meg sniffed the bag. "So, you kind of get a 'family fix' all at once, huh?"

Janell nodded. "How'd you like Uncle Ken?" She looked toward the docks. "Is he gone?"

"Yes, I just watched him go. I'm still a little bit shell-shocked from our conversation."

Jane handed the candy off to Janell. "Uh-oh. Did he try to get you to join the Libertarian Party?"

Janell took a whiff of the white bag, and moaned. "Did he give you one of his rants? We love to watch his face turn all red when he shouts about the government."

Giggles.

Meg bit her lip, and then threw out a question. "Is Ken married?"

Jane unlocked the car and they climbed in. "Oh, yeah. Aunt Jennifer is great. And quiet, compared to him. You'll meet her back at the cottage."

Janell pulled a box of fudge out of the bag and handed it to Meg with a tiny white knife. "Speaking of which, we better boogie. They're probably making the potato salad by now."

They hopped into the car and Meg dug into the fudge. Smooth, buttery chocolate enriched by toasty pecans melted on her tongue. "Mmm. It reminds me of the turtles we buy in Charleston."

"You buy turtles? Why?"

Meg chuckled. "A turtle is a pile of toasted pecans covered in caramel and then chocolate. They're to die for." She said it again. That careless phrase cut like a razor on her heart now.

Popsie's smiling face floated across her mind. What was she doing here? So far, failing. What if the others acted like Ken? What if this trip ended up in a bungled mess? She closed her eyes and drew a long, deep breath.

Jane pulled the Malibu onto Bridge Street and a clanging bell sounded, stopping traffic and indicating the bridge would be opening soon. She hit the steering wheel. "Shoot! We missed it by ten seconds. Now we're really going to be late for potato salad."

Willing herself to focus on the present, Meg dragged herself back into the conversation. "What's the potato salad for? Another tradition?"

"Yeah. We have a lot of traditions."

"I noticed."

Jane shifted the car into park and turned toward Meg. "We're going to be here awhile." Her eyes connected with her sister's. "Let's give her the schedule."

Janell twisted around in her seat to face Meg. "OK, so Friday afternoon the moms and girls make potato salad. It's always homemade, always the same recipe. We grill burgers for dinner over the fire pit." She reached into the backseat and felt around on the floor. A mischievous grin lit her face. "Wait 'til you see the grill. Uncle Jeff told us Grandfather made it when they were all in elementary school 'cuz he didn't want to spend the money on a real grill."

The bridge opened upwards ahead of them. Jane said, "Yeah. That thing's ancient. It's made from two bed rails wired to a couple of old refrigerator shelves—you know, the metal racks they used in old fashioned fridges? We lay the whole thing across the fire pit and the burgers actually taste awesome."

Janell held up the tube of lip-gloss she scavenged from the backseat floor. As she applied it, she spoke, causing her words to escape, half-formed. "So there's a campfire tonight—s'mores and talking 'til late." She capped the lip-gloss. "Saturday, we spend the whole day prepping for summer: dock goes in, boats and water toys get scrubbed down and put into the water. Sunday, we finish planting flowers and just hang out in the afternoon. Monday, we make the summer schedule: who's coming when. Then we pack up and leave."

Amusement tugged the corner of Meg's mouth into a half-smile. "It's always the same, every year?"

Two voices answered. "Exactly the same every year."

Meg examined the road ahead through the windshield. The tops of sailboat masts passed between the open bridge sections in single file. Cars lined up in front and behind the Malibu, locking up traffic past the marina and throughout the entire quaint shopping district.

Jane said, "The whole family always comes up on Memorial Day weekend, no matter what. We just wouldn't think about doing anything else."

"Except Uncle Ken." What was his deal? The twenty minutes she spent aboard Cutthroat managed to bleed every ounce of confidence from her well-trained mind.

Janell removed her hair tie, smoothed her hair back, and retied the ponytail. "Right. But technically, he was here. I think he came up yesterday and sorted out the Hobie Cat rigging for us. He always takes an early fishing trip up in the North Channel. Then he goes back again in August."

"We're in charge of the summer schedule at the cottage, so we know what everybody's doing the whole summer. Do you have any big plans for the summer?" Jane straightened as the bridge closed.

My father's dying and I'm getting married. I'm hoping the latter comes first. Meg stuffed her thoughts back into a mental closet to keep them locked away. "Not too much. Aside from recruiting new clients, I'm trying to start up a non-profit organization to help orphans find permanent homes." She felt her heart tug in the direction of the Southeast. She belonged there, not here. How could she choose to write a stranger's will over tending her sick father and planning her own wedding? Not to mention putting Orphan Advocates on hold. But remembering the pleading look in Popsie's eyes stopped the pity party.

"Orphans? Wow. That's amazing."

"How do you find them homes?"

Meg sat up straight, eager to explain the project so close to her heart. "We work with local adoption agencies and provide all the necessary legal services pro bono, to make good adoptions happen."

"Neat."

"You are so good, Meg."

"Well, I'm not so sure about that. I'm not even sure we'll be able to get the organization off the ground. I'm waiting to hear back from several large donors next week. Fund-raising is the hardest part."

Jane switched on the radio as the bridge closed and gates opened to allow traffic flow across the bridge again. The car edged forward. "Finally. Here we go."

Meg kicked off her shoes and tucked her feet under her on the seat. She wrestled with yesterday's decision, which landed her here. Tourists walked by, many carrying their own bags of fudge along with other purchases. Carefree expressions on the passing faces exaggerated the weight of Meg's concerns, adding pressure to the worries in her mind, and the possible hazards awaiting her arrival at the cottage.

The car pulled into a gravel driveway cut into the woods. It twisted through several "S" curves before branching off to the right and depositing them in a clearing. Meg felt her stomach lurch. She pressed a hand on her midsection to calm the nerves. This was it; no more bends in the road. Better pay attention.

Trampled, dead leaves lay on the damp ground in natural areas beneath tall, skinny trees, which sported tiny buds. They parked in an area carved out of the woods and lined with pea gravel.

The house looked like a 1920s or 30s era home with a deep wrap around porch and flower boxes under every upper window. Painted a dusty medium blue, the wooden siding and pointed gables gave it a regal but comfortable look. The home nestled under towering trees, and guarded an enormous, pristine lawn. The carpet-like green made a gentle descent to the lake, which sparkled in the afternoon sun. As she climbed from the car, Meg lifted a hand to shade her squinting eyes, bedazzled.

Jane and Janell led her past flats of ready-to-plant pink and purple blooms, up the drooping wooden steps of the side porch, and through a squeaky screen door. As they entered a large kitchen, the door slammed behind them, causing seven pairs of eyes to look up and fix themselves on Meg, who squirmed in silence.

The heat of the kitchen mixed with the heat of her blush

and caused Meg to sway momentarily. She grabbed the edge of the kitchen counter, satin-smooth wood, stained dark.

Seven women poised for work around a long table. Their eyes flitted amongst themselves, while their hands froze in place. Meg shifted her stance and crossed her arms. Her eyes flicked back and forth between the twins in awkward silence, waiting for them to throw her a lifeline. Were they going to introduce her or what?

Meg scanned the kitchen stretched out before her, much longer than it was wide. It must have spanned the entire width of the house. Bright white cabinets lining the walls appeared as if they had been painted and repainted many times over the years. At the far end stood an industrial size stove with at least three giant, bubbling pots on top. Steam billowed toward the white tin ceiling and into a small hood overhead. Between the stove and Meg, a blue painted, beat-up worktable occupied the vast space. Mounds of potato peels split it down the center. Blue and white metal pots and pans hung from a rack over the table.

"Hi!" Jane finally spoke. Her voice sounded an octave higher than usual. Why would she be nervous? Meg squelched the butterflies in her own stomach.

Jane placed an arm around Meg's shoulders, pulling her slightly forward. "This is Meg, everyone. Grandfather's lawyer." The bright room and hawk-like stares brought to mind an operating room with Meg naked on the table for all to see.

A low raspy voice muttered, "Party-crasher is more like it."
Meg's hot face went stone cold. Her arms dropped to her sides
and she garnered every remaining scrap of strength to keep her
mouth from falling open in disbelief. Did she hear that right?
Animosity she expected. Outright rudeness blasted her like a
cold bucket of seawater in the face.

"Mom!" The twins' voices pronounced it with three
syllables and heavy scolding.

"Oh, I'm kidding. Just trying to see what the little lawyer's
made of." A barrel shaped woman stood up, wiping her hands
on a kitchen towel. She strutted toward Meg and offered her a
rough hand. "Ruby Vanderzee-Marston."

Meg automatically shook her hand. "I'm Megan Marks. It's
a pleasure. Sorry to intrude on your weekend—this place is
beautiful."

The twins smiled at each other. Jane delivered a half-hug to
her mother. "She hasn't even seen it yet."

Ruby nodded toward Janell. "So the wonder twins haven't
shown you around?"

Immediately and in sync, the girls raised their hands in
front of them, fingers spread, in a gesture that seemed common
and often directed at their mother. "Mom! We hate that name!"

"I know girls, but you are twins and you are a wonder."

Ruby put her arm around Meg and ushered her further into the kitchen. "I'll take over from here. Meggie . . ." She paused and cleared her throat, making eye contact with one of the women at the table. ". . . Meg, let me introduce you around here."

She gestured toward the left side of the table. "First we have Amanda and next to her is Andrea. They're sisters, fourteen and sixteen, and they belong to Amy who's on the end, there." Amy waved and continued peeling the potato she held. All wore matching dark glossy hair with the same extreme bob haircuts. Each smiled and nodded as Ruby spoke their name. At first glance, the sisters did not appear to be alike except for the hair. Fingernails on the younger daughter flashed dark blue, matching heavy eye makeup, while a string of pearls circled the older girl's neck.

Ruby continued with her Vanna White moves, and gestured toward the woman standing across from Amy. "This is Jennifer, Ken's wife.

Jennifer's blond hair formed a neat bun at the nape of her neck. She held a chef's knife in her hand, a pile of diced potatoes on a cutting board in front of her. "Did you make it up to Charlevoix before he left?"

"Oh, yes. We caught him just in time. Thanks for the heads up on that one." Meg searched her docile face for personality clues. What kind of woman would marry a guy like Kenneth? A woman comfortable with a large knife in her hand.

Ruby interrupted her thoughts. "Next to Jennifer is her mother, Karen. She's the only one who can slice onions without crying, so we give her that job whenever she comes." Karen looked up from her pile of onions. A wide smile crossed her face. "Pleased to meet you, Meg."

Ruby walked over to the girl beside Karen, sitting nearest to Meg. She stood behind the chair and draped her flabby arms around the girl's neck. "And last, but not least, this is Martha, my oldest."

Poor Martha. She attempted to shake her mother away from her, but Ruby seemed to grip her more firmly than before until she stopped squirming. Only after another five or six seconds, did her mother finally release her.

Martha's face blushed as fiercely as Meg's face felt. The girl carried the exact same build as Ruby, resembling a wine cask with arms and legs. Her pretty face favored the twins, but the resemblance ended there. Ruby appeared to prefer her over the twins, but such distinction did not appear welcome.

The kitchen pulsed with heat and tension. Jennifer and Karen whispered something between them, but everyone else focused on their work. To Meg's relief, Jane scooted a chair toward her. She sat ramrod straight in the stiff, wooden chair as she looked across the room at the people whose future she held in her hands. What would she know about these people next week at this time? She forced her shoulders to relax and smiled. "I'm not much good in the kitchen, but I'd be happy to help. Is there something I can do?"

Ruby washed her hands at the sink. "We could probably make the potato salad in our sleep if we had to. We don't need the help. I'm on my way out the door, but maybe you could get started on your . . . whatever it is he wants you to do." She turned to the twins, a hard look in her eye. "Wonder Twins, meet me out front in a minute."

As they exited in silent compliance, a sudden urge to contend with this bully-mother rose up inside Meg. She pasted on an enormous and hopefully warm smile while reciting to herself the words Popsie taught her so long ago. Being nice to a bully is like punching them in the gut; unexpected and undeserved. Never bully a bully. She placed her hand on Ruby's arm as she drew near. "Thanks for the warm welcome, Ruby. You've been so kind. I hope we'll be able to sit down for a nice chat before the weekend is over."

Ruby opened her mouth to speak but nothing came out. Her face looked confused for an instant before she pulled it back into a grim and busy expression.

Meg's smile transformed from fake to natural.

Ruby bustled toward the door. On her way out, she called

over her shoulder, "See you tomorrow, everyone."

When the screen door slammed, Meg exhaled and slumped against the uncomfortable chair. She inspected the faces in the kitchen. Her gaze landed on Amy, staring at her from across the length of the table. The warmth in her eyes caused a wave of gratitude to relax the tension in her back.

Bolstered by the absence of Ruby, Meg launched into the spiel she prepared to deliver to the family, explaining her obligations and responsibilities to her client, their father or grandfather, Mr. Vanderzee.

When she finished her speech, Amanda—the fourteen-year-old with bad nail polish—asked, "So, is this, like, for just like, my mom and my aunt and uncles? Or are the rest of us maybe gonna, like, get something too?"

Meg could not stop a slow smile from sneaking across her face. She loved an honest question with no pretense. This might turn out to be a little bit fun after all.

Amy looked horrified. "Amanda!"

Amanda rolled her eyes and looked at her mother. "What? It's a fair question."

Amy covered her downturned face with her palm for a moment, probably hoping to cover her obvious deep red flush. Meg jumped in, trying to rescue everybody in the conversation. "Anyone related by birth or marriage to Mr. Vanderzee or his immediate children qualifies as a possible heir. However, it is not required that everyone should receive something. So, I would really like to get to know all of you, your stories and situations, and whatever else I need to know to make the best decisions concerning this inheritance."

Silence invaded the room and every mouth clamped shut. Why wouldn't anyone look her in the eye? Meg swiveled her head around, searching past the screen door for twin ponytails. Willing them to return.

She returned her glance to the women before her. "So, how long has the family owned this property?

Amy glanced around the room before answering. "Forget Ruby. I like this girl, so I'm talking." She crossed the room toward Meg and leaned against the table facing her. "Daddy bought the property before any of us came along. He and mother built their dream vacation house when we were still very small. I guess we've been coming up here ever since."

Meg tried to imagine Amy young and the only image she could conjure involved a small imp of a girl with a very dark, extreme bob haircut. "Tell me about your father."

"I still have this little girl mentality when I think about him." Amy stood and gathered several quart-sized plastic containers from below the sink, to Meg's left. In a frenzy, she spun like a tornado and Tupperware flew across the kitchen.

"Mouse!"

The room erupted into panic and mayhem. Women climbed onto chairs or busted out the door with shrieks. Martha and Meg scrutinized one another, two spots of calm in the chaotic kitchen. Martha moved step by careful step toward the corner where the trouble began. Meg stooped slowly to grab one of the abandoned plastic bowls, and handed it to Martha as she passed, stalking her prey.

Meg watched Martha's expert moves, cornering and capturing the mouse, as if she performed this task every day. A familiar knot tightened in her stomach. Meg's brain flicked back to the work ahead of her. So far, she averaged asking one question every three hours. Maybe she needed to approach her task like Martha—corner and capture. Based on her first day, nailing down the Vanderzees would be a lot like trying to capture water with her bare hands.

The twins led Meg along a path of sunken stones partly buried over the years and covered with moss. The path started at the back porch, crossed the back yard and entered a thicket of woods and enormous bushes. A tiny stone cabin appeared a few steps into the woods. Sheltered by tall pines, maples, and various saplings, it leaned toward the woods. The roof sagged and moss grew on the near side of the building, striking memories of an Underground Railroad school project.

Meg placed a hand over her heart. "Oh. How adorable! What is it?"

Janell reached the padlocked door first, swiping spider webs away with fern fronds she must have picked from the edge of the path. "We call it . . . the shed."

Jane rolled her eyes. "Oh, brother. Don't make fun, Janell."

Pink polish flashed as Janell rolled numbers to the correct combination and slid the lock open. Unlatching the door, they stepped into a damp, earth-scented room. As their eyes adjusted to the darkness, Jane found a string hanging from a single light bulb in the center of the room and pulled it, flooding the room and their wide-open pupils with light.

Meg scrunched her eyes closed and shivered. "Why is it so cold in here?"

"It always is. Weird, huh?" Janell crossed the dirt floor to the far side of the room, barely ten feet from the door, and started rummaging on shelves beneath what appeared to be an abandoned workbench. "I think I saw mouse traps under here last summer."

Jane headed toward an enormous deep freezer on the right wall, which dwarfed the refrigerator beside it. She opened it wide. "This is where we store all the potato salad. We make enough for the whole summer on Memorial Weekend."

"What's in the red bags?"

Jane grabbed one and tossed it to Meg. "Cherry pie. Well, it will be cherry pie when Aunt Jennifer gets done with it. Have you ever been cherry picking?"

Meg shook her head. Not too many orchards in the low country.

"That's my favorite time of year. When we were kids, Daddy used to drive his pickup truck into the orchard and Martha and Janell and I would stand in the back so we could reach the branches."

Janell spoke over her shoulder as she continued her search at the workbench. "Yeah. I think we usually got more cherries on our clothes than we ever managed to put in the baskets."

Jane pointed to the lowest freezer shelf. "Uncle Ken's fall hobby always ends up in here too. We have enough venison for burgers all summer—they're better than ground beef, for sure."

As Meg continued to survey the contents of the shed, something on the workbench caught her eye, and she wandered over toward the dusty mess. Amidst various certificates and award plaques, a framed newspaper article hung askew just above the scattered tools, pieces of wire, miscellaneous engine parts and other non-descript oddities. She reached out to dust off the article. "Who is this?"

Together, the twins cackled, "Grandfather." They looked at
each other and laughed. Jane continued searching for the
mousetraps. "He's younger there, but you should still recognize
him."

"I haven't met him, so I wouldn't . . ." She snatched the
frame off the wall to get a better look. Her insides turned to jelly
and a white-hot plane of shock sliced her soul in two as she
looked directly into a pair of familiar eyes.

Chapter Six

Her head throbbed and she gulped each breath. In a full out run, Meg zig-zagged up the driveway and veered right at the "Y" down the road. When she reached the inn, she tore around to the back of the house and collapsed facedown on a wicker couch. Situated under the covered porch on the walk-out patio, she buried her head in the crook of her arm and willed the burn in her lungs to eclipse the agony in her mind. But must and mildew from the couch cushion forced her up with a loud sneeze.

A foursome stared at her over steaming mugs, some with eyes wide, others exchanging looks full of assumptions. They sat upon carved wooden furniture just twenty feet away in a natural area beneath soaring pine trees. For what felt like the hundredth time that day, her face flooded hot with embarrassment. How many times could a person be mortified in a single day?

Leaving her dignity on the floor, Meg rose with the framed article clutched tight against her chest. She waved to the curious onlookers. "I'm sorry to interrupt your tea. I'm a little . . .

stressed." She shuffled away, employing all the strength she could muster to gather up the scattered pieces of her self-confidence. "So sorry."

She scrambled up the outside staircase, which led directly into her room. After she locked the door, she leaned against it as if she were trying to keep someone from bursting in behind her. Prying the article away from her chest, one look at the photo clinched her heart. She forced her eyes to focus on the words and read the yellowed news about the opening of a new golf and ski resort near Mancelona.

Her body slid to the floor by increments as she absorbed each new bite-size fact about the founding of Snow Cap Mountain, a major achievement in the life of Duke Vanderzee, aka Guy Marks, aka Popsie. As her fingers traced the familiar face in the photograph, a wellspring of tenderness erupted from somewhere inside. He looked good young.

After reading it a third time, she tossed the frame onto the bed and rose to pace the room. All the tenderness, which flooded her moments before, dissipated. Her mind kicked into gear and questions whirled.

She strode to the interior door, leading to the hallway. Why did Popsie hide his identity from her? She stalked towards the wall of windows and the exterior door. Why did he hide this family? Back toward the hallway. Did he intend to keep her a secret from them as well? Back to the windows. Why ask her to write this will? And how did she live with him all those years and not know about all the money?

Meg grabbed her suitcase and threw it onto the bed. She snatched up everything she brought and stuffed it into the bag. With every item jammed in, an uncomfortable angst escalated until it grew into a palpable knot in her stomach.

The man who saved her as a child, adopting her out of the foster system and an uncertain future, lied. Hurt pricked at her heart like a thousand tiny scalpels. She would not stick around for the rest of the charade. Her whole life had hinged on the trustworthiness of the man who swooped in to save her from unreliable parents. After a lifetime of learning to trust again, he chose to ruin everything in the last few weeks before his death.

With a flood of guilt, she remembered Popsie's health. Tears stung her eyes. She curled up on the bed, threw the covers over her head, and gave in to a deep-seated cry of solitary pain.

Minutes later, a gentle knock on the door roused Meg from her cocoon of solace. She turned and stared at the door for a moment. Sitting up, she rubbed her face in her hands a few times. She shook her hair out and moved to open the door. A large face with a beaming smile peered at her over a mug of steaming tea.

Opening the door wider, Meg could see the fifty-ish

innkeeper dressed in too-short khaki pants and an Easter sweater. "Hello."

"Hiyah. My name's Mrs. Dooley. I'm the innkeeper."

"Hi." She rubbed an eye. "You sound like an old Minnesotan I used to know."

She nodded her head at least four times per second. "Oh yah. I used to live there, you know. That's neat that you guessed it. Sorry I wasn't here at check-in. Didja get everything ya needed?"

"Yes, everything is lovely."

Mrs. Dooley offered an "I knew it, but had to ask" smile. She held out the mug and leaned closer, as if she meant to walk right in and wait for Meg to drink it. "It seemed like you were havin' kind of a rough day down there. I thought you might like some tea." The word "down" came out like "dough-n" tumbling out with all the other syllables. Her gaze scavenged across the room over Meg's shoulder.

Meg accepted the tea and before she could narrow the opening of the door to dismiss her, Mrs. Dooley's gaze locked onto something behind her. She looked to Meg with eyes wide. "Oh my! Are you plannin' to leave us already?"

That particular question at this particular moment stymied Meg. To buy time, she sipped the strong, cinnamon tea. Her mind wrestled between her anger at Popsie's betrayal and her sorrow at his impending loss. The tea wobbled in her trembling hand, overcome with the desire to run home and berate Popsie for not trusting her with the knowledge of his family. But a growing curiosity niggled at the back of her mind. If she chose to stay, she might learn something about her father, which he did not want her to know. Sugar. The tea needed lots of sugar.

"I'm not planning to leave. Why do you ask?" she conjured up the most innocent look she could, reaching back to the days in her youth when she had perfected the look with Popsie towering over her, hands on his hips.

Mrs. Dooley backpedaled, wringing her hands. "Oh, never mind. Great. There's sugar and cream over on the table if ya need it."

Her face projected a dire hope for more information as the door began to close. Her eager smile did not waver. "Is there anything else I can getcha?"

A time machine being out of the question, Meg tilted her head and decided to throw her a bone. "I hope I didn't disturb the other guests with my little outburst downstairs. I heard some stunning news and I wasn't quite myself. Please tell them I'm very sorry."

Eyes as round as a child's at Christmas, Mrs. Dooley nodded. "You betcha. No problem."

The door closed and Mrs. Dooley's steps clomped away

from the room. Meg chuckled and rolled her eyes, happy to provide enough fodder for at least a couple days' worth of gossip in the kitchen below.

She swiveled back to behold the mess on the bed. Pausing only for a moment, she swooped forward, yanked the suitcase off the bed, dumped the clothes out, and put the case under the bed, almost all in one smooth movement.

Meg reached for the framed article amidst the pile of clothes. She held it out before her and addressed the photo as if Popsie stood before her. "Why should I ever trust anything you say to me again? What else have you said? Or not said?"

Popsie's voice leaped out of her memory and before she could stop the thought, she sensed herself to be twelve years old again, standing on a fishing boat with a hook in her hand. Popsie removed it with ease and a gentle hand. "Do not fear pain. Fear the day you cannot feel pain."

The quote served as the perfect antidote to her refusal to fish again, but what if all the advice Popsie ever gave served only to manipulate her through the years? White knuckles gripped the picture frame. "I can't trust you now. So where does that leave me tomorrow?

The phone slid out of Meg's sweaty hand onto her lap. She snapped it up and pushed the speed dial button all in one motion.

Enough dawdling, time to get it over with. Confrontation always aroused her fight or flight instinct, usually manifesting itself with a fight, making her a better lawyer.

As the call connected, dread initiated a sudden wave of nausea; she pressed a hand to her stomach. The stuff of life played out very cut and dried with Popsie. Knowing where she stood with him at all times laid the foundation for her own black-and-white view of the world. This gray moment blinded her mind.

One ring . . . two rings . . . Maybe he's sleeping.

"Meggie!" Popsie's command of technology, especially caller ID, amused her every time.

Meg closed her eyes and forced the pleasantry out of her voice. "Popsie."

"Uh oh."

"Yeah, uh oh. Did you think I wouldn't find out . . . Mr. Vanderzee?"

He paused. "Hmm. You caught me quicker than I expected."

She paced the room, trying to make sense of it all. She squelched her desire to hang up and willed her fight to kick in. "I don't even know what to do with that. Who are you? I mean, c'mon!"

"Meg."

"Popsie, I just found out my father lived a secret life. I mean, you hardly told me anything about your life before me. You let me believe I occupied the best part of your life. Now I find out it was all round two, a rerun, leftovers. Am I so pathetic you worried I might stain your perfect past? Why did you shut them out? I could have had brothers and sisters." Her voice broke and tears spilled down her cheeks.

"Meg, I'm so sorry."

She sobbed. "Why didn't you tell me?"

Popsie waited until she quieted herself. "I'm going to start by telling you two very true things. Number one: I love you more than you will ever fathom. I will always love you as much as I possibly can. Number two: Everything I withheld from you was for your protection."

Meg peered into the trees outside the window. "That's it?"

"For now. When you fully believe those two things, we can talk more. Call me when you're ready."

"Wait! Why did you give me a different last name? Why are we Marks now?"

"Meggie, I want you to understand everything. It's why I sent you there, believe it or not. Stick to the plan. Pretend you don't know Mr. Vanderzee and do the job I hired you to do."

Before ending the call, she held the phone out in front of her and made a face at it.

"Cody."

"Hey, Megs. You OK?"

Trying to control her voice so as not to sound like a basket case, Meg switched to her Bluetooth and spewed the events of the day on Cody's sympathetic ear.

"Wow. That's huge."

She stared into the bathroom mirror. "Yeah. I think my name should probably be Megan Vanderzee. It's like I'm looking at the life I should have lived, and I wonder what went wrong."

"Wrong?"

A brush in hand, she attacked her long silky hair. "This place up here is idyllic. The family is addicted to tradition. No way Popsie decided to up and leave one day just for the fun of it. I hope it wasn't my fault."

"Hmm. So what now?"

She grabbed her makeup bag for a touch-up. "Well, I packed all my stuff and planned to leave. Then, raving mad, I called Popsie and he got all secretive and told me to stay put and stick to the plan."

"And you're a sucker for your father."

She uncapped black eyeliner. "I can't help it. Plus, I'm curious now."

"So'm I."

She leaned over the sink, close to the mirror. "He wouldn't lie to me for no reason. I want to find out what's going on. So far, his family . . . my family . . . well, my adopted family I never knew—they're pretty interesting."

"Do what you think you need to do. I'm holding things down here, so don't worry about anything."

She smudged the black across her eyelid. With dread, she asked the question lurking in the back of her mind. "So, what's your mother working on as far as wedding stuff goes?"

"She's handling the food and the minister."

One of several knots in her stomach loosened. Mama knew food. And church. Meg tried to mask her giant sigh of relief. "Great. They aren't calling you back to work tomorrow, are they? Surely there's a photographer somewhere who can cover NASCAR this weekend."

He cleared his throat. "There is and it's me. Don't worry, I can make phone calls in between shots. Give me some credit, I'm a professional."

"Of course you are. I'm just thinking about this wedding coming together and all of sudden I have family coming out of the woodwork up here and I'm kind of freaking out a little bit."

He must have been running his hands through his hair, like he always did. "Don't freak out. Trust me. Have I ever gone back on my word before?"

Finishing her eye makeup, she apprised herself in the mirror and dug into her bag for lipstick. "Of course not. I completely trust you. I just thought you had the whole week off work and would be able to focus on wedding stuff. I'm sure you'll get it done. I'm sorry I questioned you."

"It's coming quick now. By the way, I did have a couple questions about the list."

Meg checked her watch. "OK. I'm heading out in a few minutes. There's a cook-out. What's up?"

"Well, I talked to the guy at the cake place you wanted to use and he said we should have called him three months ago, at least. So I have to call around to some other places."

Meg looked at the ceiling, her hand slammed her forehead. "What? You can't take no for an answer. Did you tell him how much I love their cakes? And it doesn't have to be a formal wedding cake. Did you ask him about a smaller, special occasion cake?"

"No. I thought I we wanted a wedding cake."

Meg grabbed a sweater from the jumble of clothes she dumped on the floor. "We want a fabulous cake for our wedding. It doesn't have to be a wedding cake. Can you call them back, please?"

He huffed out a deep breath. "OK. I'll try again tomorrow."

She slipped her head into the sweater and started working on the sleeves. "Thanks, hon. To me, it's the most important piece. Did you get the caterer set?"

"Mama's on it."

"Oh yeah. Flowers?"

An edge creeped into his voice. "I'm working my way down the list, in order. I've got it covered."

She bit her bottom lip. "Sorry. I know it's a long list. Thank you."

"It is long, but you're welcome. Remember, it's my wedding too. I'll talk to you later."

"Bye." He clicked off before she finished speaking. Pursing her lips, she replayed the conversation, hoping she hadn't crossed a line.

Chapter Seven

Pounding fists on the door drew Meg out of a dead sleep. She rolled over to look at the clock: 6:45am. What now?

"Meg? Are you ready?" The unmistakable voices of the twins blasted through the door like a bullhorn.

The entire inn would be roused if they didn't stop soon. She lurched out of bed and opened the door, hair slightly mussed, but pajamas neat and uncrumpled, thanks to their silky texture. She waved them in. "Shh! What are you doing here?"

Two voices sang, "Do-nuts!" They held up a pink cake box, which undoubtedly contained piles of sugar sprinkled on wads of fried fat. Great.

Meg sat on the bed and ran her fingers through her hair. "Did you by chance pick up any multi-grain bagels while you were in town?"

The twins, in matching pale blue oxford shirts and khaki pants, looked at each other. "We always . . ."

"You always have donuts on Saturday, right?" Meg finished. She sighed and opened the pink box. At least she saw a couple powdered sugars staring up at her. She grabbed a donut, and then squinted until her tired eyes found the freckle on Jane's nose. Even if she didn't need to call them by name, she liked to know whom she was dealing with. "So, what's the plan? I still have a lot of questions I need to ask people."

Jane cocked her head. "What about last night? Did you have any good talks around the campfire?"

Meg huffed a laugh. "Not exactly. Ya'll talk and talk but I could hardly get a word in edgewise."

Janell crossed her arms over her chest. "Yeah, I guess you're right. It's been awhile since we were all together."

Jane set the box on the bed and helped herself to a chocolate-covered raised donut. "Mom's working, but she asked us to bring you over to Snow Cap this morning. She'll show you around and you can talk to her there. She's usually nicer when she's at work."

Janell swallowed and licked her lips. She swung herself around the post at the end of the bed. "That's for sure. We need to talk to her too. Our debit card didn't work this morning when we got the donuts. Good thing Uncle Jeffrey gave us some cash."

Meg brushed the powdered sugar off the front of her pajamas. She would believe in a nice moment with Ruby when she saw it. "OK. I'll be ready to go in about twenty minutes. Should I meet you out front?"

A drive lined with tall maples interspersed with flowering crab and blue spruce trees led them uphill and into the woods. Meg's eyes drank in the budding trees and marveled that she could experience spring in Michigan, hours after leaving hot, sticky summer temperatures in Charleston.

The narrow road curved as it climbed, revealing glimpses of a golf course tucked into the surrounding forest and carved into the little mountain. The woods opened up when they reached the heart of the resort.

Jane stopped the car in the middle of the road. "Ta da! This is it. What do you think?"

An alpine village appeared to have been plucked from the mountains in Switzerland and transplanted to the base of Snow Cap Mountain, northwest of Mancelona, Michigan. Meg leaned toward the window and looked up to see the summit. "Wow. I didn't know Michigan had hills this big."

The Malibu lurched forward and headed toward the main lodge building. Janell turned toward Meg. "Our mountains are just barely big enough to be called mountains, but the skiing's pretty good. Not that we've skied anywhere else." She proceeded to point out the ski shop, the pro shop, and various eateries hemming the edge of a large parking lot.

Jane pulled the car into a reserved parking place near the entrance. "Guess why it's called Snow Cap."

Meg groaned inside. "Tell me."

"Look at the top of the mountain. It's all sandy. The soil up here is super sandy everywhere, and since there aren't too many trees up at the top, when you squint your eyes, the sand kinda looks like snow up there. So Grandfather called it Snow Cap Mountain. That's the name of the mountain and the resort."

At the mention of Popsie, Meg's heart flopped for one huge beat. She wanted to forget about Popsie's involvement here so she could focus on her task and go home, but her heart, evidently, would not allow it. Raising her hand to her chest, Meg forced some cheer into her voice as they exited the car. "This place looks great. I wish I knew how to ski."

The twins slammed the car doors simultaneously and looked at her with matching shocked expressions. "You don't ski?"

"I grew up on a boat—not much snow on the ocean. I can water ski, though." That seemed to soften the blow of her ineptitude. She wasn't a total novelty. They climbed the steps to the entrance. "So, does your mom run this place all by herself?"

Janell held the door open. "She's in charge of everything—exactly how she likes it. But Grandfather makes all the big decisions. I don't know how it all works, but she has to go through an overseer and ask him stuff a couple times a year."

A wave of nausea roiled inside Meg. She grabbed her stomach and braced herself for more. It was one thing for Popsie to keep old relationships hidden from her; people he had written out of his life. But hiding his relationship with Ruby—a current, ongoing relationship—magnified the betrayal she felt. Trying not to shout, but failing to keep her surprise inside, Meg tilted her head. "She talks to your grandfather?"

The girls stared at her again. The moment dissolved with the appearance of Ruby walking toward them across the lobby. Crisply pressed khaki pants and a wrinkle-free, light green oxford shirt anchored Ruby to her resort, along with every other employee. A non-conformist pink silken scarf hid her chubby neck. She smiled a big fake smile, arms spread wide. "Welcome to Snow Cap Mountain. What do you think of our little hamlet, Meg?"

Meg turned her gaze upward and rotated, absorbing her surroundings. Huge timbers framed the inside of the lobby and knotty pine boards lined the floor, walls and vaulted ceiling. An enormous chandelier made from antlers resembled an upside-down leafless tree and hung in the center of the large room. Several cushioned rounds filled the space. They were probably filled with skiers buckling their boots in the winter. Windows lined the side of the lobby facing the mountain, interrupted by a giant stone fireplace rising two stories. Meg envisioned the view with four to five feet of snow on the ground and skiers flying down the hill toward the lodge and the long couches facing the windows.

Meg squashed her desire for a sarcastic response, and faced Ruby with an expression that might have occurred naturally in the event of an authentic welcome from Ruby. "It's the quintessential mountain lodge. I couldn't dream up anything more apropos. Will you show me around?"

"That's why you're here, isn't it?" Ruby turned to the twins. "They need help down at the tennis pro shop today."

"Mom?" Janell looked hopefully at Ruby.

"Not now. Get down to the tennis center."

Meg felt her mouth moving toward a frown and pressed her lips together to stop it. Watching this mother-daughter relationship left her with the impression that having no mother might be better than having one like Ruby. As real as the constant ache in her heart was for the mother she never knew, this woman elicited gratitude in Meg's heart for a life thus far devoid of a mother like that.

As the twins scurried off to do their mother's bidding, Ruby stalked away in the opposite direction. She cast a glance over her shoulder. "Are you coming?"

Meg shifted into motion and trotted to catch up with Ruby.

Time to start the interview. Take all you can, give nothing back. Sounding like something from a pirate movie, she chose to follow the advice anyway. "Tell me how the resort started. Did you purchase an existing company?"

"No. Duke bought the land and built the resort from the ground up. This is the main dining room. We use it for everyday resort dining and a few special occasions.

The view through another wall of two-story windows stopped Meg in her tracks. The ski hill extended up and away, covered with a slew of green textures and colors that drew the eye upward. Blue sky faded as golden rays of sunlight burst from behind the pinnacle, providing a spectacular view of the entire mountain. In a whisper, Meg let out a dumbfounded, "Wow."

Heaving a sigh, Ruby spun on the heel of her ugly brown pumps and clomped out of the room. "I'm taking you to the village next."

"Ruby, tell me about your father. What drew him into this business?"

Cobblestones replaced slate tiles on the floor of a long hallway. Bavarian facades on the wall gave way to a barbershop, a business center, and the resort gift shop. Emitting a half-laugh, Ruby shook her head. "He saw an opportunity and he capitalized on it. He's no genius."

"How long has he been out of the picture?"
Ruby spat her words at Meg. "He's not out of the picture.
Never has been."

Meg wrinkled her brow, trying to make sense of this. "I
thought . . ."

"Give it up, girlie. You're in way over your head. I don't
know what he was thinking, but I sure as heck don't need
another babysitter up here—or a baby, for that matter." Ruby
reached the end of the hall and pushed on a door, which opened
onto a sunny cobblestone square.

Meg followed Ruby outside and clutched at her elbow,
trying to approach her face to face. Ruby shook her off. "Tour's
over. I don't care what you do with his money. I'm not kissing
up to Duke and I'm not kissing up to you. Stay out of my way."
Ruby thrust a finger toward Meg before she trundled off, shoes
power clacking over uneven stones.

Meg scrutinized Ruby, who left the impression of an
armored vehicle wrecking everything in her path. Birds chirped
in argument from a nearby tree. A door slammed nearby and
Meg jumped. "Oh!" She wheeled around to see a short, apron-
clad man in his sixties struggling to secure a heavy door, opened
wide, but opposed by the wind. She moved toward him, hands
outstretched. "Let me help you, sir."

They fastened the door with an ancient hook anchored into

the stucco wall behind the door. The aroma of fresh baked goods wafted out of his shop and as Meg looked for the signage, he spoke. "Pasties & Pretzels. We're open now, thanks to you."

"Wonderful." She followed him into a small café, where newspapers and photographs lined the walls in a decoupage style. A hand painted wooden menu hung from chains over the counter. Breakfast pretzels, Lunch pretzels, Dinner pretzels. Pasties. Drinks. Meg smiled at the implicit trust required by the customer. No ingredient list, no disclaimers, no explanation. She rolled the word "pastie" over her tongue with a counter-intuitive "past . . . eee."

The man made his way behind the service counter. "How may I serve you this morning?"

"Well, I've never been here before, what's good?"

He tilted his head and looked her in the eye. "I've seen you before. You must be mistaken."

Startled, Meg shifted her gaze toward the stools affixed to the floor in a perfect row along the counter. Sparkly flecks winked at her from every other black tile and she dismissed the idea as fantasy on the older gentleman's part. People think all sorts of crazy things. "Maybe. I just need a little snack. Why don't you surprise me?"

"In that case, you must try the pasties. My mother's recipe."

Five minutes later, Meg bit into a piece of her past, long forgotten. The pastie consisted of beef and vegetables with potatoes in a savory sauce encapsulated with pastry. It tasted remarkably singular. She closed her eyes and wished for a memory to materialize. But nothing happened except for the sensation she had received a hug from the inside.

She swallowed and opened her eyes upon the proprietor. He flashed her an "I told you so" smile, turned, and disappeared into the back. Unprepared for sudden revelations from the past, Meg re-wrapped the pastie, left some bills on the counter and dashed out the door.

The tiny Bavarian-style village sprang into life as storefronts opened and tourists meandered through the cobblestone streets. Meg took in every detail, scouring the village for a hint of something familiar. Her senses reverberated with the taste of pastie on her tongue. So she'd eaten one before. Big deal. That didn't prove she ate it here. Meg dismissed the old man from her mind.

In search of the twins, Meg took stock of her situation. Day two and she felt her task slipping out of reach, like a dropped sheaf of papers on a windy day. Chance of finishing the job quickly and travelling back to Popsie on Wednesday: not good.

Just past eleven o'clock, Jane directed the Malibu into the crowded driveway at the cottage, but stopped short to avoid stacks of dock sections, metal posts, and people. The men of the family had gathered in full force, including several new arrivals since the previous night's bonfire. Most wore waders held up by suspenders. Others wore bathing suits, water shoes and looks of dread as they threw shifty glances toward what must be cold water.

The air temperature struggled to maintain itself around sixty degrees, which meant the water temperature probably hovered at least twenty degrees less. The men gathered under a huge maple tree whose tiny green leaves pushed out light brown seed packets. Every gust of wind sent 'helicopters' spinning through the air, raining around the group. The effect created a party atmosphere with a steady supply of confetti.

Jane parked the car on the edge of the gravel drive. "Oh look, they're putting the dock in already."

Having seen some of these men only by campfire light the previous night, Meg struggled to match names with faces. "Before we get out, tell me who the tall guy in the camouflage hat is."

Janell's hand froze above the door handle. "That's our cousin, Michael, Uncle Ken's son. But we call him 'Dude.' He's always grouchy, never talks to us and he wears black t-shirts and camo all the time."

"Yeah. We're pretty sure he hates us. His dad makes him come up here and usually all he does is clean his gun and listen to horrible music on his earphones. He didn't get here until late last night, so you haven't met him yet."

Meg rubbed her forehead with two fingers. She needed to write this down. Popsie failed to send a list of the extended family members. Did he even know about all of them? Surely somebody filled him in on family news. "Michael. Got it. And the bearded short guy is married to Amy, is that right?"

Jane turned off the engine and looked over her shoulder at Meg. "Yes, Uncle Walter. Don't get caught alone in a corner with him, he'll try to sell you insurance or something. And Brett, the big guy, is Michael's brother. He was in charge of the fire last night."

Janell opened the door and as she backed out of the car, she lowered her voice. "The cute blond is Aiden. He wasn't here last night either. He's Amanda and Andrea's brother and if we weren't cousins . . ."

"Janell! That's gross. He wouldn't look at us twice anyway. Remember what he said in 7th grade?"

"I know. Anyway, we like him."

"No we don't."

"Whatever."

Eyebrows raised, Meg pursed her lips to stop the smile creeping across her face. The twins disagreed on something—at last! "OK, so I know Uncle Jeffrey and Uncle Morty over on the left. Wait, Morty's your dad, right? Oh, and there's Martha too. So what does your dad do? He doesn't work at the resort, does he?"

"No!" They both laughed at the question.

"He owns a deli in Gaylord."

"Yeah, it's like a New York deli. Really good stuff."

Jane jangled the keys in her lap. "And it's a good business for him and stuff, but he really wants to move it."

"Why?"

"I dunno. I think there's more customers close to the highway or something."

Janell leaned back in the car. "Yeah, but he can't move it now anyway. Why are you guys talking about this? Are you going to sit in the car all day?"

Jane opened the door and hopped out. "C'mon, let's go. Have you ever watched a dock go in before?" She turned away from the car and waved. "Hey everyone, we're here!"

Cool air bathed Meg's face as her shoes crunched on gravel. The difference between salty ocean breezes and crisp clean lake air surprised her again, in a pleasing way. All conversation halted as she approached.

"Good morning, gentlemen! I'm told the dock is going in today." Meg smiled and prepared to take control of all interviews going forward.

Aiden stepped forward and introduced himself, taking her hand in both of his and kissing it. With a fake French accent, he said, "What a pleasure to meet you, Mademoiselle. I've heard so much about you already. All good, of course."

This guy needed a cold shower. Extricating her hand from his warm, soft embrace, Meg cleared her throat and addressed the group with her best syrupy smile. "The pleasure is all mine. However, my job requires me to spend some individual time with each of you, and I am looking forward to getting to know you better today. In the interest of 'getting this over with,' is anybody willing to go first?" Long pause.

A look of surprise spread across each face in the driveway, like a wave travels around a stadium, when Michael removed one of his ear buds and walked toward Meg saying, "If it gets me out of dock duty, I'll do it."

His negative work ethic stood out against the backdrop of a family who seemed to relish every annual task involved with opening the cottage. Plus, his attitude prevailed as the only one with disdain for tradition and family; he would either be interesting or a predictable, rebellious teenager. With briefcase and laptop at her side, Meg walked in the direction of the front yard. She looked over her shoulder at Michael. "Is that a horse shoe pit down by the water?"

Michael shrugged. The remainder of the group kicked up their banter again and soon Meg heard an organizing voice give orders. Michael followed in her shadow, loud, metal music leaking from his ear buds. For the first time, she observed her surroundings by daylight. The front porch of the house boasted black wicker furniture with bright red cushions and pillows. A close-clipped, wide lawn sloped down to the water; pairs of black Adirondack chairs dotted the green. It reminded her of a scene from a movie where tea was served on the lawn to people carrying parasols.

At the far side of the yard, near a thick hedge bordering the property, half-buried horseshoes lay scattered around a metal stake in a sand pit framed by rotting wooden boards. Like everything else up here, it appeared an ongoing game had been played for years and years, interrupted briefly by winter snows. Who played the previous game? Who won?

Hands shoved deep into his jeans pockets, Michael stared at the ground and waited for Meg to say something. Teenage boys were a pain in the neck. Cody sprang to mind. Had he acted like this? She tried to imagine Michael in the future, after he shed his attitude and decided to participate in the world around him. She reminded herself that she shouldn't feel intimidated, and willed her heartbeat to slow. "Would you like to play while we talk?"

Pointing to his ear he shot her a look that said he didn't hear her. Meg propped her briefcase up against an old locust tree. She approached Michael and pulled the ear buds out of his ears. "Can we turn it off for 20 minutes and play a couple games? Please?"

He shut down the iPod. Meg accepted his grunt as assent.

The metal horseshoes felt icy to the touch. Meg hoped this game would loosen Michael's tongue. And make him less rude. But her aspirations for a worthwhile interview drooped when she saw the extreme ambivalence on his face. Taking a deep breath, she handed him two horseshoes. "You throw first."

He took the shoes from her and tossed one after the other, glancing only a second to see where they landed. Stuffing his hands into his pockets again, he turned away from Meg and the game to watch the others carrying dock pieces down toward the water.

The cold metal clutched in both hands, Meg prepared to throw her first shoe. "Tell me what you know about your grandfather."

Meg caught him rolling his eyes in her peripheral vision. As her shoe took flight, he said, "That's a joke. Pretty much nothing."

The shoe fell wide of the pit. "Well, tell me any scrap you

do know."

"Pfft. He started Snow Cap. He left and doesn't call. Dad says he's a coward. That's it."

Taking aim with her second shoe, she tried to focus on a good throw to avoid embarrassing herself. "Why did he leave, anyway?"

Michael scraped together a pile of leaves with his foot. "Who knows? All I know is he built this place and he loved it, and now we all have to take care of it 'cuz he doesn't come anymore."

Meg let her second shoe fly and turned to face him. "OK, so are you the only one who hates coming up here? It seems like everyone loves it here and can't wait to do the same thing together year after year."

They walked toward the far pit to retrieve the shoes. Meg's second shot beat one of Michael's. "More like they're afraid to do anything different to the place. You know, bad luck and stuff."

Grabbing the horseshoes, Michael handed her two and threw his horseshoe at the metal post, taking an extra three seconds to aim this time. Was he starting to care just a little bit? Probably not. "What do you mean, 'bad luck'? Is your family superstitious?"

A snide half-laugh burst through the rock wall of indolent teenage boy standing before her. A genuine reaction. Better pay attention.

"Yeah. Way superstitious."

Meg threw her shoes, forgetting to concentrate. "That's why they do things the exact same way every year?"

"Well, one year I guess they did their own things, not everybody came up here, and stuff didn't get done and something really bad happened."

"What was it?"

They walked back toward their horseshoes. "I don't know. I wasn't born yet."

Meg's shoes lay far outside the pit. She looked at Michael's face, long curls covering his eyes. "I'm a pretty bad horseshoe player, aren't I?"

Peeping at her through his dangling locks, Michael agreed. "That's supposed to be unlucky too. It's so stupid."

Meg bent to grab the horseshoes again. "So you think superstitions and traditions are stupid."

"Yeah."

"Why?"

He held up his horseshoe and took his time aiming at the far stake. "Traditions are like prison. You get stuck in them and then you can't get out."

Metal clanked on metal. The sound surprised Meg and she whirled around. "You got a ringer! Great job!"

"Whatever. Are we done here?"

Holding a horseshoe in each hand, Meg faced him. "Tell me who should get the best inheritance from Mr. Vanderzee."

"Me." The earbuds emerged from a pocket somewhere and Meg knew the interview was over.

Perfect. Meg's hands fell to her sides, the heavy metal weighing down her shoulders.

Whoever invented wicker furniture should be punished. Never failing, it looked more comfortable than it felt, every time. Meg shifted in the chair as she typed notes from Michael's interview. She caught sparkling glimpses of the lake between budding trees at the shoreline. What looked like a beautiful summer day actually stung her skin with a chill which began in her sandal-clad feet, crept up her legs and proved to her uncomprehending eyes that Michigan spring fully intended to keep summer waiting.

Voices rang through the air. "Next one!" Two men carried a section of dock toward the water like a stretcher. Hammers struck wooden dock sections, seating them in place on metal frames. "Yow! Every year, more splinters." Ruby's husband, Morty picked at his hand and shook it out.

A tall gangly man lumbered past the front porch, crossing her line of vision. Uncle Jeffrey's shoulders hunched forward, as if he labored under a heavy pack, each step thumped like a heavy statement on the softening, moist ground.

Setting her work aside, Meg moved to the steps. "Jeffrey, isn't it?"

He grunted assent, head down, and continued his pace around the side of the house. Meg rolled her eyes. People should speak with words. They were easier to understand than grunts.

Not put off by his gruffness, Meg followed him. "Mind if I tag along?"

No answer reached her ears, and when she reached the corner of the house, he was gone. Stepping it up, Meg jogged to the back corner and almost tripped over the twins, who bent over a flowerbed, bordering the back of the house.

Giggling, twin voices overlapped each other. "Meg!" and "What're you doing?"

She halted and looked across the backyard to the parking area. "Where did he go?"

The twins looked at each other and then toward the back shed. "Who? Uncle Jeffrey? Why?"

Meg walked in a circle, eyeing the girls. "I'm trying to ask him some questions and he walked away from me like I was invisible."

Jane knelt over the bed and with bright pink, gloved hands, gathered dead leaves into a pile. "He does that to us too. He doesn't really like anybody."

Janell bent and scooped weeds into a garbage bag. "Yeah. He's been like that since Aunt Anne left him. His kids hate him and we never see them anymore."

Jane twisted to look Meg in the face. "He works for Mom. Did she tell you? He's in charge of the grounds. The one thing he seems to like is being outside. Even in the rain."

Janell stood with most of her weight on one foot. "Yeah. He's always out in the rain. He looks spooky sometimes, tramping around in a huge raincoat with the hood up—kinda like the grim reaper or something."

Meg laughed. Drama. "So do you know which way he went?"

They pointed toward the stone shed. "Try back there."

Sighting the shed through the trees reminded her of Popsie's huge lie she discovered there only yesterday . . . and renewed a pang of hurt. Why didn't he trust her with his family? Who kept secrets like this? She trudged into the woods.

A loud crack split the air and squashed her questions as she rounded the corner of the shed. Uncle Jeffrey stood before a giant stump, a sturdy ax in his hands, split wood lying where it fell on the ground. Maybe the grim reaper reference wasn't all drama.

Meg approached, but kept her distance. "Jeffrey, could we talk for a few minutes?"

Heaving the axe high in the air, he brought it down with a grunt and another loud split. "Go ahead."

Great. Another man of few words. Meg grabbed an old metal chair sitting in the shadow of the shed and pulled it out into the sunshine, a safe distance from the stump where Jeffrey mutilated the logs. "Tell me about your father."

Jeffrey looked at her, shook his head and grabbed the split logs with gloved hands. At the edge of the clearing and between two trees, stood the remains of a large woodpile, presumably from last year. More likely, from every year since the cottage had been built. Jeffrey stacked the wood, shifting it until everything was square. Two split logs at a time, he methodically built a neat stack of firewood. "He's smart. Cunning. Cowardly."

Meg felt the cold metal of the chair through her jeans. How could she draw this guy out? What would make him talk? "Are you like him?"

Jeffrey looked up, eyes wide. "I'm not. I put down roots and stay true to them. I work hard. I'm proud of who I am, even if nobody likes me. I email my kids every day to remind them who they are. And I tell them I'll be around if they ever change their minds about me. My father and I are not alike in any way. He left." The axe swung high in the air again.

Meg leaned back in the chair and examined her hands. She felt Jeffrey's words in her soul. Left by her mother before the ago of two, abandonment rankled her to the core and made her a good advocate for orphans. The "O" word left a pit in her stomach, recalled snapshot memories from foster care, and almost every time, caused her heart to thunk hard in her chest.

Cold from the chair seeped through to her bones. Jeffrey's life mirrored her own. A dead mother and a father who left versus a dead father and a mother who left. Except Popsie left his own kids and then went on to save her. Why? He would never abandon her, would he?

The rhythm of the axe, the splitting, and the stacking soothed Meg's nerves and numbed her thoughts. Distant voices coming from the lake side of the house broke her reverie. She had to ask it. "So tell me who deserves the most from your father?"

Jeffrey paused, the axe in midair. Regathering strength, he swung down hard. The log split, each piece flying in opposite directions from the force of the blow. The axe head stuck in the stump, Jeffrey's hand still gripped the end of the shaft. "My kids. Ruby's kids. All the grandkids. Skip a generation, maybe that will teach us." He circled around the stump, yanked the blade out, and walked off into the woods, axe in hand.

Meg wrinkled her forehead and stared into the woods after Jeffrey until her phone beeped. The text message blocked the sender and read: MEET ME AT YOUR B&B. COME ALONE.

Chapter Eight

Visions from suspense movies danced in Meg's imagination as she digested the text message. Would there be a serial killer waiting for her? Had the Vanderzee family hired a hit man? Warning bells rang.

With a shake of her head, she followed her curiosity up the driveway toward "Call of the Loon." Surely the "loon" referenced a bird. Surely. Unexpected doubts fought against her usual "be nice" attitude.

As she entered the lobby, a woman conforming to Snow Cap company attire threaded her arm through Meg's and steered her back out the front door, and around the house on a grassy path meandering amidst extensive flower beds. Meg struggled to shake herself free, but her captor offered only a smile and a firm grip. Confused, Meg turned to view the kidnapper. In her younger days, she could have been a supermodel. Tall and thin, beautiful, and Meg noticed again, very tall.

They weaved their way past a stone-rimmed pond, beds full of perennials waiting their turn to bloom, and a fenced-in swimming pool. The woman clutched her arm and nearly dragged her into the woods at the back of the property. Shocked that her worst imaginations might actually be realized here, Meg wracked her brain for a way to escape. She remembered a news reporter from a program years ago saying something like, "If the perpetrator can get you to an isolated area, the chances of authorities catching him drop dramatically." This sent a shiver up her spine as she searched the ground for a possible weapon.

Then just as suddenly as it began, the escapade screeched to a stop. Meg found herself standing at a pair of Adirondack chairs tucked into a small clearing beside a flowing creek.

The tall woman released Meg's arm and stood back with her arms out to the side. "At last, we meet."

The familiar low timbre of her kind voice sent shock waves through Meg's brain. She held her hand up, pointing. "You're . . ."

"Sophie. I knew you'd recognize my voice, so I didn't call. You don't mind a surprise now and then, do you?"

Relaxing, Meg drank in the appearance of this woman she spoke with often but never laid eyes on until today. Although her clothing did conform to Ruby's idea of a uniform, she wore wide-legged ankle pants and an oxford made from fine-gauged cotton. A Pashmina, jewelry, and what looked like expensive boots served as accessories, elevating her style beyond every other employee at Snow Cap.

Meg drank in her scent. Musky with a touch of rose. "A surprise every now and then would be fine. So far this entire weekend has been nothing but surprises. What's with all the stealth?"

Sophie tweaked her sassy, graying coif and held her hand out to Meg. "I'm so sorry about that. Let's start the weekend over. I'm Sophie Wilcox, pleased to meet you."

One of the knots in Meg's stomach released. She smiled. "Meg Marks. And I can't believe I'm finally meeting Popsie's 'go to girl' in person! Speaking of which . . . Did Mr. Vanderzee send you to make excuses for him?"

"No excuses. But he did ask me to explain the situation a little bit. He planned for us to meet all along, but he thought it would occur either after his death or at least after you finished the will."

Meg shook her head. "He does always hope for the best. You have to love that about him."

Sophie motioned Meg toward the chairs. "Shall we sit? I ordered some tea. Meanwhile, let's start at the beginning. Your . . . father . . . "

"Popsie."

"Yes. Popsie hired me over twenty years ago to handle his business interests here in Northern Michigan."

"When he moved away."

Sophie nodded. "Yes."

Questions flew around Meg's mind faster than she could think. Crinkling her brow, she pressed her lips together. "Why did he move away in the first place?"

"You will get that answer, but we need to start elsewhere."

Meg tucked one leg under the other and faced Sophie directly. "OK. No offense, but I have a million questions right now."

"Of course you do. I'll do the best I can to fill in the gaps, but some things need to come first."

Ignoring her words, Meg gripped the rough edge of the chair and picked at the peeling paint. "I don't know who my father really is, which means I don't know who I really am."

Sophie took a breath to speak, but Meg continued. "Why would he orchestrate such an elaborate farce? And why did he hide this family from me? Is he ashamed of me?"

Sophie pulled an accordion-style file from behind her chair and set it on the ground between them. "I think we should start with these records. I'm acting CFO at Snow Cap. Though most employees think I'm a consultant working for Ruby, she actually works for me. I report to your . . . Popsie."

Placing a hand on the dusty file, Meg said, "So what is all this stuff?"

"I made some copies my first week on the job, before Ruby

destroyed the originals. To my knowledge, she does not know they exist."

"So they're financial records from the ski lodge?"

"Actually, they are financial records from Snow Cap's Development Company." She flicked her eyes up at Meg.

"There's a development company?"

Sophie opened the file and took out a thin folder from the front. "I expected nothing less from Ruby. She gave you a tour of the resort, but neglected to even mention the land development."

Snapping twigs caused Meg to swivel her head around. Mrs. Dooley tramped down the trail between the creek and the house, toting a large woven picnic basket. "Well now, how do you like our little lookout here in the woods? I hope this snack will be okay for you. There's no cake. I barely had time to bake some cookies. I could have done more if I knew ahead of time." She set the basket on the ground in front of them and clasped her hands in front of her. Her eyes searched out the treetops thoughtfully. "I think I'll start keeping some extra cake on hand—maybe in the freezer—just in case." Her head nodded once, punctuating her decision with certainty. "You two enjoy now." And just as quickly as she had come, she disappeared into the woods.

As soon as she was gone, Meg mouthed to Sophie, "No cake?" Grateful for the release, they shared a conspiratorial smile.

But a sudden serious tone descended between them when they remembered their purpose.

"So why doesn't Ruby like me? Amy insinuated that Ruby lambasted the whole family before I got here and told them to keep quiet. Are they hiding something?"

"If you knew Ruby, you'd assume she's hiding something. Your . . ." she corrected herself. "Popsie hired me as his watchdog for all the holdings he owns and operates here in Michigan, so he could enjoy being with you."

Meg picked at a thread on the tablecloth. "I heard him speaking to you on the phone all those years, and I never really listened. I knew you talked about business, but how could I not know it was a family business? Honestly, I'm not sure I know anything about Popsie anymore."

Sophie's face smiled a tight-lipped smile everybody wears when they feel sorry for you. "He loves you more than anything—you have to know that."

"He told you to say that, right?"

"He did tell me to say it, but I've known it's true since the day he picked you up. He's fairly obvious."

Meg tried to stop the small smile, which lifted the corners of her mouth. Popsie would never be accused of containing his emotions. He shouted from the mountaintops (or at least from the flying bridge) what he felt and almost never apologized for his opinions. "Did he ever tell you about the time my tutor complained about my history studies when I . . . ," she made quotations with her fingers in the air. 'Refused to write when so directed?'"

"What did he do?"

Meg sat back in her chair and stared at the leaves undulating in the breeze high over her head as she remembered the scene from seventh grade. "He demanded to see the history book. After looking through it, he told Mr. Funditeen, 'This is what I think of the material you are teaching my daughter.' And he threw it over the side of the boat into the water. Then he said, 'And would you like to know what I think of you, Mr. Funditeen?' You know that look he has, with his hands behind his back and he stands on his tippy-toes?"

Sophie nodded repeatedly, placing a hand over her mouth.

"I never saw a tall man like Mr. Funditeen run so fast. He rushed out the door and onto the dock in about three seconds. Never looked back, didn't even clear out his stateroom. The next morning, Popsie told me, 'I'm hiring a governess. It seemed to work for most of those English people back in the 19th century, and I'm sure it will work for you.'"

Laughing, the two women settled into a quiet reverie as they drank their tea and nibbled on the last-minute cookies. Moments later, Sophie started packing her things to go. She slipped the folder she had removed from the file into her brief case. "He asked me to leave you with these documents as a start."

"But wait! I still have so many questions. Let me ask you just one more thing before you go." She grasped Sophie's arm.

"You've been wise to keep your connection to Popsie a secret from the family. Ruby is less than fond of me, since I represent her father's interests. The family knows nothing about Megan Marks. Or Guy Marks. They only know Duke Vanderzee. To preserve that, you should not be seen with me." She removed Meg's hand from her arm and squeezed it. "Look at those documents. Call me. I'll do whatever I can to help."

A business card had been pressed into her palm. Meg stared at the green swirls on the card, impressed by Sophie's stealth. Still seated, she looked up to see the heels of Sophie's boots fluttering down the wooded path, each step falling softly like leaves on grass.

The creek water babbled, filling her ears and numbing her mind. The empty woods pressed in on Meg in Sophie's absence.

She leaned back into the cold, hard chair and stared at the embossed, four-color business card in her hand.

> Sophie Poppingraff
> Snow Cap Mountain Resort
> Chief Financial Officer
> 231-555-4242

The file stashed safely under the bed, Meg sat down before a blank sheet of paper. Time to make a family tree. She drew the tree she had always made. Popsie at the bottom, a long vertical line to the top of the page, and Meg's name above it all. In her past, the sparseness of the tree gave her lots of time to embellish it by drawing an actual tree around the diagram. Sometimes an apple tree, other times a giant live oak or a flowering crepe myrtle.

Today, she drew a line through Popsie's name and replaced it with Duke Vanderzee. She stared at the name, separated from hers by a long thin line. Was her name even right? If his name was Vanderzee, who was Megan Marks aside from the only person she knew with that last name. Learning Popsie's real name thinned her connection to him. She fought the urge to erase the line connecting them on paper. The distance between the two names on the page applied itself to the physical distance between them. Meg's heart ached from the pain of knowing Popsie had other children to love. She scrambled to stop the expanse opening between them as she learned about this family.

Powerless to stop the avalanche of new information hurtling her way, she strove to organize it, to grasp what change life might pummel her with next. The family tree grew before her eyes.

She recorded Popsie's children first, starting with Ruby, married to Morty, (Jewish deli owner). She decided to write tiny notes beside the names to keep everyone straight. She drew lines to each of their three daughters, Martha, Jane, and Janell.

Kenneth married Jennifer and had two sons, Brett and Michael. She penciled (horseshoes) beside Michael's name and (Libertarian) beside Ken's.

Jeffrey (wife Anne, left, find out her name), and (find out how many kids).

Amy married Uncle Walter (beard, Insurance). Her son Aiden (guitar) and daughters Amanda and Andrea (dark bobs).

She wrote Rachel's name beside Duke. (what year did she die?) Off to the side, she wrote Sophie, but drew no lines. She circled the name and added several question marks. Drawn to her own name at the top of the page, Meg noted the single line connecting her to a person. Everyone else on the diagram belonged to multiple names. Her empty heart thunked in her chest and she wrote Cody's name beside her own, connecting them with a dotted line. Though no one would see the difference, her heart lightened at the thought of her future. She fought off a desire to draw Cody's family tree and focused on the one before her.

Satisfied that everything she knew stared back at her from the paper, she worked to memorize what she saw. She inhaled a deep breath and released it with a loud huff. Popsie robbed her of more than eight cousins, maybe ten or twelve. How many kids did Jeffrey have? Popsie probably didn't even know. Before her thoughts tumbled further into the downward spiral, hunger twisted her stomach and drove her out the door.

Meg headed back to the cottage for lunch, which apparently operated like a twenty-four hour smorgasbord every day. She carried her plate outside, laden with potato salad among other things, and noticed Martha sitting alone on one of the Adirondack chairs.

"May I join you?"

Swallowing, Martha smiled. "Sure. Yeah. Sit down."

Settling into the familiar chair, Meg looked toward the lake. How come everyone has the same kind of chairs up here? "What a view. You picked the best spot in the yard for lunch."

"Well, actually Grandfather did that. He placed these chairs strategically around the yard, capturing all the best views. This one's my favorite because it's closest to the water and the sound of the waves lapping up can sometimes drown out noise from the house."

"Hmm." Meg abandoned herself to the curiosity pounding her consciousness. Desperation steadily built inside her to the point her knuckles nearly glowed white, curled around the plastic fork in her hand. Throwing professional decorum out the window, she avoided the proper questions she needed to ask for the will and instead asked the question she wanted to know for herself. "What else do you know about your grandfather?"

Martha tilted her head back against the chair, gazing toward the infinite blue sky. "He kind of owns everything we have. The cottage, the ski lodge, the other stuff. And he doesn't talk to anybody anymore. Nobody really likes him, especially my mom. I never met him, though."

Meg struggled to extinguish any defensive notes from her voice. "Why doesn't she like him? Is it because he left?" She stole a furtive glance at Martha, hoping for a clue.

Martha's face clouded over. "I don't know. It's not like she talks about him very much—she never does. But I think he made her mad before he left. Then he left and that made her madder. She likes being mad, though, so it all works out."

Sarcasm hung in the air between them, ugly and poignant. Meg crunched a carrot. A test formed on her tongue. "Whatever happened to your grandmother? Have you met her?"

"Oh no. She died way before I was born. Mom said she had a weak constitution, but Grandfather never believed it."

Meg finished her potato salad, savoring the confirmed truth that Popsie's wife died years ago. She twisted in her seat. "I'm asking everyone this question: who do you think deserves an inheritance from your grandfather the most? And who deserves it the least?"

Martha leaned over, placing her plate on the ground. She crossed her arms over her chest, and stared out at the lake, taking her time. A gust of wind blew maple seed packets down around them and a hint of warmth from the sun filtered through the clear air. In a low voice, Martha began. "I would like to say Mom deserves it because that would mean I might get something from it at some point too. I would also like to say that Michael should get nothing, because he's a loner and never helps out around here. But what I think the truth is—"

"There you are!" and "Here you are!" The twins burst onto the scene sharing a bag of potato chips. Each perched herself on an arm of Martha's chair.

Meg watched as Martha's face closed, like a curtain drawing over her soul. What words had she just swallowed?

The twins managed to interrupt her thoughts as well as conversation. Their brows wrinkled in sync. "Guess what?"

Martha sighed. "What's up?"

Speaking together, they said, "Our identity's been stolen!"

Meg bit her lips and looked from one to the other. "What happened?"

Jane sniffled. "We lost it all. I mean all."

Janell twisted her ponytail. "They took the Alaska money. We've been saving for so long and now we'll never get to go."

Lips quivering, Jane said, "We saved $3,473. We were so close. We would have been ready next April."

Martha rose and faced the twins, hands raised, palms out. "OK. We're going to calm down first. I'm sure the bank has procedures for this sort of thing. We'll start there."

Two heads nodded, bewilderment leaking from their expressions.

Martha grabbed a hand from each and pulled them toward the house. "Let's get to the bottom of this right now." Over her shoulder, she spoke to Meg, an afterthought. "Sorry. Maybe we can finish up later."

Like an empty dingy adrift on the ocean, Meg meandered toward the house, injured self-esteem in tow. Home called to her like a distant memory—the tiny world aboard Gilda where her priorities lay. Her heart longed for the time when Popsie told her things and she believed him. That life—life before Mr. Vanderzee—had slipped beyond reach.

Guy Marks lay in a hospital-type bed rigged up in the salon, facing aft. The bed, the nurse, all part of the compromise he made with the doctor. His gaze traveled around the room, around his home, and tripped over at least a hundred foreign items, medical equipment, supplies, death paraphernalia. No more privacy. No more trips to the head on his own. Only a shred of dignity left.

Yet this trip ensued. He would spend his last day on his boat. He would see his last sunset over the water, even if necessity required he watch it from this industrial-sized, awful bed. The only question remained Meg.

Marcie walked into the room, arms full. "I thought you might need some exter pilla's to prop y'up."

"If I get any more propped up, there won't be room enough in this bed for a patient!"

"Now, Mr. Marks, I'm only tryin' to help ya feel more comf-terble. How's that pain medication doing?"

"I feel pain, if that's your question. Is it time for another pill?"

"The doctor left orders for you to have a pill as soon as the pain is a problem."

Guy rubbed his abdomen and winced at the extra pain he produced. He spoke in his best Southern drawl. "I reckon I've arrived at the junction of pain and problem. If there's a pill to be had, I'd be much obliged, ma'am."

With a smile and a chuckle, Marcie bounced across the room and headed toward the galley and her stash of narcotics. She looked back over her shoulder. "You sit tight, I'll be back in a jif!"

The smell of hand sanitizer and antiseptic cleanser clung to everything in the room. Marcie would be back in a jiffy. How long before Meg returned? Would she? He opened and closed his hands. His lips smacked, focusing his thoughts.

He set her up by sending her to Michigan. It probably looked bad to her. Really bad. The plan might fail. Had he risked too much? He set his jaw, clenching his teeth. Nothing risked, nothing gained. His plan, worked to the end, would give Meg the choices she deserved to make; the choices Joey had deserved.

"Okay, Mr. Marks. Here we go." Marcie returned with his favorite white mug and a tiny white pill. "It'll go down easy as pie."

He swallowed the pill and clung to the white mug. "I'll just hold this for now."

"Is there anything else I can do for ya right now?"

"Marcie, do you have children?"

Her face broke into a grin. "Sure do. Four of 'em. And they're spread all over the country."

Popsie placed one hand on the pain. "Would you say you know them pretty well?"

"Nobody knows a child better'n his mother. We go see 'em every chance we get. And now we're startin' in on grandchildren."

Popsie forced a smile. The familiar ache of regret throbbed in his gut beside the new pain. It felt like a boulder he carried around with him, rubbing his insides raw and slowing his progress forward. Mistakes made in life seemed to follow a man toward death. And the decisions he made to right a wrong carried severe consequences; namely, his lack of grandchildren. Or rather, his lack of relationship with his grandchildren. "How many do you have?"

Marcie sat in the chair near the foot of the bed. "Two and a half. Everybody got married in the last coupla years, so it's baby time now. And I love it! How many grandchildren do you have?"

Guy pursed his lips and held them there a few moments. A difficult question. How should he answer? He hated the complexity of the seemingly simple question. With nothing left to lose, he opted for the truth. "Eleven, I think."

She ignored his long pause, smoothed the pale, worn quilt at the end of the bed. "Oh my! That's a lot! I can only hope my kids will keep 'em coming that long. Doncha just love those lil' grandbabies?"

He smiled and shifted his gaze to the water churning behind the boat. In his mind's eye, his beautiful wife sat at her sewing machine in the old house near Gaylord. Rachel quilted like a crazy woman, usually working on three or four projects at once. The day Joey called with news of a baby on the way, their first grandchild, she locked herself in the sewing room, choosing fabrics and making plans for what she would make to welcome the little one. "My wife lived for them. Couldn't get enough."

Guy reached for the little quilt near his feet and Marcie popped up to help him reach it. "Oh, let me get it for you. Are you cold?"

"Thanks. I'm fine." He pulled it near, and clutched it like a lifeline. As he ran his fingers over the small pastel printed squares, he imagined his hand caressing Rachel's hands. Her handiwork provided a shallow but true link to the woman he loved and lost too young. Fresh heartache bloomed in his chest. What would she think of the mess he made of their family? The fact she knew nothing of the fallout soothed his worried mind.

Marcie looked at him with huge, blue eyes. Her cool hand rested lightly on his. He could tell she was concerned. "Mr.

Marks, is something bothering you?"

He spread the quilt over his lap. "You'll have to excuse this old dog and his old tricks. You set me off day-dreaming about my sweet wife."

Patting his hand and then fluffing her artificially auburn hair, Marcie said, "Well, I hope those're happy thoughts."

He smiled and rubbed his hands on his thighs. "Very happy." Folding his hands in front of him, he cocked his head. "Do people in hospice always talk like this? Thinking about their whole lives, wondering how they could have evaded all the bad decisions?"

"Always. It's completely natural for you to think about the past. I like to tell my patients they are blessed, blessed, blessed. When you know your end is near, it's easier to make peace with all the people in your life. You have the advantage of hindsight and time to share it with all the people you love."

She started coughing, almost like it was on purpose. She stood and motioned to him, then coughed her way to the galley for a drink. Despite the wind, sea gulls, and all the other sounds surrounding them, the silence left in Marcie's wake ricocheted off the walls. All the people in his life were hundreds of miles away.

Chapter Nine

Jeffrey backed the trailer into the boat launch like he'd probably done four hundred times before. Meg and Amy unstrapped two long narrow hulls from the trailer and guided the Hobie Cat into the water, holding fast as small waves pitched and jostled their ride.

Icy water stung Meg's legs. When Amy asked her to help launch and sail the Hobie back to the cottage, joy bubbled inside her and the stress of the weekend waned a bit. She didn't speak for fear this luck might dissolve into a figment of her imagination.

Unlimited interview access to a key player in this family with no interruptions, plus she'd be on the water. Never mind a complete lack of experience on a catamaran. She could professionally dock any motor yacht 110 feet in length, she could hold her own on an offshore racing team, she could even handle a cruising sailboat with a spinnaker. This eighteen footer would be a piece of cake. And Amy had already rigged the whole thing herself.

Grateful for the windbreaker she wore, Meg looked up to

see Jeffrey plodding toward them from where he parked the truck and trailer. "Hop on. I'll give you a shove."

With life jacket buckles snapped into place, both women jumped onto the boat. Amy took charge right away. "Meg, I need you to handle the jib for me up front. Once we get going, you'll need to release the furling line and haul the jib sheet to starboard."

A rush of warmth oozed under her skin. Her facial muscles ached from the giddy smile, still in place. "I love a girl who knows the meaning of starboard. No problem."

"The cottage is only about a mile from here. If it's not too cold, we might want to tool around a little bit."

The wind drove them away from shore, hurtling over sparkling waves. Though the chilly air raised goose bumps on her skin, a rush of freedom and ease fed Meg's soul. She checked the jib and scooted onto the pontoon, leaning back against the wing seat. After a deep breath, she dove right into the interrogation. "I get the feeling everybody's ticked at your dad for leaving."

"Oh, well, I guess some of them are. I might have been a little hurt when he first left, but I couldn't hold a grudge if my life depended on it."

"Why did he leave?"

"Hmm. I wondered myself for a long time." She paused

and looked up at the mainsail with keen interest. "Mother died. That's what started everything."

Meg could hear the longing in Amy's voice as she spoke the word, mother. "What do you mean 'everything'?"

"Well, this is what Ruby's been trying to cover up—all the money troubles and the trial."

"You better start from the beginning. How did your mother die?"

"It was a heart attack in the middle of the night. She woke Daddy and told him she didn't feel well. Her arm hurt. He encouraged her to rest and they would see how she felt in the morning." She looked Meg in the eyes. "She never woke up. Daddy found her in the morning, already cold." Her eyes misted. "Kenny and Ruby said that Daddy killed her. Even Jeffie thought they should have called someone and they all blamed Daddy."

Meg's mind staggered. A sick feeling percolated in her stomach. They thought Popsie killed his wife? Not possible. For twenty-one years she watched Popsie grieve the loss of his wife. Meg grew to love Rachel from the stories he told. Like a favorite character in a book.

She felt again, the same inner prick she felt when Popsie had told her this same story years ago. Meg mourned the loss of the mother Rachel might have been to her. Popsie had told her so many times, she reminded him of Rachel. "It's your spirit," he would say, "Your spirit is so like hers."

Meg gripped the edge of the pontoon. She wanted desperately to share these feelings with someone—anyone—but as soon as she told them her secret, the animosity they felt toward Popsie would shift to her in his absence. She swallowed the acid in her throat and threw out the question she didn't want to ask. "Do you believe he killed her?"

Amy trimmed the mainsail and they picked up speed. "I kinda went along with the rest of them, not knowing what to think. I'm the youngest and I wasn't used to thinking for myself. Only Joey stood up for Daddy."

"Joey. He was the oldest, right?" Meg leaned forward and strained to hear Amy's words over the wind.

"Yes. Ten years older than me. I was only eighteen when Mother died. I barely knew what kind of clothes to wear, let alone what I should believe about my parents. I believed everything revolved around me back then and my parents just helped me along through that cloud."

Meg dipped her hand into the water below her and yanked it out as fast as she could. "Freezing. Sorry. Go on."

Amy nodded, adjusted the tiller and scanned the lake all around her. "When Mother died, I learned about loneliness, first-hand. Dad sort of crumpled without her."

Amy shifted the tiller and turned the bow into the wind. "We're coming about. As soon as the jib is back-winded, I need you to release the jib sheet and haul it in to port."

Meg moved to the center of the tramp and waited on her knees as Amy directed the boat into the strengthening wind.

Amy's glance skirted across the mainsail. "The jib might flop around a bit, but it'll catch."

When the boat turned, and wind filled the backside of the jib, Meg released the jib sheet on the starboard, following Amy's instructions.

Meg and Amy switched sides for the ride along the shoreline. "So, you thought your dad might be responsible for your mother's death?"

The boat picked up speed. "Yes. At least, that's what my siblings wanted me to think. So I did."

"Do you still believe it?"

"Whether it was his fault or not, I've come to the conclusion he certainly didn't try to kill her. He loved her. We all know it. Plus, Mother would have told him if she wanted him to take her to the hospital. And if she told him, he would have done it. That's the way it was with them."

"Did the others ever come to the same conclusion?"

"I think they all missed her and they wanted someone to blame. And it got easier and easier to blame him."

Meg's mind swished with the blue water rushing past. She thought of all the times she blamed her mother for leaving her natural dad. Memories of her dad appeared patchy at best, but they all elicited warm fuzzy feelings. Whatever caused her dad to give her up at age six must have been her mother's fault. She knew all about blame. "Why did it get easier?"

"Well, after Mother died, I left the country. I dropped out of college before I even started. I had to roam the world and find out who I would be."

"Really."

"I travelled to France and I started to paint, on the street. Then I met Robert." In a breathy voice, she trilled the "r's" and didn't pronounce the 't.' "He took me into his studio, where I really learned to paint. I arrived back in the States, a starving artist engaged to a Frenchman."

Meg bit her tongue, trying to hide her surprise. "Walter?"

Bursting out with laughter, Amy took a moment to catch her breath. "No. No. No. No. No. Walter is the opposite of French. He's the one who saved me from Robert."

Meg played with the jib line in her hand. "Wow. Your life sounds like a movie."

Amy flashed her huge smile. "I know! But trust me, it calmed down with Walter at my side."

Her original question about Popsie still unanswered, she

tried a different tactic. "OK. So, what do you think about your father now? Do you ever miss him?"

The smile disappeared from Amy's face, like she shifted into neutral. She looked up at the clouds, blinked a long blink and then looked back at their double wake. "I miss the idea of a father being in my life. I missed out on the ol' safety net my roommates called 'Dad' during my crazy years. But honestly, I'm kinda over him leaving us on our own. And he didn't really leave us on our own. The business is still here. And the cottage." She looked up at Meg. "I mean, I love my life. I love my work and my family. I don't have a huge hole in me named Duke Vanderzee crying out to be filled. I hope that doesn't sound crass." She raised her eyebrows.

"Oh no. I think I understand what you mean."

"But I miss Mom every day. That still hurts." The words tumbled out, like items from an overturned purse.

"I'm so sorry." Meg hated when her job dredged up pain for someone else. She looked up and yelled, "Hey! Isn't that— Turn!"

Amy screeched when she noticed the boat racing straight toward the cottage, and several people stood on the newly installed dock, waving their arms, yelling at them. "Shoot!" She pushed hard on the tiller, turning the boat into the wind with a lurch.

Meg crawled across the tramp to release the mainsail. She found the line wrapped around the tiller, locking it in place and the end dragging in the water—impossible to release. Meg's eyes met Amy's as she sat up on her knees to look for a solution, but the boat turned past the neutral position and the mainsail flopped hard. The boom smacked Meg on the side of the face and knocked her down. She fought the urge to pass out, shook her head and rubbed her stinging face.

A sudden gust caught the sail and propelled the boat forward. The starboard hull lifted into the air. Caught off guard while trying to free the trapped line, Amy tumbled backward into the lake. Meg heard the group on the dock yelling and saw them scatter to help Amy, but the tilting of the Hobie dragged her attention to her present situation. She scrambled to the high side of the boat, righting it, grabbed the trapped tiller and held on for dear life. She sailed toward the middle of the lake with limited steering, jib flapping, and no way to stop.

Dark gray clouds scudded across the sky, blocking the cool sunshine, which had started the day. Wind whipped the waves into miniature mountains of water and Meg gripped the tiller with all the strength left in her frozen fingers.

She flew across the water. The boat gained speed as the wind increased. She knew she needed to turn the boat into the wind to change direction or else let out the mainsail to reduce her speed. But until she released the mainsail line tangled around the tiller, she could not steer or slow down. If she failed to turn or stop the boat, she'd be forced to run aground somewhere on the far side of the lake.

Hoping to free the mainsail, Meg inched herself toward the center of the tramp. Water splashed up with every large wave she crossed. Spears of icy pain shot across her bare legs, and chilled her entire body to the bone. She reached for the line, knotted and wrapped around the tiller. Her frozen hands refused to cooperate. Clumsy fingers struggled to grip the rope as the boat moved faster, and the starboard hull rose up out of the water again.

Meg leaned back, trying to balance the boat. Her one hundred twenty pound frame accomplished little at this speed. She lost her grip on the tiller and as if in slow motion, she felt herself rise up into the air and watched the mast tilt toward the water. Aside from her dread of submersion in the frigid lake, a flash of embarrassment passed through her mind a second before she hit the water. Even on her own turf, she had failed to control the situation.

Waves jostled Meg under the water. She pulled hard, swimming away from the boat as fast as she could, afraid she'd be knocked out any second. When at last she broke the surface, the overturned boat rose high above her on a wave. Adrenaline coursed through her body, giving her enough energy to get out of the way, and avoid another bonk on the head. She twisted in the water and saw one pontoon in the air, black rudder stark against a gray sky. The tramp tipped slightly from vertical as the boat slid down into the trough of the wave. Meg noticed the mast floated along the surface of the water. The sight reminded her of a toy boat flicked over in a puddle by a careless six-year-old.

Her leaden clothes dragged in the water. Meg's muscles responded slower with each passing moment as she tried to swim toward the boat. She needed to get out of the water to avoid hypothermia. Like the Titanic movie, guy in the water dies, girl on top of the water lives. Her mind wandered. What month was it? May? Should Michigan be this cold in May? Should anyplace on earth?

Her arms tired. She reached for the boat and the back of her hand hit a pontoon, sending a shot of pain up her arm. Mustering all her strength, Meg stretched her arm as far as she could, grabbing the edge of the overturned pontoon. She could not even hope for the strength to pull herself up; she held on, but her fingers slipped a moment later.

Crashing waves pulled her back into the lake. The life jacket kept her afloat, but she closed her eyes and wondered if she might beat Popsie in the race out of this life. What if she didn't make it? What would Cody do? As waves splashed on her face, she thought about swimming for shore but she didn't even know on which side of the lake safety lay.

Hugging her knees to her chest to retain body heat, Meg listened to the waves on which she floated. They packed less power than similar ocean surges, but their chaotic lashing and tumbling aroused a wish to be stranded in the middle of a warm ocean, rather than here. All feeling fled from her bare legs and her hands. Would she actually die here? Death alone in a strange place with not even a friendly face in sight. She marveled that this situation might be even worse than her childhood fear of living a long life of loneliness only to die alone.

Just as despair edged its way into her mind, the sound of a motor reached her ears. Twisting with great effort, Meg looked up to see Morty on a jet ski headed straight toward her.

"Oh, thank God! Over here!" She tried to wave, but could barely lift her arm out of the water. So she yelled instead. "Over here! Here I am!"

Morty, Ruby's husband, appeared the unlikeliest of heroes. As he drew near, she noticed his thick, shaggy legs, which disappeared into rain boots mid-shin. He wore a Yankee's baseball cap, a teal life jacket and bright colored plaid shorts. Cutting the engine, Morty drifted toward her, and reached out a hairy, muscular arm.

She heard his gravelly voice for the first time. "Grab hold."

With all her might, she reached for his hand and somehow managed to hold on. "Oof!"

Morty dragged her onto the flat mini-platform on the back of the jet-ski. She landed hard but full of gratitude. Meg took care as she forced frozen muscles to turn herself around. With great effort she eased herself onto the seat. Advancing waves threatened to tip them over. Not again. On a calm day, she might have thought twice—or three times—before placing her arms around Morty's waist. Not today.

Morty started the engine. Looking over his shoulder, he yelled, "Hold on."

She hadn't noticed the rain while floating in the water, but now icy pellets peppered her face. The jet-ski pounded hard on the waves, bouncing Meg off the seat over and over. The repetitive jolting loosened her grip around Morty. He reached his arm back, trying to hold her on as they zoomed ahead. Lightening flashed across the sky. Thunder rumbled in the distance.

Out of habit, Meg scanned the horizon for land. But on a lake, land is nearly always visible, so she squinted toward shore, recognizing nothing. Unsure how long she could last, Meg closed her eyes and squeezed Morty around the waist with the last bit of strength she could muster. If she could hold on for two more minutes . . . Waves crashed over the front of the jet-ski and Meg wished for land like never before.

Chapter Ten

When they reached the cottage, Morty beached the jet ski beside the newly installed dock. They landed with a jolt and Meg's arms fell to her sides, every ounce of strength depleted from her death grip around Morty's waist. Face leaning against Morty's back and unable to move, she looked at the grass beneath her rescue vehicle in wonder. Her gaze crept up the lawn until it landed on the house, gables pointing toward the stormy sky. Meg's attention fell back to the waves washing over the back of the machine, urging it further up the lawn and nudging her off balance.

Amy and Jennifer crossed the grassy landing carrying umbrellas and dry towels. Lacking the strength to stand, Meg allowed Morty to hoist her in his arms and hurtle up the hill toward the house. Her body shivered violently, despite the towels. As Morty adjusted his grip, her head swung out and her eyes searched for Cody. Grey clouds hovered above trees with emergent beginnings of leaves. Where was he? She couldn't remember. Her brain struggled in slow motion, as her head bounced with every step. Her gaze took in dandelions sprinkled throughout the grassy lawn. Her ears ached from the gusty wind. The corners of her vision speckled black. She closed her eyes and sensed an ocean swell sweeping her under.

Voices drifted through the fog of returning consciousness, reaching her ears in muffled tones. She strained to hear a familiar voice.

"We have to call an ambulance."

"She'll be fine."

"She's got thin Southern blood."

"Didn't she say she's from Mississippi?"

"Soon as she warms up she'll snap back."

"I'm going to make her some tea."

"Are there any donuts left from this morning?"

Meg forced heavy eyelids open. She looked straight into the fire on her left, blazing in a huge stone fireplace on one end of the large front room. Her chest felt heavy, like at the dentist's office when the assistant brings out the leaden shield to protect against x-rays. As she regained her senses, she realized someone had laid her out like an "X" on the floor and covered her torso with a pile of blankets. Not fully aware of herself, she wondered what she must look like. Did they leave her in wet clothes?

The thought sent panic coursing through her body, which rallied enough adrenaline to roll onto her side. She heard a moan before she felt the pain in her throat caused by the effort.

"She's moving. Aunt Jennifer! She's moving."

Twin faces appeared less than twelve inches from her face. "Hi Meg. We're here. You're going to be okay."

"Do you feel okay?"

Meg tried to draw her head back from the twins, but the floor prevented it. Their frantic attention launched her into wakefulness. She struggled with the multiple layers piled on her chest as she pushed up to a sitting position. Her eyes roved around the room, trying to identify an annoying, clattering noise. But realization struck. Her teeth chattered like applause from a roomful of strangers. Meg pressed her lips together in an attempt to arrest the vibration.

Across the room, Morty came into focus, hands stuffed into the front pocket of his baggy sweatshirt. Through her rattling teeth, Meg managed to speak, though too softly. "Thank you. For saving me."

Morty's warm brown eyes looked sad. He gave her a single, curt nod and turned aside to speak to Martha at his elbow.

The twins swaddled her upright figure with quilts around her shoulders and across her legs. "Aunt Jennifer, is it okay to warm up her arms and legs now?"

Jennifer stepped forward. If she's moving her extremities on her own, it's okay. Meg, take it slow. I think you're suffering a mild hypothermia."

Her face must have looked confused, because Jennifer offered a maternal smile and spoke again. "I used to be a nurse. We see this a lot up here. How do you feel?"

Meg shivered without pause. "Cold. I can't stop shaking."

"You're going to be fine. We're going to get you something warm to drink. Would you like to move closer to the fire?"

Nodding, Meg moved to get up. The twins jumped to help her and eased her into an arm chair and ottoman set beside the fire. Not used to such ministrations, Meg shifted in the chair and rubbed her feet together beneath the quilts.

The twins knelt next to the ottoman and spoke in hushed tones. Meg watched their mouths move, but caught only bits and pieces of the conversation.

"We've been so worried."

"Good thing we learned. . . Alaska . . . Eskimos . . ."

"Cold up there . . . blankets . . . survival . . . Aunt Jennifer"

"Good thing . . . your shoes . . . the boat . . ."

She blinked and looked around. The whole family crowded near and every eye seemed to rest on Meg.

Jane bounced on her knees. "We saw Aunt Amy fall off the boat and then the boat took off. You were flying!"

Janell leaned in toward her sister. "How did you stay on for so long?"

"Yeah. Why didn't you jump off?"

Meg shrugged her shoulders. The general buzz of conversation hit a lull as Meg's words tumbled out. "I was trying to save the boat."

A silent moment passed and then everybody started talking at the same time.

The front screen door slammed shut and a husky voice rose over the cacophony of sounds offering encouragement or expressing surprise. "You're lucky you didn't get yourself killed. What were you trying to pull out there?"

Meg followed Ruby with her gaze as she waded through family members and stopped when she towered over Meg. Meg leaned her head on the back of the chair. "What do you mean?"

Amy came forward, wrapped in a huge green towel, hair damp, but holding to its usual shape, the immovable bob. "Oh Ruby, give her a break. It was my fault for not paying attention."

Ruby's face grew red and she raised a pointed finger toward Meg. "I'll tell you who's at fault here. The moment you arrived, I knew you'd be trouble. We don't want you here, can't you see that? We don't need Daddy's money. We're doing just fine on our own, thank you very much. So stop dripping on our carpet and get out of our house."

The shock of her statement drilled into Meg's gut. Her face burned, rejection like this was hard to find. Ruby clearly hated her and she could not fathom why. Her entire being wanted to run away and leave this place and this crazy family. Popsie had even tricked her into coming. He probably knew it would be horrible. Reasons to stay flew away from her mind. She wracked her brain for a comeback. "Is that true? Would you all forfeit your inheritance to be rid of me?"

The room stood still. Jeffrey stepped forward and broke the silence. "Ruby stands alone. You should stay."

Meg glanced around to ascertain the consensus. Heads nodded and quiet voices agreed with Jeffrey. Ruby elbowed her way toward the kitchen. "You guys have no idea what's happening. The old man is cheating us! Can't you see that? I tried to warn you about this move. You're on your own now." She shot a hard look over her shoulder: narrow eyes and a scowl mean enough to send a chill through the bones. Passing Morty, she asked, "Are you with me or not?"

With his back to Ruby, the quickest of winks flew toward Meg, then he turned to follow Ruby out of the room.

The twins huddled in a corner, whispering to each other. Martha marched out of the room behind her mother. Aiden corralled the teenage contingent onto the deep front porch to watch the storm. Amy eased herself onto the couch across from Meg. "I'm so sorry about Ruby. She's bossed us around since the day we were born, so she really doesn't know how to react when we cross her."

Slumping back against the cushions, Meg pulled an old quilt tight around her shoulders. Guitar music drifted in from the porch. "She hates me. Why does she hate me?"

Jennifer walked into the room carrying a tray of steaming mugs. "Now, don't worry yourself about Ruby. She'll simmer down."

Amy grabbed one of the drinks and tucked her feet beneath her. "You've had quite a weekend already. I hope we haven't driven you away."

Meg shook her head. Surprising herself, she said, "I'm here for a single purpose. I intend to finish the job." The steaming tea beckoned to her as she added milk and sugar.

Jennifer sat in a straight-backed chair beside the fireplace, balancing her tea on her knees. "We'd like to help you. Tell us what you need."

Meg toyed with a corner of the quilt drawn around her shoulders. She studied the tiny squares meticulously sewn together by caring hands. "Maybe I could give you a list of people I still need to talk to." Her voice trailed off as her eye focused on a single one inch square in the quilt. The pink print looked oddly familiar, and next to it, a pale yellow floral.

Jennifer cocked her head. "That's it?"

Meg heard the question but the words did not sink in.

Placing her tea on the table beside her, she pulled the quilt off her shoulders and into her lap to get a better look. She stood and spread it across the floor. Upon seeing the entire design, she took in a quick, loud breath. A quivering hand covered her mouth as she stared at the quilt.

Amy sat up straight. "What is it?"

"Where did you get this quilt?"

Amy and Jennifer shared a puzzled look. Amy shrugged, then pointed across the room. "It's from that trunk over there. Mother made it. She made all of them. We use them for everything; picnics, sleepovers, movie nights, campfires . . ."

Meg stopped listening, grabbed the quilt and sat down with it in her lap. She studied the fabrics square by square, sometimes holding it close for inspection. Over Amy's continued commentary, she spoke to herself, in a voice barely over a whisper. "It's the same one. Why is it the same one?"

Amy stopped when she heard Meg. "What did you say?"

"This is my quilt. I mean—I have a baby quilt. When I was adopted, I brought three things with me. My teddy bear, a picture of my dad and that quilt. Mine's smaller, but this is exactly the same and they're both handmade. Are you sure she made this one?"

Her mind grappled with the possibilities, but she grew dizzier as she tried to reason. In her memory, the smile of the man at the pastie shop triggered a nervous quivering deep inside her. If Rachel made this quilt, then how could she have the same one? Rachel died before Popsie adopted her. Maybe someone purchased her quilt from Rachel. But that did not explain the identical fabrics sewn together in an identical pattern.

Jennifer toyed with the pearls around her neck. "Are you sure it's exactly the same? Maybe you're mistaken."

"I am not mistaken. That blanket was my best friend for years. Every inch of it is etched in my brain. Whoever made this quilt must have made mine. Did your mother sell her quilts?"

Amy sat on her hands. "No. She would not sell anything she made with such love. I know that Mother made this one, because I helped her. Summer after my junior year in high school, my best friend worked at a camp the whole summer, so I became a nuisance with nothing to do. Mother decided to apply my annoying energy to this project. I cut out hundreds of tiny little squares. I hated being forced to help, but I loved the fabrics. They all came from Mom's stash. We chose the fabrics together and she let me play with the colors and arrange them into that zig-zag water-color pattern."

Amy stared at the gray rag-knit socks on her feet. Meg watched her, waiting. "So . . ."

"So, we made an exact copy of that quilt. For a baby." She looked into Meg's eyes, holding the gaze.

All five heads in the room swiveled back and forth, scanning the shocked look on every face. The room seemed to spin. Meg placed her palm on her forehead. "What baby?"

Amy continued to stare at Meg. She opened her mouth soundlessly a few times, her eyes flicking all around the room until she forced the words out, tumbling over each other. "Mom's first grandchild. My first niece. Baby Maggie Daisy, we called her. Joey's daughter."

Musical twin voices breathed out in stunned awe, the same words running through everyone's mind. "No. Way."

Chapter Eleven

Marcie frowned at Guy Marks. "You do NOT need to work right now. I don't like it. This phone call can wait until morning."

"My little girl . . . I need to find out . . ."

Marcie faced him, hands toying with the stethoscope around her neck. "The doctor said rest. My job is ta help you rest and not get over-excited."

He gripped the phone in one hand with all the strength he could garner and pointed at her with a shaking hand. "Never you mind. I'm calling." His attention shifted to a voice on the phone.

"Hello?"

"Sophie. Good. What happened? Did you meet Meg?"

"Yes."

He sat up as straight as he could on the mountain of pillows. "Is she OK?"

"She seems to be holding up well, under the circumstances. Are you sure you want to continue with this as planned?"

Guy nodded until his head hurt. "Don't argue with the plan. You agreed to it. It's better if she learns it all on her own."

He held the phone away from his ear as Sophie released a loud sigh. "Well, it's not going to take very long. She's already farther along than we ever thought she'd be. I feel so bad for her. I wish I could tell her everything."

"Stick to the plan."

"I will."

Popsie rubbed his leg. "Does she hate me?"

Sophie's voice warmed. "No. But she's a good lawyer. She keeps firing questions at me. She wants to know why. Thinks you don't trust her."

"No! That's not it!"

"Guy, I warned you this way would be hard. If you want to stick with the plan, then you have to let her think you don't trust her for now. Like it or not, the truth will out. Your best bet is to sit tight."

Popsie's hand shook. His grip on the phone loosened and the phone dropped into his lap. Marcie jumped up from her perch across the room, where she propagated the illusion of giving him privacy, but probably hung on every word. "OK, young man. That's enough for now."

Popsie leaned against the pillows and closed his eyes. He heard her talking to Sophie. "I'm sure he's fine, but he needs to get some rest. Yes. A little weaker. He can't handle too much excitement."

Turning her back, she edged toward the pilothouse and lowered her voice. "He's better in the morning, right after he wakes up. Yes. I'll tell him. Bye now."

Popsie pulled the blanket over his face as she walked up to the bed.

She gently pulled the blanket away from his face. "Mr. Marks, I know you don't want me to say it, but I think you need to hear it. I told you so."

"I know. But there's no messing with me when it comes to my little girl. I had to find out about her."

Marcie sat on the edge of the bed. "Tell me the story."

His tongue examined each tooth and slowly made its way around the outside of his top teeth. Keeping everything inside hadn't worked too well so far. Might as well come clean with somebody. "I'm not much good at stories. And this one's a kicker."

She patted his hand. "Do you need to tell it?"

Catching her eye, he felt something inside him release. He tried to stop, but it felt like a dam had broken somewhere. "I really messed up when I was younger."

"OK. So far, that's the exact same story as everybody else I know."

Her comment washed over him like a cool breeze. He took a deep breath. "Well, I messed up so bad, my son died. I tried to fix things the best I could. I even found a way that might bring his daughter a little justice. Problem is, she has to learn a bunch of secrets I've been keeping from her, and she thought we didn't have any secrets."

Marcie cocked her head. "I thought the phone call was about your daughter."

His hands began their familiar track up and down his legs. Here goes. "Only you and one other person in the world know this . . . my daughter . . . the girl everybody thinks is my daughter by adoption . . . is really my granddaughter by birth."

"And she doesn't know that either?"

"Not yet. But she's a real firecracker. She'll figure it out before long."

Marcie folded her hands in her lap. "So that's why you had to make the call?"

Guy nodded once. He pressed his lips together. "I sent her to my family under false pretenses. They don't know her and she doesn't know them. I left them behind when I got Meg. But it's all going to come out now."

Shaking her head back and forth, Marcie looked at Guy's hands. "So how many children do you have then?"

He rubbed the arthritic knuckles in his left hand. Afternoons by the lake flitted through his mind. Pulling five kids on water skis at once, making kites and flying them in the yard, running with Amy on his shoulders in pursuit of the older kids and even sleeping under the stars in the front yard. "It's a complicated answer. I've been a different dad to different kids. Had five of my own with my beautiful wife. Lost one. Adopted another one, alone. I guess what smarts at this moment, is I'm not on speaking terms with even one of them right now. Might as well have none. I deserve as much."

Marcie batted his arm and stood to lecture him. "Mr. Marks, don't say that. I'm sure you deserve much better. I can see plain as day on your face how sorry you are for what you did. Have you tried talkin' to 'em?"

"I abandoned them once, a long time ago. Calling them now and dying on them would only repeat the offense. They don't need that. They don't need me. I do wish Meggie would call me, though. I worry. I'm hoping she'll come back to see me before . . ."

"Can I call her for you?"

Popsie struggled to hold up a hand in protest; it shook in the air before his face. "No, you may not. She will call when she's ready. You don't call her."

"OK, OK. Calm down, for cryin' out loud." He rested against the pillows. "I promise I won't call anybody unless you tell me to. I didn't mean for you to get all worked up. Some kind of nurse I am. Let's get you comfortable again. Do you think you could sleep for awhile?"

The plumping of pillows and shifting of blankets took over. He wondered at the child-like state of his existence. If he didn't keep a sharp eye, Marcie might tuck a teddy bear under the covers. "I'll sleep if you say so. But I get to keep the phone in my lap. Just in case she calls."

Marcie smoothed the last wrinkle out of the top quilt. "I can live with that. I'll be right close if you need me."

The quilt lay in a heap on the bed. Meg kept her eye on it in the mirror as she brushed her hair. It almost seemed to breathe. How many stories she longed to hear lay trapped in its fibers? She almost wanted to poke it with a stick to see if it would disintegrate like a dream at dawn. The heap of fabric scraps resembled Meg's brain—a million tiny pieces of information, patched together, but not yet recognizable as anything cohesive.

"But your name isn't Maggie." The twins' words rang in the air and now the conversation played over and over in her mind.

Meg had rubbed her arms with her hands, trying to warm them with friction. She wondered at the same thing. "So it can't be me."

Janell had grabbed Meg's hand and said, "Oh, I wish it was you! You would be our cousin!"

The comment landed like a branding iron on her soul. The familiar sting of "does not belong" burst like a blister in her chest. Tears flooded her eyes and she brushed them away with the quilt, stood, and excused herself, seeking solace and warm clothes in her room.

A hot shower cleansed the tears and cleared her mind. She pulled on her jeans that fit like an old friend. *As if I understood old friends.* She replayed in her head the moment she realized the quilt matched her own. Revelation of the second identical quilt pleased her, but the idea "Bankie" might have been intended for someone else dealt a crushing blow to the fragile concept of her past.

With great care, she had preserved the three items she arrived with on Popsie's boat. Together they comprised her entire history, a small square on the tableau of life which represented Megan Marks. Or Megan Vanderzee. The tableau blurred and she felt her history smearing like oil on teak. Messy at first, and then vanishing all together.

She slipped into a sweatshirt and appraised herself in the mirror, hands in back pockets. Tossing the early years to uncertainty, Meg now began to doubt the years she spent with Popsie as well. He lied about his name, his family, what else? Her quilt? The girl in the mirror drifted farther into the darkness of ambiguity.

Scanning the room, Meg eyeballed the bright red suitcase. She loved red. In fact, as a teenager, Meg asked if they could add some color to Gilda. Popsie special-ordered a bright red Bimini because she loved the color so much. The canvas stretched over the fly bridge atop the boat and stood out like a beacon. Most boat owners prided themselves in maintaining their boat's original features, but Popsie took orders from Meg. When he showed it to her for the first time, he said, "How do you like that? *Gilda* looks like an ice cream sundae with a cherry on top!"

The memory grounded her rational mind enough to think. Popsie loved her, she could not deny it. But he had made a royal mess. Now this thing about Joey's daughter nagged at her. The very thought her quilt rightfully belonged to someone else provoked a wave of nausea in her gut. Fearing a drift into loneliness again, Meg chose to consider the other possibility.

Everyone assumed Meg's quilt had been stolen or sold or lost. It might be the one Rachel and Amy had made, but only the twins even considered the idea niggling Meg's brain. Maybe the baby quilt never switched hands. Maybe the quilt's original owner still owned it. Maybe the owner changed her name . . . like her father.

The pinks, yellows, and greens blurred in her peripheral vision as she bent to retrieve the cell phone from her bag. Five calls from Cody. Three voicemails. Tucking her guilt away, she dialed his cell.

"Meg!"

"Hi. I saw you called, what's up?"

"Did you get my messages?"

Meg walked to the window and fingered the lacy curtains. "I saw you left a few. I just got back to my room. You won't believe what happened to me."

"You won't believe what I've been dealing with down here. Is everything alright?"

"Not really, but you go first. Mine's going to take awhile to tell."

Clearing his throat, Cody paused. "OK, I'm just going to say it. I can't find a caterer for the wedding, so Mama and my sisters have offered to cook for the reception."

Meg fell into an armchair beneath the window. "What?"

"I know. It sounds bad. I can't believe in all of Miami there isn't one place who can cater a wedding this week. June weddings."

Deflated, she pulled a thread from the upholstery. "Did you try Triple Crown?"

"Booked."

"What about the hotels?"

"Double booked." An edge of frustration crept into his voice.

She bit her lip, but plunged ahead. "Come on, there has to be someone."

"Megs, Mama already spent all day on the phone. I'm working my tail off trying to make this wedding happen. Unless we get a call back in the next day or two from a miracle chef with time on his hands, I think Mama's our best option. You like her cooking."

With a deep sigh, she threw her head back against the floral wing chair and stared at the quilt across the room. "How are the other things going? Thank goodness I picked out flowers last week. What did they say? Can they do everything we talked about on such short notice? Did you get an estimate from them yet?"

A pause and shuffling of papers. "Yeah. Not good. Wasn't the budget for flowers like, $3,000?"

She glanced at the forsythia branches standing in a tall vase on the bedside table. "Oh, no. Is the estimate more than that?"

In his goofy car commercial voice he said, "Everything you've ever dreamed of can be yours for the bargain basement price of only $15,000."

She sat up straight. "What?"

"That's what I thought."

She stood and padded a barefoot figure eight in the middle of the room. "What are we going to do? I know I gave him a budget when we picked everything out." She chewed on her lower lip for a few seconds.

Cody cleared his throat twice, but did not speak.

His discomfort spread to her through the phone, souring her stomach.

"Don't tell me there's another fiasco."

"I wouldn't call it a fiasco."

Stopping for a moment, she said, "Seriously, there's something else?"

"Well, it's the venue. We knew it might be tough to pull off."

"So the church said no?" His reluctance to explain grated her already tender nerves.

"Not exactly."

Meg's free hand flew into the air, as if she could make him talk by gesturing to an empty room. With great effort, she drizzled some patience into her words. "So . . . what then?"

"There are five weddings at the church on our date. When they heard our story, they agreed to work us in, but our time slot is three o'clock, hottest part of the day. And we have exactly one hour, including set-up and tear down."

Meg fought a desire to pull out her hair by the roots. The plans she carefully dreamed over the course of the past twenty years spun out of control before her eyes. "This wedding is falling apart! I can't deal with it right now, Cody. I could've died from hypothermia today. I flipped a Hobie Cat on the lake."

Cody's voice registered genuine concern for the first time. "Seriously? Are you OK?"

She fell backwards onto the bed, and propped her knees up. "I'm not really OK, no. The family is bizarre and I'm still freezing and there's some stuff I learned today I don't know what to think about and, and . . . I'm gonna kill Popsie."

"Whoa. Take it easy. Slow down."

She fingered the quilt beside her on the bed. "I'm serious. He kept all these secrets and Ruby hates me and I have to read all these files and probably one or two of these people are crazy and I'm so alone up here!"

Cody's voice filled with tenderness. "Baby, I'm sorry. Should I come up there and help you?"

She sat up and pulled the quilt over her lap. Meg did not hesitate to answer. "No. You're helping me in Charlotte, and we all know how that's going."

Silence.

"Sorry, Code. I didn't mean it."

His voice came out strained and business-like. Almost

paternal and condescending. "Meggie, I love you. I want to marry you and I am going to move heaven and earth to make sure it all turns out as close to perfect as possible. But right now, I think we better hang up before either of us says something else we might regret, OK?"

She froze. "'K."

"Bye."

Cody hadn't called her Meggie before. A violent shiver shook her body.

She leaned against the tall post at the corner of the four-poster bed. Popsie used the nickname when she was very small. She never gave it any thought until now. It was only one letter different. Meggie and Maggie. Twin voices in her head echoed the words she spoke out loud. "No way."

Chapter Twelve

Meg marched up the front steps of the cottage. Armed with a shower, warm clothes, and an idea, she entered the living room with her head held high. Guitar sounds strummed in a corner by the window where Aiden and a few others huddled. Amy sat staring into the fire in the same place Meg had left her. Laughter trickled into the room from the kitchen along with the aroma of . . . lasagna. Lasagna?

"Meg!" The twins accosted her and dragged her toward the fireplace.

"Hey. Am I in time for dinner?"

"It's hard to be late for dinner. We're always eating something or other up here." They sat her down on the couch and flanked her, blasting questions.

"Are you still cold?"

"Did you get a hot shower?"

"Do you need some warmer clothes? I could lend you something."

"What do you think about that quilt?"

"I know, it's so weird!"

They both paused for a moment and Meg seized her entrance. "Yeah, I've been thinking about that. Tell me about your Uncle Joey."

They looked at each other for a moment. Amy shifted her eyes toward them. Jane said, "We didn't know him. I think he died when we were really little. Or maybe before we were even born."

Janell agreed. "But let's see, Mom told us his wife took off on him. And she left the baby. It was like she just turned into another person and disappeared. Nobody ever heard from her again."

This new piece of information flew into place in Meg's mind. She looked up as Ruby approached her from the kitchen. "Oh. Hi."

"Don't believe anything the twins tell you. They don't remember things very well."

"Mom!" Two syllables, loud.

Meg looked at Ruby, giving her a dazzling smile. "They're full of information. It's so refreshing when people answer your questions."

Ruby grunted and headed back toward the kitchen.

Emboldened by her successful barb, Meg called after her. "Would you like to give it a whirl, Ruby? Answering questions?"

Ruby turned and stalked back toward Meg, finger pointing. "Listen here, Missy. I am here DESPITE your presence. This happens to be my family and as I said before, we don't want you here!"

Meg stood and faced Ruby. "I'm curious. Would you ever throw a member of your own family out of this house?"

A look of confusion turned into annoyance on Ruby's face. "Of course not. But I'd like to throw you out."

Meg felt the right side of her mouth curl up in a wry half-smile. "Aunt Ruby, I don't think that's very nice."

Her visage contorted into an angry sneer. "Don't you dare call me Aunt. You audacious little . . ."

Meg interrupted and looked around the room. "Does anybody have a photo of Joey? Cuz I have a photo of my real dad with me. I'd like to compare the two, just for fun."

Conversations halted. Everybody looked at Meg. Amy stood with her mouth open, but it broke into a smile as she skipped across the room to her mother's quilt trunk. "Mom's journal's in here. There's a photo of all five kids taped in the back of the book."

Digging the journal out from the bottom of the trunk, Amy smoothed her hand across the front cover. She looked up at Meg. "Are you ready?"

Meg's heartbeat almost blocked out all other sounds. If the photos proved her wrong, not only would she look and feel like a fool, but she would render herself powerless to continue this job. Popsie's final request would be ruined by a jump to conclusions. But if the photos matched . . . she could hardly hold herself together at the thought.

Meg pulled the familiar photo from her back pocket. She ran her finger along the crease running vertically, just off center. Wear and tear from so many years had almost erased the details near the fold, Daddy's ear and part of his shirt. Time faded the colors, but his blue eyes still seemed to sparkle on the paper. She held the photo against her chest and nodded to Amy.

Amy opened the back cover of the journal and five or six photos fell out. The family pressed in close while Ruby stood back, arms crossed over her chest, eyes examining Amy.

One of the twins pointed. "Is that one him? With the little girl?

Jeffrey nodded curtly. "That's Joe."

Amy held the photo out toward Meg, whose gaze fixed on it, eyes like a laser beam. Speechless, she turned her photo around for all to see.

Everybody talked at once.

"Where'd you get that photo?"

"How do you have his picture?"

"What?"

"It's him!"

Ruby clapped her hands together, staccato-style, slow and precise. The room shushed. "Oh, very nice. Where'd you find that? Did you pull it off the internet from some old newspaper story? Did you bribe one of the grandkids with a hefty inheritance?"

Meg's face burned, her muscles threatened paralysis. But new truth galvanized her courage. "No. I've kept this photo with me since I was six."

Ruby strutted across the room. "Just because you have a picture of Joey does not mean you are his long lost daughter. Ladies and gentlemen, I believe we have a pesky little con-woman in our midst."

Amy stood. "Ruby, she has the quilt."

Eyes wide, she turned to Amy. "She has the quilt or she knows about the quilt?"

Jeffrey swung his arms as he walked across the room to a leather chair. "Give it up, Ruby. This is the girl. Look at her pluck—you knew it the second she spoke. Sounds just like him."

Meg spun to look at Jeffrey. "Really?"

The twins looked like they were about to burst; and then they did. "Meg! We're cousins! We're cousins!"

Meg's heart gushed under multiple hugs. Excitement ricocheted around the room. Surprise, smiles and kind words passed between all except Ruby, who stood shell-shocked, hands clenched at her sides.

The feeling she had chased all her life fell like a warm blanket over Meg's shoulders and rested like a mantle. Her heart beat steadily, not a worry flitted through her mind. Time spent with Popsie gave her the same feeling, but this was so much bigger. She belonged. To people, to a place, to a family. She couldn't speak, so she smiled while the family she always dreamed of spun before her eyes like a merry-go-round.

From the corner of her eye, Meg saw Ruby turn to walk down the hall toward the kitchen. Over her shoulder, she said, "I'll believe it when I see a birth certificate or DNA evidence."

Hand after hand patted her on the shoulder. Voices echoed, "Don't worry about her." Meg's shoulders relaxed. She basked in the warmth of the group, amazed to suddenly be counted as one of them.

Jennifer entered from the kitchen. "Dinner's ready!"

The loud group talked constantly as they filled their plates and commandeered seats all around the house. Meg found a footstool near Walter by the living room windows. She balanced the dinner plate in her lap.

Scratching his head, he looked at her. "So, your grandfather hired you to write his will for him, and you didn't know he was your grandfather?"

Meg swallowed. "This is how crazy my world has been over the last day and a half. I thought I was doing this job for a friend of my father. Twenty-four hours later I find out my father hired me, and he's not only my adoptive father, but also my biological grandfather. Plus, instead of no family to speak of, I'm related to all of you. I thought it was just me and Popsie this whole time."

He stared at the ceiling and ate quietly. After mopping up tomato sauce with his garlic bread, he turned to her, bread poised in the air, dripping sauce to the plate. "So why didn't he tell you anything?"

An icy chill filled her chest; breathing required extra effort. She bit her lip. Anger and sadness and wonder played like a slideshow inside her mind. "I don't know."

Morning light seeped into the room through pink and yellow Waverly curtains. Physically speaking, Meg's body awakened well-rested and energized, but her emotions hung in tatters. Heavy revelations from the previous night crashed back into her consciousness. With her identity on the line, Meg determined to learn about her real father. Her biological father. And more about her other father . . . grandfather. The will inadvertently slipped to a lower priority. Did he really want her to write it in the first place anyway? Or did he use it as a ploy to lure her to the family?

Processing everything would be easier on the move. Meg threw on her sweats and headed outside for a brisk walk in the crisp air. Her stomach communicated it might be better to keep a little distance from today's annual Vanderzee pancake breakfast.

She struck out northwest, away from the cottage. The scent of spring traveled on the breeze: freshly turned earthy mulch, clean air, and sweet wildflowers. Meg power-walked up a slight incline until she reached the main road. She picked up speed on the pavement and her body shifted into automatic mode, her mind churning. Everybody seemed to like Joey. But even though the family talked about him frequently, no specific information ever materialized.

A flicker of red caught her eye in the woods to her right. Before she could shift her brain back to her present surroundings, Jennifer appeared, wearing a red quilted barn coat and holding a bouquet of tiny spring flowers. Pieces of blond hair had escaped from her indelible bun and she wore a guarded smile. "Hi, Meg."

Meg passed her by before she gained the presence of mind to stop. "Hi. Sorry. My mind runs about two minutes behind my body this early in the morning."

"Oh, that's OK. I was just picking some flowers for my room." She held up the bouquet.

Meg shifted her weight to one leg. Her genteel upbringing raged inside against the intense desire for solitude. "Would you like to join me? I thought I'd walk a couple miles to clear my head this morning."

"I'd love to. The kitchen back at the cottage gets a little oppressive now and then. Right now, it's full of people who think they know how to make the best pancakes in the world. I don't even eat pancakes."

"Neither do I. French toast is way better."

"Definitely."

Meg stared off to her left. The lake appeared in patches of blue between trees and cottages. The surface of the water rippled and hair escaped from Meg's ponytail and wafted in the rising wind. "So, I'm not sure I got the whole story on Kenneth. Why did he have to leave so suddenly?"

Jennifer shook her head. "He planned this fishing trip with his buddies about a year ago. They finally found a week they could all get away and now he's afraid the weather will mess it up. They're meeting in Rogers City next Friday, so he needs to move the boat over there and if we have storms like they are predicting this week, he'll never make it. I hate we have to miss him this weekend."

"I hope I didn't chase him away. We had an interesting little chat on his boat before he left."

"Did he proselytize you?"

"What?"

"Did he try to get you to join the Libertarian party?"

Laughing, Meg kicked the gravel. "The twins asked me the same thing. No, he didn't. But now I'm curious. I'd kinda like to hear his spiel."

Jennifer crossed her arms to hug herself. "No, you don't; although he makes a pretty good case for it. He might come across as a little bit crazy, but he really just loves his country and he wants other people to love it the same, so it doesn't get messed up any more."

Meg bit her lip. Might as well use this opportunity. "Speaking of things getting messed up . . . what can you tell me about Joey?"

Jennifer stuck her free hand into her coat pocket and focused on the ground ahead as they walked. "Hmm. You must be curious. What do you know already?"

Meg kicked gravel pieces ahead of her on the road's shoulder. "I know that my mom left him before I could remember anything. I know that he loved me. I remember a super squeezee hug. And then he had to leave. That's when Popsie adopted me and I went to live on his boat with him."

She looked up at Meg. "You lived on a boat?"

Smiling, she nodded. "An unusual upbringing, but really fun."

"Do you remember the year of your adoption?"

Meg pressed her lips together and looked at the sky, thinking. "I guess it would have been 1988. The year I turned six."

"1988? Let's see, we got married in 1983. Brett didn't come along until 1990. Ken was just starting his own company and Joey gave him a contract. Oh, that was a hard year, '88."

Meg perked up. "Why?"

Jennifer looked over at the lake for a minute. "Well, since you're family now, I guess it's OK to talk about this stuff. I don't want you to be disappointed."

In order to keep her talking, Meg placed a hand on Jennifer's arm. "Look, before yesterday, I had one family member. One. I missed out on having a real family my whole life. It doesn't matter what you tell me. No matter what, it's got to be better than not having any family at all."

She sighed. "Here goes. 1988 was the year Rachel died and Joey got caught."

A memory of Rachel's photograph flashed in Meg's mind. Popsie always kept it on the table beside his bed. In junior high she used to wonder if he kissed it before he went to sleep every night. "Oh. Rachel. I bet Popsie was crushed."

"Crushed. Devastated. Incapacitated. Yeah. He took it really hard."

"And what happened to my father?"

Jennifer scratched her upper arm. "Do you remember your dad?"

Wind blowing across the lake hit them from the left as they proceeded past a lot cleared for new construction. A chill traveled down Meg's spine and she hugged herself, rubbing her arms. A few scattered impressions, darkened by time and distance, took her to a familiar place. She used to wrack her brain trying to remember him better, but aside from a few vague impressions, she forced herself to give up as she grew older. "I remember sitting on his shoulders and spinning around. When I looked up I saw tall trees. I remember a blue plaid shirt. And I have the photo I showed everyone. Sadly, that's about it."

Jennifer's shoes crunched the gravel for several steps before she spoke. "I hate to tell you this, but he was arrested and convicted for embezzling money from Snow Cap."

Meg stopped and turned toward Jennifer. "What?"

Jennifer kept walking. "Yeah. It was in all the papers. He created a time-share property scheme to siphon profits from Snowcap into his own cap, so to speak. They thought he might be buying drugs or gambling it away, but never found any evidence."

Hurrying to catch up, Meg imagined Sophie's secret file exploding all over her flowery hotel room. "My father did that? I can't believe it."

A slight chuckle popped out. "Most people don't 'seem' like they are capable of violence or deceit or crime before they get caught. Like I said, I really hate to ruin your image of him. But when you break the law, you obviously have a great disrespect for this country and all the great opportunities it affords us. Cheaters never win. You were probably better off with Duke than you would have been with a father like him anyway."

Whoa. A slap in the face would have hurt less. A root took hold inside her, a driving force that when fully grown, would blossom into a mission. The disdain in Jennifer's voice spattered on Meg's heart. "You said he was convicted. So he went to prison?"

Jennifer scanned the road ahead avoiding Meg's face. "It's not even the worst part. He went to prison and died less than three months later."

A tiny explosion of pain in the back of her brain punctuated the new information. "That's why my dad *left* me?"

"I'm sorry. You never knew?"

"I never knew." Meg's voice broke and quieted.

Jennifer stopped and turned back toward the cottage, motioning for Meg to follow. "Not a proud moment in Vanderzee history. Kennie won't discuss his brother at all. In fact, I learned more from what the papers printed than I did from him. I'm sure Duke never told you because he wanted you to have a good impression of your dad."

Meg shoved her hands into her pockets. "Hmm." She wondered why Popsie would bother to reveal the truth at the end of his life. It didn't fit with Jennifer's theory. He knew it would hurt Meg. Was he feeling guilty? Guilty for what?

Meg nodded slowly as a wave of emotion crested in her chest. She choked out some words. "I think I'll run on the way back, if you don't mind." Without waiting for an answer, she sprinted away from Jennifer.

My dad died a convicted felon. Meg typed it on her screen in an effort to process the news. She discovered the covered back patio while walking around the house to cool down from her run. Finding it deserted, private and comfortable, she grabbed her computer and set up camp for the morning.

A pristine lawn met the edge of the flagstone patio and swooped around a natural area containing three soaring white pines. Beneath the trees, mulch defined the area and supported a

Lincoln log loveseat and matching swing to form a cozy setting for conversation. The lawn swept down to a beautiful fenced in swimming pool, and a small grassy path sneaked between rock-bordered perennial gardens. Beyond the maze of blooming beds, the yard backed up to a hardwood forest mixed with evergreens. Bright lime green needles popped out on the edges of all the piney trees in stark contrast to the darker, older growth. Wind swayed the tops of the hardwoods, creating a rainy sound, even though sunshine shone bright through the high, newborn leaves. Young fern plants opened one by one on the floor of the woods, creating a wobbly green carpet beneath the greening tableau before her. The air smelled like new dirt mixed with an unfamiliar malodor. Meg's view bespoke serenity, but her inside world teetered on the brink of a dangerous cliff.

She couldn't look at the statement she had typed, nor could she erase it. Her gaze wandered to the woods again, and her eyes fixated on the path to the right, which seemed to lead away from the trouble staring back at her from her computer screen.

She packed up her laptop and stowed it behind her wicker rocker. She decided wicker must be the state chair of Michigan as she strolled toward the path which promised diversion and escape from her . . . family.

Odd, that. Running away from family. Her chastisement of Popsie on this very subject burned a guilty spot in her chest. She had said family was a gift and she believed it. But what about felonious family? Or cantankerous family? To believe in something is to live it. Popsie drilled that axiom into her head over the years.

She rounded the flowerbeds and followed the path to the edge of the woods. Movement on the ground to the left froze her feet where they had fallen. Something appeared to scurry away from her. She watched the ferns bend and jiggle as the creature sped further from her and then stopped at the base of a tree, about twenty yards away.

Meg stepped with care, heel-toe, heel-toe, in an effort to sneak up and discover what kind of creature she had frightened. Decomposing leaves rotting on the moist ground softened her footfalls. Even so, her gait mimicked one walking on eggshells. Everywhere she treaded this weekend seemed to be fraught with potential drama. Especially where Ruby injected herself. How could a complete stranger hate her so? Did Ruby's hatred run deeper? Extending back in time to her feelings toward Joey?

Meg stood six feet from the tree where her mysterious prey stopped. Assuming it had long ago disappeared, she squatted to peer beneath the lilac bushes, hoping to see a fox or a rabbit hole. The scent of the lilacs elicited such joy in her spirit she could not inhale enough of the sweet, provocative scent. About to follow Jennifer's example, she moved to pick a few of the blooms for her room while searching for the source of the unfamiliar odor. From the corner of her eye, she caught a movement. In a flash, the black and white creature turned its back and raised its tail.

Meg dived away with all the strength she could muster, but a pungent stench filled the air in an instant, creeping across everything in the vicinity. She held her breath as she ran to the edge of the woods and when she reached the Loon's well-kept lawn, she sucked in a deep breath. Hands on her knees, she panted, gasping at the putrid smell clinging to the trees, the grass, and worst of all, her.

As if she didn't feel foolish enough already, as a restored member of a family who forgot her long ago, now this. Her pathetic voice rang out, "Help!" Meg hoped she wouldn't need to enter the house to be heard. Or smelled.

Mrs. Dooley burst out the back door from the upper level glassed-in porch, her face covered in concern, her sweater covered in giant sunflowers. She stopped short when she smelled the fresh skunk spray and saw a humiliated Meg kneeling in the back yard. "Land sakes!"

"Mrs. Dooley, I'm covered in it. What do I do?"

She gripped the railing at the edge of the porch. "Just sit tight. I know exactly what to do." Then she hustled back inside.

"Thank you." Meg unfolded her legs beneath her,

stretching them out in the grass. She leaned back on her hands and concentrated on breathing through her mouth. Apparently life at sea did not prepare her for life in the woods. So much for trying to make friends here. Who would talk to a skunky lawyer? The irony did not amuse. Every time she turned around this weekend, something blew up in her face. The trend grew more literal by the day.

Her stomach roiled and emotion riled her. She prepared to grab her situation by the horns and wrestle it into submission. She rejected the stigma of her dad's crime. She would not believe it until she found proof. There must be one piece of truth about this family that she could hold on to, a singular true piece of gold that could once and for all define her. And hopefully exonerate Joey Vanderzee. Was it too much to ask?

Reappearing through a sliding glass door in the walkout basement, Mrs. Dooley trotted across the yard, carrying a heavy bucket as fast as she could without spilling the liquid inside. A clothespin pinched her nose closed, nasalizing the sound of her voice. "Okay, here we go now. This concoction is sure to do the trick."

Meg grabbed an outstretched clothespin for her own nose. Instant relief tempered the nausea rising from her stomach, though she still tasted strong remnants of the odor. She peered into the bucket at a frothy, bubbling liquid. "What is it?"

"Hydrogen peroxide, baking soda and Palmolive. We have to use it while it's still bubbly, though, so let's get to it." She plunged a sponge in the bucket and squeezed it out over Meg's head. "Rub it into your hair, fast as you can."

"Uck." Meg closed her mouth then, afraid of the dripping liquid possibly poisoning her. No need for further mortification or hospitalization.

Mrs. Dooley proceeded to sponge Meg's entire body with the bubbly mixture, clothes and all. "I can't promise this won't maybe change the color of your clothes a little bit, but I figure you'd rather have them smell normal than look normal, am I right?"

Meg nodded. The scent of the cure reminded her of an old drug store Popsie dragged her into somewhere in the Bahamas. They needed disinfectant for a five-day-old gash on her knee, grown very red, puffy, and oozing pus. The entire place reeked of disinfectant, like the inside of a can of Lysol. Happy to smell something other than skunk, hope took hold and she helped rub the mixture with zeal over her clothes and skin.

Meg rubbed her neck and face. "I'm so sorry. I had no idea." The sound of her nasal voice made her giggle.

Joining with her mirth, Mrs. Dooley bellowed out a belly laugh. "I'd take off the clothespin, but I still can't stand the smell."

They both shook with laughter until Mrs. Dooley finally spoke again. "Don't you worry about this one bit. I'm glad I had all the ingredients on hand for you. Let's get you hosed off right now and I'll make you another batch of this stuff. We'll get you upstairs so you can clean yourself head to toe."

"I can't thank you enough."

They stood to cross the lawn. "Don't mention it. That's what I'm here for." She paused and then launched the full force of her curiosity toward Meg. "You seem like you're having quite a time with those folks across the road. Has it been a nice visit so far?"

Meg laced her laugh with heavy sarcasm. "I have to admit, it's been a little rough."

"I can imagine. We've been neighbors for almost twenty-nine years now. They're a quirky bunch." Mrs. Dooley handed the hose to Meg and moved toward the spigot to turn on the water.

The irony of Mrs. Dooley labeling anyone "quirky" drove Meg to turn her face away to avoid broadcasting her amusement. "You've been here that long? Do you know them well?"

"Nobody knows them well, but I s'pose I know them as well as any."

Meg doused her head under the freezing water, willing herself to endure the cold for the sake of a normal human smell.

Clearing the water from her eyes, she asked, "Did you know Duke? I mean, before he left?"

"Oh now, I liked Duke. He walked right over to say hello soon as we bought the place. And Rachel. We might have been great friends if . . ."

"I know the feeling." Meg rubbed her arms and legs under the spraying water.

"But those kids were something else. I guess I shouldn't call them kids, I'm the same age as Joey. Was, anyway."

"You knew him?"

"Of course. We were in school together in Gaylord. His folks convinced my folks to buy this place."

Stunned, Meg stared at her. "What was he like?"

"Fun. Happy. Like the world kept doing him favors. But the rest of them weren't the same. I could hear that Ruby yelling clear up here, across the road once in a while. Lots of squabbling, especially after Rachel went. Course, they're only here in summer now."

Meg held the hose in her hand while she stared at Mrs. Dooley. Water poured onto the grass unchecked. "Has it been like that ever since?"

"Oh, no. When they sent Joey off, things quieted down. Then Duke left and they've kept to themselves since then."

Mrs. Dooley picked up her feet from the water pooling in the grass.

Meg jumped to turn off the water. "Oh. Sorry. I guess I'm ready for round two upstairs. How do I smell now?"

Mrs. Dooley unclipped the clothespin from her nose. Her smile faded, but she said, "Okay then. You head upstairs, get out of those clothes, and I'll whip up another batch for round two."

Chapter Thirteen

Meg sniffed the towel at intervals as she dried her hair. She smelled mostly apple shampoo. The other scent barely peeked through. Wishful thinking? Hopefully not. Regardless, Sunday morning slipped closer to noon and the driving desire to address the shame of her dad's conviction stampeded to the front of her consciousness, trampling Popsie's plans for a new will.

Her mind bounced from one father to the other. For a girl without a family, she found herself in a rare spot. Pulled between two fathers, one dead, the other dying, she struggled to prioritize the interests of the two men. To which man did she owe greater allegiance? The man who gave her life or the one who taught her how to live it?

Mrs. Dooley disappeared with her skunky clothes and Meg luxuriated in the smoky campfire smell of her sweatshirt. Anything but skunk. Meg dropped her hair towel and when she bent to pick it up, the accordion file from Sophie caught her eye from under the bed. She pulled it out and set it on the bedside chair. Biting her lip, Meg stared at the file, half-expecting it to speak. Why would Sophie ask her to sift through all those papers? Meg glanced at the alarm clock by the bed. No time. Too many interviews remained undone.

She grabbed the handle on top of the file and swung it behind her, ready to shove it back under the bed. But the clasp broke loose. All the papers dumped out and littered the floor. Meg stood stunned amid the chaos, still clutching the handle of the empty file.

She slumped to the floor, landing on top of the scattered papers. Her eyes scanned the papers strewn across the room and then flicked to her watch. A groan escaped her mouth, but her hands started pushing papers around in a hurry. She slid some papers into a pile and uncovered a yellowed newspaper clipping. The headline read, "Not Her Brother's Keeper." The article quoted Ruby condemning her brother's selfish crime, which came on the heels of his taking control of the company upon their father's retirement. Ruby went on to explain her new leadership role in the company, and tried to distance Snow Cap and her siblings from their felonious brother. No love lost there.

Meg's interest in the company piqued as she tried to reorganize the papers. Her sense of time dulled and she paused to read the papers as she sorted everything into piles, gleaning a basic understanding of Snow Cap's financial information over the past few decades.

Heaps of paper carpeted the floor around Meg. She

stretched to place another memo on its stack and the tension gathering across her shoulders flashed down her spine like slow lightening. As lunchtime passed, her hopes of discovering magical evidence on behalf of her dad evaporated.

She easily discovered the scheme in the documents. A new property management fee appeared one year, with no additional revenue reported. The Time Share purchase records included no information on down payment check deposits, yet photocopies of those checks remained on file. Obvious money siphoning. But why would he do it? The article about Ruby burned in the back of her brain. Before this happened, he took control of the company when Popsie retired. Why steal from himself and his own family?

Maybe he was framed. As childish as it seemed, she couldn't help wishing her fairy tale father really did measure up to everything in her imagination. Up against the stigma of a criminal father, in desperation she hoped for a different end to this story. Her story. Her history. Even as she pieced together shreds of the past, could she make it right before she launched into the future with Cody?

Her cell lit up across the room. Cody's ring tone chimed—excellent timing. The end of their last conversation pricked her conscience. Meg owed him an apology. She had spewed her frustration in his direction at the exact wrong time.

She unfolded herself and rose from the unyielding wood floor. Meg grabbed her phone, butterfly wings beating inside. "Hey! I miss you. And I'm sorry for what I said last time. I know you're doing your best and I completely trust you with all the wedding details. I want you to know I think you're amazing."

"Oh." He paused at her long hello. "I miss you too and it's OK. I . . . uh . . . are you doing OK?"

Meg brimmed over with the need to process. "You won't believe everything that's happened here since yesterday. Popsie's my grandfather and his son Joey, my dad, died in prison, a convicted felon."

"Whoa. What? Prison? What'd he do?"

"They say he embezzled money from the ski resort, but I don't believe it. My dad wouldn't do that. I don't want my dad to be a bad guy."

"But your true dad is Popsie, right? He adopted you and raised you."

Meg ignored the comment. "I told the whole family who I am and I think Ruby hates me even more, but some of them are really nice. They're my aunts and uncles. I have aunts and uncles, Cody!"

"That's super."

The effort in his voice raised questions in her mind. Was he really not happy for her? Was something else bothering him? "I can't believe it. But I have to find out more about Joey. He can't be guilty."

"You said he went to prison, right?"

"Yes. But maybe he was framed."

Silence. "Hmm."

She tried to keep her voice even. "I'm not crazy."

"I never said you were."

Meg huffed. "Trust me. I'm going to prove his innocence, even though I can't bring him back. He's my family and I'm a lawyer. I have to try."

"What if he's guilty?"

"He's not." But that worry hovered in the back of her brain.

Cody grunted. "Didn't he already go to trial? He probably hired a flock of lawyers to defend him back then. How are you going to resurrect a case that's been decided for years when the defendant isn't even alive to help you? Who would have framed him, anyway?"

Meg plopped on the bed. "That's what I can't figure out. It's a family-run business. Why would he steal from himself and his family? And I don't know of anyone outside the family capable of stealing the money because everyone with access to the money at the time was a Vanderzee."

"You better watch yourself, then. If you go after other

family members, you might turn your happy family reunion up there into something ugly."

Meg propped herself up on an elbow. "I hadn't thought of that."

"Yeah. Well, if you like those people up there, you might want to back off. Justice for a dead man might not be worth it."

She ran her finger along the stitching on the quilt covering the bed. "I better think about that." Shifting gears, she said, "Oh you wouldn't believe what happened to me in the woods this morning."

Cody cleared his throat and interrupted. "Meg. I need to tell you something. It's actually the reason I called. I mean, I called to talk to you, but I kinda have a question for you."

Meg closed her eyes, hoping to ward off another wedding disaster by refusing to look. "Uh oh."

"Yeah. Anchor took off on me today."

Something snapped inside her. "What?"

"I'm so sorry. I was walking him through Uptown and you know how hard he pulls sometimes. Well, he saw a cat on somebody's stoop—you know those townhomes, across from the church? And he just took off chasing it. The leash slipped out of my hands. I ran and ran, but I lost him."

Hot tears ran down Meg's face. The dog carved a place in her heart the day she found him at the pound. In a pathetic sort of way, he became her family. Popsie and Anchor, some family. She sniffled and wiped her nose on her sleeve. Popsie would be gone soon. She counted on Anchor helping her through that loss. Now what?

"Meg, I'm so sorry. I've been all over your five-block route. Where else do you think I should look?"

Meg struggled to find her voice. "Did you check the greenway? I hope he didn't cross over the highway."

"Yeah. I keep going back there. Don't worry, I'm not going to stop looking. I made some signs and I'm gonna hang them up now. I called the police and asked them to keep a look out. He still has his collar on. I'm sure somebody will find him and call."

"Hopefully."

"I hate this happened."

"It was an accident. I know you didn't let it happen."

"No way. We actually started getting along for the first time. I know what he means to you and I'm gonna find him. Soon."

Meg sniffled again. "Cody, I need that dog."

"I know. I'm going to do everything I can. I bet he'll be back by this afternoon. Don't worry about it. If you think of anywhere else I should look, or anybody else I should call, let me know."

Nodding, Meg forced an answer. "OK. Bye." She tossed the phone into the chair and collapsed on the bed, tears flowing from an eternal reservoir somewhere deep inside.

Chapter Fourteen

Rain poured over the eaves of the front porch. Meg glimpsed swaying trees through the watery curtain as occasional wind gusts sprayed her face, mingling tears from heaven with her own. Standing in a corner, she leaned her back against the log wall.

Far from home, Meg longed to snuggle with Anchor on the couch, his head on her leg. Facing the loss of her dog paled in comparison to the impending loss of Popsie, but somehow, the news telescoped her emotions, injecting future grief into her already overwhelmed system.

Sure, Cody never liked the poor dog, and if Anchor didn't come home, Cody wouldn't have to deal with the dog when they got married. Did Cody even try to hang onto the leash when the dog ran off? How far did he keep chase? A block? Half a block? She should have begged the kennel to keep him on.

Meg watched a spider spinning a web under the eave of the porch. The solitary creature commanded complete control of its entire world. With her fingernails, Meg scraped at the finish on the log home. Maybe Anchor would find his way home. But what if he didn't? Things like this always came out right in Disney movies, but so far this week felt more like *Dynasty* than Disney.

Oblivious to the deluge, the spider tracked back and forth across the web, swinging precariously, creeping with little apparent caution. Meg scratched her neck and rubbed her arms. Cody would never find Anchor. For Cody, the only thing better than married life would be married life minus Anchor. Not that he ever complained. No. She needed to stop that line of thought.

The spider descended on an invisible vertical zip line and disappeared from view behind a pot of spring flowers at the edge of the porch. Meg shifted her attention to the smooth gray sky. Rain pelted her world, relentless. How could she have helped Cody like Anchor better? She dropped her face in both hands. Probably too little too late.

Endeavoring to squash her feelings, Meg rehearsed the list of assets Popsie intended to give to his family:

- $10 million
- Deed to a property in Gaylord
- 29% stock in Snow Cap
- Rachel's jewelry
- Painting—LeRoy Neiman, "Sunset Sail"

She tapped her feet on stained wood, no idea who should receive what. If she packed right away, she could feasibly be home by dark. Maybe Anchor would return if he could catch her scent. Let Popsie write his own will.

The sound of plastic flip-flops smacking bare feet at a run splashed through the rain and burst into Meg's quiet moment. Two very wet ponytails dripped onto bright pink rain jackets. Dark skinny jeans drew her eye toward the ear-offending footwear. "Hi, Meg. Where've you been all day?"

"Yeah. We kept thinking you would come down. We have a big question for you."

Meg shifted forward, transferring her weight from the wall to her own feet. "Sorry, I had a little run-in with a skunk up here."

"No way!"

"I smelled it walking up the road. Did it getcha?"

"You could say that. Thank goodness Mrs. Dooley knew what to do. Can you smell it on me now?"

The twins leaned close to sniff and each took a seat on a wooden trunk against the wall beside Meg. Janell swung her legs back and forth. "Hardly anything."

Jane waved her hand. "You're good." She tilted her head to the side. "So what're you doing out here?"

Meg sighed and rubbed her eyes, sore from crying. She

leaned against the railing at the edge of the porch and faced them. "Honestly, I'm thinking about going home. Today. Right now."

A loud response drowned out the rain. "What?"

"No!"

"Why would you leave now?"

"Did you write the will already?"

"You haven't even talked to everybody yet, have you?"

"Is something wrong?"

"But, we're cousins!"

"Did Mom tell you to leave?"

"I'm going to . . . "

Meg's head turned back and forth as if she were at a tennis match. "Girls!"

They silenced themselves and blinked big questioning eyes. Meg noted the bigger eyes sat to her left, Janell. She leaned forward, hands on her knees. "Thanks for being so great to me. You made me feel very welcome here."

Jane looked her straight in the eye. "You're family. You belong here just as much as we do."

Janell shook her head back and forth, sending her ponytail swinging. "We just found out we're cousins. You can't leave now."

Meg chewed her bottom lip. Their mom hated her. Could

she trust them with her thoughts about Joey's innocence? She cleared her throat. "I just found out my dog ran away from home. He's my best friend, and I can't do a thing from up here. And I'm not so sure I can handle writing the will. I think I'm too small for this job. Do you know what I mean?"

Jane nodded, ponytail bobbing. "We feel too small for everything we do."

Janell agreed. "Yeah. Like this bank thing. We've been saving for years to go on our dream trip and now somebody stole our dream. It seems too big."

"That's why we came looking for you. We want to hire you as our lawyer."

Janell nodded, ponytail bouncing. "Will you help us?"

Jane's face fell serious. "We need lots of help."

Closing her eyes, Meg searched all her faculties for a good excuse. But a warm sensation started growing deep inside her and the harder she tried to ignore it, the stronger it became. Her family needed her. She opened her eyes again to identical hopeful faces.

"So?"

Meg sensed the self-pity draining from her system. She steadied her facial features to stop any semblance of a smile. "I can't say no to family. Of course I'll help."

"Yay!" The twins cheered and clapped.

"Let's sit down tonight after dinner and go over your bank statements line by line to see if we can figure out who bled your account dry. And when. And how." She looked up with a smile. "Then we'll get 'em."

Jane clasped Janell's hand. Her hopeful eyes met her sister's and then turned toward Meg. "So you're staying?"

With her raw emotions still hovering in the back of her brain, Meg forced herself to focus on the twins. Both sets of blue eyes stared at her with what seemed to be concern and a hint of desperation. She couldn't abandon these girls.

Even if she decided to get off Popsie's emotional rollercoaster and wash her hands of the will, she would follow through on their case. Surely Cody would be able to find Anchor. He loved them both, undeniably. She swallowed a lump in her throat. "For now, I'm staying. And consider me hired. We're cousins, aren't we?"

"We knew you'd help us. And we know you can write the will too. Why else would Grandfather ask you to do it?"

The rain had stopped, and bits of sunlight filtered through the damp air. Why did he ask her to do this?

Together, the twins stood and buried her in a double hug. "Thank you."

Meg relished the warmth of their acceptance and wished it would rub off on Ruby. "I'll see you back over there in a bit."

"OK, see ya there." Their heads huddled together. "Janell, we have to finish planting those petunias." They waved to Meg and walked off arm in arm, interrupting each other.

"And the border over by the woods too."

"Where'd we leave our gloves?" Their voices faded before the sound of their flip-flops.

Meg squinted in the wet sunlight, and reconsidered her decision to stay. With Anchor on the run, Cody weighed down with her list, and Popsie traveling south toward . . . what would come, she couldn't shake the logic of leaving right now.

Relief poured across Meg's shoulders as she spied her friend. As good as her word, Sophie traipsed across the lawn in knee-high blue and brown paisley wellies, skinny jeans and a matching short blue trench coat. She ducked under the porch roof of the mini-cabin set away from the main house. Mrs. Dooley had recommended the quiet spot tucked behind the gazebo and greenhouse.

Meg stared at her, eyes wide, a goofy smile stuck on her face. "No wonder Ruby hates you. Look how gorgeous you are in the rain!"

Sophie dismissed the comment with a wave of the hand as she sank into the other hand-carved log chair. "Oh please, nothing to see here. I'm glad you called, though. What's up?"

"Well, an hour ago, I almost packed up and left the premises." Her hand rose to stave off any commentary until she finished speaking. "But I've decided to stay on, for now."

Sophie's eyes filled with concern. "What happened?"

"It sounds kind of ridiculous, but my dog ran away." She blinked back tears that threatened to spill.

"Oh my dear."

Meg cut her off. "That's not really the reason. It's kind of the straw that broke . . ." She shook her head, and placed both hands, spread open wide on her lap. "I'm staying." Sniffling, she pulled herself back together and took a deep breath. "I asked you to come over because I have some questions. I want to get this thing over with.

Sophie nodded. "What's it going to take?"

"I didn't want to take another extended drive with the twins so I'm hoping you can tell me about a piece of land I'm supposed to give away."

"That would be 802 West Main Street in Gaylord."

Meg raised her eyebrows. "Exactly. What can you tell me about it?"

"It's prime real estate. Used to be an auto parts store. The second owner started to convert it into a restaurant, but he had a stroke. Duke entered the highest bid at auction following foreclosure. It's close to the highway, close to the heart of town.

It's a great location." Sophie fingered a bloom fallen from a vase stuffed with spring flowers.

"Why did he buy it?"

Sophie hesitated, entranced by the flower. "Because somebody else wanted it."

Meg's head shot up, trying to read Sophie's face. "That doesn't sound like Popsie." Her heartbeat sped up, and she dreaded where this conversation might take her. Curiosity plunged her into it anyway. "Who wanted it?"

Sophie rose and traversed the lawn, heading toward the greenhouse. Meg hopped up and scampered after her. As they entered the green house, wet warmth reached out to grip their senses. Dirty windows blurred the outside world, distorting reality. They idled halfway down one aisle until Sophie stopped and spun around to look Meg in the eye. "Ruby."

"What?"

"Morty's Deli is a big success for the locals in Gaylord. In fact, he's outgrown his current space. He and Ruby bid against Duke for the auto parts store—the location is perfect for him. And the building needs minimal work."

Meg fingered some baby tomato plants. "And Popsie outbid them? But that's mean. Is he even using it?"

Sophie continued along toward the back of the green house. She crossed the end and stopped at the corner. "No. Morty and

Ruby don't know it was him. For five years now, they've tried to buy the property."

"And Popsie won't sell it?"

"No. Rumor has it, rather than looking for a different location, they've hired someone to examine the possibility of legal recourse."

"And now he wants me to give it to someone. But not Ruby?"

"Did he say that?"

"No." Meg shivered in the hot house. Why all the secrecy? Why stop Ruby from buying the property?

Striding toward the front of the greenhouse now, Sophie moved to leave.

"Wait!"

She twisted to face Meg. "I'm not running out on you. But I think you need to sit down for the next piece of information you are going to ask me."

Meg followed her through the door and around the back of the building to the rose garden. Under a dripping arbor, they found a bench and despite the damp, perched on the edge. She searched Sophie's face.

"So go ahead and ask. The one thing you keep wondering."

She chewed her lower lip. Not believing it to hold much consequence, she babbled out a simple, but nagging question.

"What's your role at Snow Cap? I mean, why do you work here?"

Sophie nodded. "This is all I can tell you. On her twenty-sixth birthday, Ruby received stock certificates amounting to twenty percent of Snow Cap."

Meg stared, willing Sophie to put more pieces together for her. When she didn't make a move or offer any further explanation, Meg pressed her. "Popsie is giving away 29% of the stock in his will. So who owns the remaining 51%?"

The look in Sophie's eye told Meg she had asked the right question. But the same look also portended an unsatisfactory answer. With a relaxed smile, she breezed off the bench and wended her way through the rose garden. She called over her shoulder, "My client."

Guy Marks sat up in bed. Bustling city garbage trucks rumbled over cobblestone streets a few hundred yards away. A swampy odor permeated the air, cut infrequently by wafts from the candy shop on the corner—fresh pralines, or as Savannah natives call them, praaah-leens. No problem remembering what city he woke up in today.

No other city sounded, felt, or even smelled like Savannah. He used to tell Meg it resembled Charleston in its obsession with history, but the swamp and the people juiced it up a bit. He smiled at the early morning sounds of the city and remembered jogging through all the squares with Meg at dawn. Sweet scents from jasmine-laden garden walls alternated with the sour odor of trash. People slept on park benches. Old, regal homes stood watch over the decades passing by like dead wood on a stream. The squares marched on, mapping the city like a checkerboard of mysteries.

Two days passed since Meg left, and he'd only reached Savannah. Time loomed before him, a threatening enemy. His body seemed to operate on a timeline entirely apart from his plans, slowing down just as his need to move quickly toward Key West intensified. The stress of "when" death would hit had long ago replaced the uncertainty of "if." He would press Captain Steve to go faster. Would Meg meet him in Key West? Would he see her before his . . . last sunset?

Marcie bounced into the room. "Good morning, Mr. Marks. Didja sleep okay last night?"

"I'm sleeping more than usual lately." He ended with a question in his voice and threw his gaze toward her.

She reached behind him and started plumping pillows. "That's the beauty of prescription meds, my friend. Don't worry. Your body is slowing down, which means you have less energy and you need more sleep. The medication dulls the pain so you can actually get the sleep you need."

Popsie rubbed his legs with his hands, up and down. "I don't like all this sleep. If I'm alive, I want to live, not sleep. Can I take less medication?"

Marcie's eyes softened and she tilted her head as she reached a hand out to grasp his hand. He could see a hundred other patients like himself in her eyes. He directed his gaze away to avoid her efforts at masking her sympathy.

She placed her hand on his. "How 'bout we play it by ear? You tell me when you need another pill. If you wanna wait longer in between pills that's okay with me. I'm here ta make ya comfortable, so you just need to tell me how yer doing and I'll help you get through it."

Popsie nodded once. "Thank you."

Squeezing his hand, she said, "Yer welcome. Now how about some breakfast?"

With hope, he looked up at her. "Can I have something other than dry toast?"

She stood and clapped her hands together once, holding them in front of her chest. "Well! I just spoke with the doctor this morning." She paused for dramatic effect. "He said you can eat anything you want, from now on."

Smiling, he rubbed his hands together. "I realize this means I'm dying even more, but I can't tell you how happy I am to hear this news. Tell Sheila cheesy grits and eggs, please."

She smiled. "Comin' right up!"

As she walked away to find Sheila, he called after her. "Oh, and before we leave harbor, let's get some pralines to go! This is my last day in Savannah, after all."

"Yessir."

He reached for a photo frame on a shelf beside the bed. Duke and Rachel Vanderzee, newlyweds on top of the world. How far he had fallen since that day. He would see her soon— sooner than he had anticipated. Time to come clean.

Replacing the frame, he pulled a folder from the shelf below and opened it on his lap. A yellowed letter lay on top. Tattered edges and well-worn crease lines betrayed the angst with which it had been carried all these years. Seeing it caused the exact same reaction every time: a giant pit opened up in his stomach, and regret swirled out, stinging his eyes with tears. He snapped the folder closed and rang the bell Marcie had left him.

A moment later, she came bustling up the steps. "Everything OK?"

Nodding, Popsie held up the folder. He swallowed hard and willed his voice to sound normal. "Would you fetch Skip for me, please?"

Skip popped around the corner from the wheelhouse. "Speak of the devil. Morning, Mr. Marks."

Breathing a sigh of relief, he held up the folder. It was like ripping off a band-aid; best to do this quick so he wouldn't have time to rethink it. "Skip, I need you to fax this for me. The cover sheet is all set. It's at the back of the folder. Be careful, one of the pages is falling apart. Oh, and would you call to make sure it goes through? It's a B&B up north, and you never know with those little mom and pop shops."

Skip smiled a golden smile and flipped the hair off his forehead. "No problem, Mr. Marks. I'm heading out with a list from Sheila. Looks like somebody threw the healthy diet out the window." He winked. "I'll do this on my way."

"Thank you. It's very important." He caught Skip's eye. "And private."

He turned to go, but said over his shoulder, "I gotcha covered. We'll be hoisting anchor in sixty minutes. See ya!"

Popsie turned to Marcie. "A real go-getter, that one. And he'll make a good captain at some point. Do you think that's what he wants to do?"

Marcie stared at the empty doorway. "I'm not sure. He doesn't seem like a guy who's oper-ate-in' on a plan."

Popsie adjusted the sheets and blankets over his legs. The boy's moods changed erratically, that much he noticed. One day he would be very polite and the next, he couldn't dredge up a "Yes, sir," to save his life. But his mood never affected the work. Up or down, he worked like a driven horse.

"Kids move so fast these days. Everything moves fast. I thought I moved at a pretty good clip, but for the first time in my life I think I'm in the slow lane."

She took the quilt from the bed and folded it with great care, replacing it over his legs. "Welcome to the slow lane. You see more when you slow down. It's a good place to be."

Popsie grasped the edge of the quilt and ran his fingers along the edge. Rachel's fingers flew across patches of color in his mind then blurred to the quilt before him. "Now. Tell me what else the doctor said this morning. How much longer have I got?"

Chapter Fifteen

A knock on the door startled Meg. She finished tying off her ponytail and peeked through the peephole to find Mrs. Dooley's wide face filling the view. She pasted on her best fake smile and opened the door. "Oh, hello."

Mrs. Dooley stood, toes on the threshold, in a bubblegum pink sweater with a white bunny embroidered on the front. Hands behind her back, she snooped over Meg's shoulder. "Hiyah. Don't you smell nice."

Meg received the compliment as it was intended, but with a dollop of chagrin. At least no one else had smelled her foolish mistake. "What's up?"

Mrs. Dooley's hands flew up, one of them containing some papers. "Well, this came for you. It's a fax. From Georgia." Her emphasis on the word Georgia made it sound like a foreign country, or a crime.

Meg's heart fluttered. So Popsie woke up in Georgia today. Probably Savannah. Would Sheila make room for some pralines on his new diet? They shared the same weakness. She took the papers from Mrs. Dooley. "Thank you very much. Do you know what time it arrived?"

"Oh, just now, it did. Just now."

Backing into the room slightly, Meg began to close the door. "Thanks for bringing it up right away."

Through the narrowing opening, Mrs. Dooley scrambled to ogle the room again, as if it might enlighten the contents of the fax, which she had undoubtedly read. "You're welcome. It was nothing at all. Let me know if there's anything else you need. Anything at all." The last of her words faded behind the closed door.

Meg lifted the coversheet to reveal some legal documents and a personal letter. Her gaze traveled around the room, as if Mrs. Dooley's prying eyes somehow lingered. Convinced of her privacy, she settled into a wing chair, grateful for the luxury of bracing herself for the unexpected.

Margaret Murray Vanderzee appeared in bold type across the top document and like a diesel engine starting, Meg's heartbeat thundered in her chest. The document recorded the legal name change of Margaret Murray Vanderzee to Megan M. Marks.

Meg had always wondered why she'd been given no middle name. Popsie pulled Southern tradition out of a hat and used it as an excuse for why she'd been given only an initial. She still mourned the loss of a chance to choose her middle name. Her given middle name versus her maiden name. The signature at the bottom told it all. The handwriting belonged to Popsie, but the name read Duke Vanderzee. In giving her only a middle initial, he had changed her name while retaining a piece of the old.

Meg smiled and shook her head as a life puzzle piece locked into place. But on the heels of solid proof, a hundred questions battered her brain. Why did Popsie change their names? Why did they leave? Why did he send the information now? Why did she feel worse instead of better at this news? With reluctance she pushed her curiosity about "Murray" to the back of her mind for another time.

"Ring around the maze-y, pocket full of daisies, ashes, ashes, they all fall down." The song from long ago rang over and over in her consciousness along with the memory of smashing daisies into a jeans pocket, yellow crumbs lodged under her fingernails, staining her skin.

Before she became Megan Marks, the dad she longed to know named her Margaret. And called her Maggie Daisy. A formal, official, and legally binding document stared her in the face, proved the point, and made it truly true.

She shuffled the papers to examine the rest. The second document read across the top, Last Will and Testament of

Joseph Jay Vanderzee. Meg's head popped up, her gaze locked onto a photograph hanging over the bed. A blue jay in the snow. Did blue jays usually stay for the winter, or was he caught unaware?

Meg stared at the photo, refusing to cross an imaginary line represented by the will she held in her hands. She weighed the moment, fearing it might become a milestone in her life, from which she could never return.

She looked around the room, searching for an emergency, anything to distract her attention away from the inevitable. Lilacs filled a narrow vase on the vanity in the bathroom. Housekeeping? Or Mrs. Dooley? Seeing them awakened her to their scent, suffusing into the bedroom along with stinky regret from the last time she allowed herself to be distracted by lilacs.

Meg squeezed her eyes tight and took a deep breath. She blew it out and opened her eyes to read the will. Better fast and painful than slow and tortuous.

Joseph Jay Vanderzee, divorced from Stacie Lynn Vanderzee in 1984. I have one living child, Margaret Murray Vanderzee. I hereby appoint Duke Vanderzee as her legal guardian and request that he adopt her as his own daughter in the event of my death.

I leave everything including my stock in Snow Cap to be held in trust for Margaret Murray Vanderzee until she reaches her twenty-eighth birthday, at which time she may decide to keep or sell all stock. The terms require that such an inheritance be revealed on her 28th birthday, June 13, 2010, or upon the death of Duke Vanderzee, whichever comes first.

To judge a man by his will seemed a lot like judging a book by the last chapter. Meg squirmed in her seat, trying to escape the voyeuristic quality of the moment. The wing chair boxed her in. She stood to pace. A good walk across the floor cleared the mind, and churned her thoughts, and helped her cope . . . a little.

This situation required a longer walk than the room could provide. She rolled the papers up and shoved them in her back pocket on her way out the door, keenly aware of the remaining unread page. A sick feeling crept into her stomach like the moment in a movie when the bad guy turns down a chance to be good.

Her body unerringly led her to the family dock and the water, a combination which served to soothe her under normal circumstances. Her feet swung ten inches above the water and she leaned back on her hands, poised to absorb multiple splinters from the ancient dock. She stared, unseeing, across the clear sunny lake, but dragged her mind back into the present.

A blue and white striped sunfish sail fluttered as her pilot struggled to catch a breeze in the middle of the lake. To the left, a classic wooden runabout cut through the water throwing up a huge wake and pounding the air with what sounded like at least a 120hp engine. A pontoon boat chugged away, cruising the coastline at a sleepy pace. It dipped when the runabout's wake intersected its path, taking the turbulence in stride.

A family of ducks swam twenty feet past the end of the dock, following the shoreline. Well, a mother and her ducklings, anyway. Where did the father ducks go? They never seemed to be around.

Peace and recreation all around her, Meg's heart floundered in utter turmoil.

"Yah! Scat!" The dock shook as heavy footsteps thundered toward her at a sprint. A burly man drew up, his foot grazing Meg's backside. He braced himself by leaning his leg into her back, and she jumped at the loud crack of a BB gun firing over her head.

Her scream echoed as she ducked, but also craned her neck to look up at the man who would terrorize baby ducks. Uncle Kenneth.

"What? Why?" Meg sputtered.

He released a few more shots. Most landed just behind a ducktail, propelling them away at a fast swim. "Oh come on. A BB won't kill a duck. We don't want them hanging around here and bringing swimmer's itch with them."

Meg's hand pressed her heart, willing it to slow. "You scared me."

"Couldn't be helped." Kenneth yelled at the ducks again as they paddled on toward the next dock. He lowered himself and placed the gun between them like a dare. "Bet you're surprised to see me, huh?"

Meg eyed the gun. "Surprised, perplexed, and a little freaked out, thank you very much."

Kenneth punched her upper arm with a playful jab. "Yup. You've got ol' Joey's spunk, alright."

"So you heard."

"Yeah. Ruby called me cussing up a storm. Told me to get my butt down here and kick you off the property."

The pit of her stomach yawned open and threatened to suck what remained of her confidence away. "Really?"

His shoulders shook with silent . . . giggles. "Not really. Well, the cussing part is true. I made great time to Rogers City on Cutthroat, so I figured I'd come over and finish out the weekend with everybody. How's the will coming?"

Meg fixed her gaze across the lake. Boat motors hummed in the distance, burning through the summer's first tank of gas. "There's a question."

Kenneth's hands gripped the edge of the dock and he leaned forward, investigating the rippling water below. "My guess is Duke Vanderzee's conscience finally caught up with him. Must be gettin' close to kickin' the bucket. Am I right?"

His bright blue eyes flashed a look of certainty that stole the question mark off his inquiry. Meg's mouth fell open. She clamped it closed, sitting like a glass of water, filled to the brim. One move either way and everything would spill.

Kenneth picked up the gun and placed it on his other side. "Are you stickin' around, or leavin'?"

Meg's hand slipped and she felt a splinter pierce the palm of her hand. She raised it to investigate how far under the skin it had lodged. "I started packing right after I read all of this." She grabbed the roll of papers from behind her and tossed it into his lap. "The last page."

He read the page and grunted. "If this letter is real, then he knew it and . . ."

She finished the sentence, her voice rising with each word. "He. Did. Nothing."

Meg slammed a fist onto the dock. "I wanted to believe my dad was innocent. So bad. Then I find out Popsie figured it all out and what did he do?"

Kenneth shook his head side to side. "He sent Ruby a letter. A letter?"

In a whining tone, Meg interpreted the words of the letter. "Please Ruby, turn yourself in. It's not right."

"Yeah."

"Yeah. And then he died. My dad died in prison a convicted felon for a crime he never committed. A crime his own sister set him up for. And Popsie let it slide."

Kenneth leaned his elbows on his thighs, stared down into the water.

Meg picked at the sliver in her palm, trying to grip it with her fingernails. "You were right."

His head swiveled toward her. "Huh?"

"You called him a coward. So you knew."

His hands flew up in defense. "Oh no, you don't. I never heard Joey was set up. I called him a coward because he liked Joey best and never tried to hide it. Gave him half the business with no shame, but wouldn't answer a single question. He never admitted to one mistake, and wouldn't listen to a word of criticism."

A deep churning began inside Meg. A rumble of sickness threatened to erupt, but she swallowed, holding it at bay for a moment. "Why? How could he? And if he liked my dad best, then how could he just let it lie?"

They sank into a silence heavy with personal trauma and mixed emotions. Water rippled against the shore, and smoke from a neighbor's fresh bonfire drifted across the water toward them.

"Coward." They breathed, almost at the same time.

Heat like a wildfire built up inside Meg and she rose to let it fill her entire body. Hands shaking, she balled her fists as she stomped down the dock toward land.

Chapter Sixteen

"Runnin' won't solve anything, you know."

Meg stopped at Kenneth's words. The trees overhead roofed her in, and she stood still as he walked around to face her. She flung her words at him. "I think it might actually solve my problem. If I go back to my old life, the only thing I have to deal with is a dying father." And a lost dog. And a wedding. But still.

Ken rubbed his hand over his brush cut. "So he is dying."

Shoot. The lawyer in Meg internally kicked the daughter inside her. Granddaughter. A sudden clarity of thought bathed her brain as she experienced her first official "conflict of interest." The cost of Popsie's little social experiment increased every couple hours. The effects threatened to render her life an irreversible mess. She needed all of her faculties running at full capacity, which meant all the emotional stuff would have to wait.

Meg took a deep breath and blew it out. "I can't believe I said that out loud. Will you keep it to yourself for me? For a couple days?"

Kenneth smirked. "How are we doing on that will? Have you written up the boat yet?"

Meg closed her eyes and shook her head. Unbelievable. "I need to know more about Ruby."

They walked toward the front porch, and Ken put his arm around her. "I'm just kidding about that. I'll keep your secret. But we should probably see if that letter is legit."

Meg's undying trust of Popsie, even after all she had learned over the weekend, stood stark against Kenneth's mistrust of the same man. Popsie wouldn't send her phony evidence. If she didn't believe it, she couldn't believe anything. "It's real."

"You want to believe it's real."

She led him up the front steps. "I'm telling you, it's real."

He remained silent, and she received it as a truce.

Thorny wicker furniture crowded the porch, but Meg's gaze fell on a hanging porch swing at the end. They sat side-by-side and eased into a gentle swinging motion. Cool air swirled past their faces.

Meg adjusted her weight on the swing, sliding toward the outer edge in hopes of balancing their weight difference. "Tell me about Snow Cap. Everything must hinge on what happened with the business."

"Everything always comes down to money. Follow the

money and you'll find the source of any problem. Look at every political move in the last . . ."

Meg cut him off. "Can we stick to Snow Cap right now?"

Kenneth regarded her for a quiet moment. "Sure. Pop was grooming Joey to take over the business. We all knew it and we assumed Joey would follow Pop as Snow Cap's CEO."

"Did Ruby work at Snow Cap during that time?"

"Well, yeah. She had the fancy business degree from Ferris State. She kept the books."

"She worked full time?"

"Yeah." He huffed. "She'd be there all hours. Couldn't get enough filling in those ledgers. She likes filling out forms as much as I like shooting deer. She was made to crunch numbers."

Meg felt her eyes rolling, and tried to hide her disgust at the obvious Vanderzee blind spot. "So what happened that changed everything?"

Kenneth kicked to push the swing into a wide arc. "Joey's thirtieth birthday party. Pop planned a nice dinner in the resort dining room. I drove up from Grand Rapids for it. We all gave him birthday cards. He opened Pop's card last—a legal-size envelope. That should have tipped me off, but I guess the wine numbed my curiosity. When he opened that last one, he pulled out stock certificates. Pop gave him 51% interest in Snow Cap."

A fly buzzed by her ear. "Huh. No strings attached?"

"No strings. Joey didn't know what to say. He wore a big dopey smile for the rest of the night."

"What did Ruby do?"

"She stood up at the table when he opened it. We all looked at each other, trying to figure out her deal. I remember because it felt so uncomfortable. Almost like she had whipped us with an angry speech, but she never spoke a word. Then she sat down and didn't say much for the rest of the night. Six months later, the cops arrested Joey at work."

Meg planted her feet on the floor and stopped the swing. She bored her gaze into Kenneth's face. "And the whole family believed Joey embezzled money from the family business. And he owned more of it than anybody else. Come on."

Kenneth stood and threw his hands in the air. "A court of law found him guilty. Why would we doubt it?"

"Do you realize how obvious it sounds with Ruby cooking the books and Joey getting set up right after he received—free and clear, mind you—controlling stock in the company? How did this not come up in court?"

"Overwhelming evidence. Lots of evidence with Joey's signature on it. You can't argue with a paper trail."

The screen door creaked open, and Ruby sauntered out onto the porch, a smug smile on her face. "You got that right, soldier. It was one of those 'open and shut' cases every lawyer dreams about."

The air between them filled with unspoken bitterness. Like
a can of soda in the freezer, only an explosion would end it. The
pit of Meg's stomach fell, like a brick of lead had lodged itself
there. How long had Ruby listened in on the conversation? The
challenge she offered beckoned. "How long have you been in
the forgery business, Ruby?"

Ruby laughed, tipping her head back. "Little girl, this
family is no place to play Perry Mason. You might as well pack
your things and leave right now. You are about to be sunk. Fair
warning."

Kenneth sidled toward the steps. "Ruby, don't be a bully.
Let her do what she came to do. If you play nice, she might save
you a little something in the will."

Ruby sat in the rocker to Meg's left. The wicker bent under
her weight with a crackle as she leaned back into a slow rocking
motion. Her aunt's gaze felt like a poker in Meg's side while she
responded to Kenneth. "If she plays nice, I might save some
semblance of her reputation."

"You two need to talk this out. Ruby, she has a decent point
and Daddy's letter implicates you. Meg, she might have an
explanation. Regardless, you need to get to the bottom of it. I'm
not surprised ol' Pop left us another mess." He descended the

steps and headed toward the back of the house. He called to them over his shoulder. "I don't want to hear any snarling."

Meg pushed herself backward on the swing, but it swung crooked because she still sat on one end, and Kenneth had vacated the other end. "So now you're going to spread rumors about me to ruin my reputation? Are we back in sixth grade?"

Ruby stared out at the lake. "You're going to wish for sixth grade, my dear. Have you heard of a little charge called 'tortious interference'?"

"You think I forced Popsie to give me control of his will? I wouldn't wish this task on my worst enemy!"

The smug smile on Ruby's face did not waver.

The wind picked up, blowing the neighbor's blue bonfire smoke across the front yard. The smoky scent burned Meg's nose as she dredged her mind for tort details she learned in law school. Did Ruby have a case? No. Would she actually file a suit? The claim was ludicrous. "How do you plan to prove such a thing? We both know it's not true."

"You seem so confident. I guess you don't need to worry, then. I'm filing suit Tuesday morning, as soon as the courthouse opens. And I also plan to spread a little information down in the Charlotte area, to make sure everyone receives full disclosure before they decide to donate to a charity started up by a devious criminal mind."

She wouldn't. She couldn't. "Do not touch Orphan Advocacy. You have no right."

"Well, you have no right to traipse in here and shake up my family. And my inheritance."

Meg shuddered at the brutality in Ruby's eyes. "Actually, Popsie gave me that right. And it's not your inheritance unless someone bequeaths it to you."

A slow smile skulked across her aunt's face, revealing a lipstick smear on one of her front teeth. "Go home, little girl."

The twins urged Meg forward. They shared a dubious glance and turned back to her with uncertain expressions. "Mom said to bring you to the kitchen."

They had found her where Ruby left her, on the porch swing. Ruby's command to go home kept her glued to the spot. Now she faced round two with Ruby, her next move hovering in the room ahead of her. Meg braced herself and strode from the front door through the gathering room, down the hallway leading to the cottage kitchen. Photos lined both walls. One end began with framed black-and-white images, and progressed to more recent photos in vivid color at the end of the hall. Every shot included the lake in some way. Family history at the lake completely devoid of Joey and Meg taunted her with every step. "Why do I feel like this is a set up?"

Janell hugged Meg's arm. "Mom told us to bring you to the kitchen, that's all we know. Well that, and Mom looked kinda mad, but not much more than usual."

Jane patted Meg's shoulder. "It's our favorite room in the house. We'll make you some coffee."

"Or hot chocolate."

"Yum."

Meg shook off her concern and opened the swinging door. The unmistakable aroma of cherry pie hit her like a wave, but then she stopped and gaped at the sweltering, crowded kitchen. Some of the family sat on the countertops, some on chairs, many stood. All scrutinized her with varying scowls and discerning gazes. Meg stopped and considered a hasty retreat, panic rising in her chest.

Meg pursed her lips, holding back angry words. Ruby knew how to pick a fight. And apparently, she knew how to stack the deck in her favor.

Janell dropped Meg's arm. "What?"

Jane spoke over Meg's shoulder. "You guys! Why's everyone here?"

Meg scanned the room for Ruby. She blocked the door leading to the side porch, hands folded across her bulging midsection, head tilted slightly, a smile stretching her rotund face into an expression reminiscent of the Cheshire Cat. Meg's urge to fight rose inside her. Bully tactics or no, she would stand her ground. She clasped her hands behind her back. "Hello, Ruby. I believe you sent for me?"

Every face in the room—sixteen, if she counted right—focused on Ruby. "We sent for you, Margaret, and I'll tell you why."

Her old name. Her father's face flashed before her eyes. The room seemed to shift as if a giant hand shoved the house over two feet. Everyone in the room became preoccupied with the floor, their fingernails, the four cherry pies forming a line down the center of the table, anything other than Meg. This family—her family—stood together against her, on the other side of the table. Despite the stifling heat in the room, Meg felt her insides freeze, brittle as thin ice. She stepped back, bumping into the twins, whispering behind her. Ruby used them like pawns in this process, so in Meg's mind they remained her only allies.

Ruby raised her hands, palms together, fingertips pointing at Meg. "We should have done this years ago with your father. But since you seem to have inherited his gold-digging tendencies, we are hoping to settle this family dispute once and for all."

Meg's stomach flopped and her heart pounded in her chest. Gold digger? She opened her mouth to protest, but Ruby steamrolled her with more accusations.

"How you convinced Daddy to let you write his will is something I wish I could have seen. As I told you earlier, I'm filing a civil suit on Tuesday claiming you have exercised undue influence over our father regarding his final will and testament."

Meg could not remain silent. "I didn't ask for this! In fact, he tricked me into taking this job. I thought a friend of his hired me, and I only learned the identity of my client after I arrived."

Janell squealed. "Oh, the picture in the shed!"

Meg nodded. "Yes, that was the moment. I didn't even know Popsie's given name until this weekend. I know him as Guy Marks."

Ruby huffed. "That's a fine story, dearie. But it's too little too late, I'm afraid. Your real father stole from this family years ago."

Meg cut her off. "You set him up. I have proof."

Questioning faces followed a whispering roar as it travelled around the room. Meg stood up straighter. Had she landed a point? She felt her hands trembling.

Ruby's hands settled across her wide girth again. Her face looked down on Meg with something akin to pity. "Nice try. You can't have proof of something that never happened. It makes you look rather desperate, which I suppose you are."

Trying to edge her way closer to Ruby, Meg's foot bumped

a chair leg. She looked around the room, meeting awkward stares. "I know what you did, Ruby. You can't get away with it."

Meg turned to face the crowded room at large. "She framed my dad for embezzlement out of pure jealousy." When the entire family met her accusation with only silence, she shot a look around the room. "Doesn't anyone believe me?"

Ruby grunted and spoke to her family. "Remember when Father gave half the business to his precious Joey? Well, little Maggie Daisy stands to inherit that little nugget on her twenty-eighth birthday, which, coincidentally, is this year—next month, in fact. So now that she's established herself as an official 'family member,' she can write herself into Daddy's will, give herself everything Popsie owns—including his remaining 29% of Snow Cap stock—and we all get hung out to dry."

Ruby's bombshell hung in the air, unchallenged. Meg staggered backward until she stepped on the toes of a twin. A cold sweat oozed from her brow. The possibility hadn't dawned on her before. Surely Popsie never meant for her to bequeath anything to herself. "I would never do that. Why would I?"

Ruby snarled a laugh at her. "Payback. We sent your daddy to jail for ripping us off. You want retribution. It makes perfect sense."

The room spun around Meg. "She's poisoning you against

me. I'm not the one gunning for retribution." Her eyes swept across the faces, landing on Amy's. "Aunt Amy. You have to believe me."

Kenneth cleared his throat. "Missy, you better keep your mouth shut for now." To the rest, he said, "Meg does have a letter, supposedly from Daddy. We should probably call the lawyers in on it."

She noticed a stiffness in his jaw as he spoke. How could Kenneth turn on her like that? Only an hour ago, they shared a mutual disgust for Ruby and Popsie's lack of courage to expose her. What did Kenneth stand to gain by taking Ruby's side on this? Or better, what did he stand to lose if he didn't? Meg shook her head in defeat. The room and every person in it seemed to grow tall around her. Evidently, Ruby practiced her blackmailing skills regularly and often.

The room broke into a jangling racket of questions and accusations. Meg caught various comments through the din.

"What if she is trying to steal our money?"

"Where did she get the letter?"

" . . . Joey's dead."

"We don't even know her."

" . . . might be harmless."

Placing two fingers in her mouth, Meg whistled the room into silence. Grateful for the entire day Popsie spent teaching her this skill, she longed to sit beside him with an undying belief in him as her perfect, if eccentric, father once again.

But that ideal lay shattered on the ground. Popsie let Ruby off the hook. Ruby's actions stole too much from her: a stable life with her Dad, an extended family, and summers on Lake Charlevoix. She alienated Popsie from the rest of the family, forced him into a struggle to replace Meg's early life with a reclusive, transient life on the ocean. Meanwhile, Ruby usurped Joey's position and lived the life he should have enjoyed. Until now. No wonder Popsie kept me away from Ruby all these years. Joey's will appeared to be the last obstacle standing between Ruby and her precious control over Snow Cap.

Revenge lurked in the corners of her consciousness, but Meg's desire to get out tamped it down. She addressed the room, her words oozing with sarcasm. "I believe I have gathered all the information I need in order to write the last will and testament of Duke Vanderzee. Thank you for your gracious hospitality this weekend."

She spun on her heel and fled.

Chapter Seventeen

The red suitcase bumped into the doorframe, jostling Meg so her shoulder bag knocked into the other side. Thrown off balance, she stood still in the doorway a moment before she reached back and pulled the door to her room shut. Now, to find Mrs. Dooley. Dread rose up inside her at the thought of taking her leave from the nosy woman.

She descended the staircase without further luggage incident and dumped her bags in the foyer. Heavy quiet padded the front hall like thick oriental rugs. Meg checked her watch and decided to make a foray into the kitchen in search of her hostess.

The decision to leave inoculated her with a supreme sense of relief. Sometimes it just felt good to run away home. Especially after Ruby's cruelty splashed in her face. How did Popsie imagine this escapade would end?

The warm and cluttered kitchen oozed with the comfort only a seasoned cook could achieve. Cast iron baking forms covered the wall, which stretched up to a cathedral ceiling, lit by skylights. Wood lined the entire room, except where brick accented the cooking areas. Collectible plates were mounted everywhere and carefully tied bunches of select spices hung upside down over the window, drying in the warmth of a truly comfortable room. Meg moved to the window overlooking the verdant backyard, but back-pedaled right away as Mrs. Dooley burst through the back door, arms full of groceries. "Oh my dear! How are ya?" She held a bag out to Meg. "Wouldja mind?"

"Yes—I mean, no." She accepted the bag, placed it on the counter top, and unpacked the groceries on autopilot. Mrs. Dooley ran out to the car for another load. Meg contemplated walking out the front door without a further word, but couldn't bring herself to do it. The skunk rescue merited a proper farewell.

Mrs. Dooley returned with another armful and set the bags on the counter with great fanfare and a huge sigh. "Well now, that sure was good timing. Thanks for your help. I almost dropped that bag. You saved me! What were you looking for in the kitchen? Didja need something?"

Prattling. The word perfectly described her manner of speech. Meg smothered the temptation to smile and concentrated on the task at hand. "Mrs. Dooley, I need to check out this afternoon."

Her wide face thinned as the smile drained from her

expression. "Oh, that's terrible. I'm so sorry to hear it. You know, check-out time was supposed to be 11am. Wouldn't you rather stay the night and be on your way in the morning?"

Meg's stomach revolted at the thought of one extra minute near Ruby and the family that might have been. A sense of dread spread in her chest at the thought. "No, thank you. I'm sure the Vanderzees will cover the fee. I'm sorry for the late notice, but I really have to get back to Charlotte." An urgent need to distance herself from this beautiful, painful place built up inside her.

"North Carolina?"

"Yes. So, is there anything I need to do before I go? My key." She slid it across the counter, avoiding the hawk-like eyes boring into her.

Mrs. Dooley slid the key to the side, and took Meg's hands in hers. "I've enjoyed your stay with us here at the 'Call of the Loon.' I hope you'll return some day. I'm working on some new cake recipes for afternoon tea."

Meg barely kept her eyes from rolling. "You've been so kind. Thanks especially for the skunk potion. You saved me, there."

"Oh, that was nothing. Now you know what to do, don'tcha?"

Meg smiled and extricated her fingers from the innkeeper's grasp. She couldn't imagine a scenario where she would need the de-skunking recipe again, living as she did, in the city or on a boat. Of course as soon as she married Cody, her idea of "home" would shift from wherever Popsie docked to their townhouse. At least that's what she planned. She hurried across the room and turned back to say, "I'm going to wait for my ride on the front porch if that's OK."

"Oh yes, by all means." Following her out the door, Mrs. Dooley chattered on. "I'm so glad your important business brought you here. I hope you'll remember us to your friends and family. Maybe next time you can visit for vacation and enjoy the scenery a little bit more."

Nice idea. Bad timing. Meg gripped her suitcase and lodged the strap of her other bag onto her shoulder. Mrs. Dooley held the front door open. With her head down, Meg marched through the door, but stopped short when she noticed a pair of banana colored pumps planted shoulder-width-apart on the porch in front of her.

Meg followed the khaki pants up the trash-can shaped body, past the light green oxford and yellow silk scarf. Her shoulders slumped when her gaze met Ruby's. The bags she carried grew heavier. "I'm going. You won. There's no need to gloat because I already feel like crap. Stop kicking dead horses."

The smug smile lasted a moment before Ruby spoke. "I don't need to gloat. I came to inform you that my lawyer suggested we also file a formal complaint with the North Carolina State Bar Association. I'm sure they would be mortified to learn that one of their bright young lawyers has broken the law for personal gain. That never looks good on the ol' resume. I had a nice chat with a beat reporter this afternoon too. Let's see, where was he from? Oh yeah, he lives and works in Charlotte, North Carolina." Ruby pointed a chubby finger her way showing mock surprise. "Hey, that's where you're from, isn't it?"

"You managed to screw up the whole first part of my life already. Thanks for following through on the rest. I never could have messed it up this badly on my own." Meg's hand slipped on the handle, but she managed to heft the suitcase into a better grip, as she sidestepped around Ruby. She aimed all of her attention on the monumental task of reaching the bottom of the porch steps with dignity.

Meg crossed her arms over her chest, leaned her head back on the front seat and with closed eyes, released a sigh of defeat. Sophie's BMW 7 Series Li Sedan hugged the curves of Boyne City Road as it sped them toward Charlevoix Municipal Airport. Meg surrendered her body to the smooth speed of the high performance vehicle and her mind to the comfortable silence Sophie's perspicacity provided.

As she sank into the cashmere and black leather interior, Meg allowed the elegant neutral colors to soothe her like a warm sandy beach. Soft arias played on the radio, insulating her from the harsh reality she had fled. Aside from the battering suffered by her ego, Meg's intellect struggled to form a response worthy of consideration against Ruby's malicious actions.

The hope which buoyed her through so many lonely nights on the water, law school, even as she traveled to Michigan for Mr. Vanderzee, vanished like a nickel tossed into the darkness of an impossibly deep well. Except this well granted no wishes. And even it if did, she couldn't formulate a wish if she wanted to. Popsie's words from just days before echoed in her head. "Everything I withheld from you was for your protection." Protection from Ruby. Maybe ignorance really was bliss.

Sophie cleared her throat, bringing Meg back into the present. "Your father arranged the private jet for you as soon as you arrived. They've been waiting for your call. You'll be wheels-up fifteen minutes after we arrive."

Meg inhaled the new car smell and shifted in the soft leather seat. Though Popsie sent her into the lion's den, at least he prepared an escape route. He obviously knew she might need it.

"Thanks for picking me up, Sophie." Meg stared out the window at the ends of driveways disappearing into thick woods, mailboxes blurring past her window. Occasional flashes of lake appeared between the trees, sometimes close and others times from a greater distance. They touched the hurt places inside her as if the water beckoned to her, don't go, let me fix it.

Sophie reached over and grasped Meg's hand. "It's okay that you're leaving. You didn't fail."

Meg half laughed. "Well, maybe I didn't fail, but three days with the Vanderzees have altered my life such that I can see no recovery on the horizon . . . ever."

Sophie placed both hands on the wheel. "What did she do?"

"Ruby? She's suing me. For 'tortious interference.' It's sort of ironic, though. Against my will, but wanting to honor my father's dying wish, I fly up here to write his buddy's will and end up served with a lawsuit and public humiliation. She's spreading lies about me in Charlotte to ruin my career and my non-profit organization, not to mention turning my entire family against me, a family I never knew existed until this weekend."

Sophie took a breath as if about to speak, but Meg cut in. "And aside from the professional wasteland created by Ruby, Popsie launched my own personal identity crisis. Problem is, I can't go back and the idea of moving forward hurts too much."

Sophie glanced at Meg and then pulled out onto Highway 131, the two-lane highway leading straight through Charlevoix. "I hate to press you like this, but what are you going to do now?"

Thus far, her only thought had been home. She needed to be where her heart belonged. She would fly to Charlotte, but home always seemed to be somewhere else. And today it felt like wherever Popsie and Gilda were—and she didn't know where they were.

Guilt tugged at her mind. Why did she long for Popsie more than Cody? Cody should be her home. His family would be hers after Popsie . . . Meg twirled her ponytail around her finger and steadied her gaze forward. "I'm getting married on Saturday."

"What? Are you kidding? And you're up here this weekend?"

"I know. I thought it was a job. And I did it for Popsie, because he needed me."

"Hm."

"I know. Talk about a crash landing. I think I need to forget about this whole weekend until after the wedding. We plan to postpone the honeymoon until Popsie's . . . you know. We'll spend the last days with him on the boat."

"But what about the will? Are you going to do it?"

Meg bit her lip. "I haven't decided yet."

Sophie pressed her lips together and let Meg's response hang in the air a moment. Her grip on the steering wheel tightened till her knuckles turned white. "Meg, this whole crazy weekend hinged on the will. You have a chance to set things right. Use the will to do what's best for you."

"It's not about me. It's Popsie putting his affairs in . . ." Meg's voice trailed off at the end.

Sophie shot her a look. "Tell me you get this."

She turned her head to the right and watched bright mounds of flowers at the street's edge blurring together. In her mind's eye, Meg held an image of Popsie sitting in his old director's chair on the back deck, drinking hot water from his stained, white coffee mug. She loved his smile and his bright blue eyes when he winked at her. She loved him better than anyone else in the world, but he shouldn't love her best. He had five other kids. And lots of other grandkids. Ken's blunt words replayed in her head. He liked Joey best and he never tried to hide it.

Popsie's motive for initiating this whole fiasco finally lay in chunks before her. Like a puzzle on a table, two-thirds finished, she started to see the big picture. One part guilt, one part favoritism, one part revenge…or was it justice? But he left the justice to her discretion. All the years she spent feeling sorry for herself, and more years spent training for a job that would enable her to stand up for those whom life had treated unfairly, failed to prepare her for a moment like this. Justice for herself lay at her fingertips and she was running away.

"I think I just did."

The road turned slightly southward and sunshine streamed through the side window like a blinding spotlight. Meg flipped the visor down and switched it over to block the sun on the passenger side. She blinked away dark spots passing across her vision and felt the weight of her impending decision draped across her shoulders like a heavy robe. A judge's robe.

Chapter Eighteen

The small plane's descent awakened Meg. She blinked her eyes to clear them and leaned toward the window. The plane hovered over the runway at Concord Regional Airport. Trees and small buildings rushed past. Heavy thoughts tamped down the thrill of private jet transportation like a sudden rainstorm kills a picnic.

As they taxied, Meg powered up her phone and checked for messages. She shook her head as if it could clear the sleepy cobwebs lingering in the corners of her consciousness. The speech she planned to dump on Popsie played through her mind again, poised on her tongue.

"Welcome home, Ms. Vanderzee." The pilot opened the door and lowered a folding set of stairs.

Meg's head snapped up. The name pounded her brain and chilled her heart. She wore the wrong name for most of her life, and today this false name rankled her to the core. But what did it matter? In less than a week, her name would change yet again—to Megan McKenny. Or Margaret McKenny. Or Margaret Murray McKenny? Or should she use one name from her real dad and one name from Popsie to make it Margaret Marks McKenny?

Meg gathered her things from the plane and descended into heavy air, which wrapped around her body like a plastic suit of armor and curled the ends of her hair into instant frizz.

Learning her given name called her very identity into question. Who would she be if not for the name change? If not for Popsie? Her next (and hopefully final) name change could set her life on an entirely different course. She muttered aloud to herself, "Best choose wisely."

As she entered the tiny airport, she automatically scanned the scarcely populated lobby for Cody, fully anticipating the looming disappointment of arriving unaccompanied and unannounced. Should have called him. What would he think when she showed up? Hopefully, he'd understand. Then again, she'd hoped he would understand quite a lot since last Friday.

While no familiar faces appeared, a man in a short-sleeved plaid shirt held a sign bearing her name. One of her names. Sophie had hired a driver. The thoughtful gesture pricked tears in her eyes and her heart ached to share this moment, this next couple of days, with somebody who would understand and tell her exactly what she should do. Would Cody be waiting at the townhouse? She imagined his happy surprise as she walked through the door. Her heart beat faster.

Meg approached the older gentleman. "I'm Meg Marks."

"Glad to hear it. I'm Peter Macowen. Call me PeteyMac. Are you ready to go?"

Nodding, she surrendered her suitcase to his outstretched hand and followed him out the door into a steamy evening with thunderclouds gathering on the horizon. "Glad I didn't see those clouds on our approach. Are we supposed to get a big storm?"

"You never know with evening storms. Sometimes they blow in and out and sometimes they stay all night. I haven't checked the forecast today." They drew up before a long black limo, and he opened the door for her with a smile. "Where are we going today, lass?"

She loved his manners—definitely a lost art with men her own age. Cody excepted. Of course, this particular vocation probably required it. She pegged him for an early retiree who couldn't take the monotony and decided to drive part-time to fill the days. "Uptown area. I'm near 11th and North Davidson."

"Ah, those new townhouses that face the freeway?"

"Exactly."

"All-righty, you just sit back and relax. We'll be there before you know it."

He closed the door and made his way around to the driver's side. As the car moved, she cringed at the notion she was stuck in between real places where real people lived and loved. Popsie cruised on a boat in the Atlantic. The Vanderzees lounged by the lake up north. When she arrived home, she expected the loneliness to expand. Unless Cody was there.

The car drove past Concord Mills Mall, North Carolina's number one tourist attraction. Trees and traffic whizzed by the window and though she longed to, she could not postpone the call any longer. She gripped her phone, dragged the first line of her speech from memory and dialed Popsie.

He picked up on the first ring, his voice a little crusty. "Meggie."

"Popsie." She swallowed hard and plunged ahead. "You knew what Ruby did and you did nothing. My father died in prison for her crimes, and you ran away from the whole situation."

Popsie broke into a coughing fit.

Did her harsh words cause it? "Are you okay?"

More coughing. "I'm fine. Did you have more to say?"

Meg squirmed on the leather seat and looked out the window at the gathering storm clouds darkening the sky. She evaluated her words for their hurt potential, but couldn't restrain them. "Do you really want me to avenge my father and myself with your money?"

Silence.

She unclenched her fist and with great effort, relaxed the

hand holding the phone. "In my mind, I grew up with the perfect father. You loved me unconditionally and sacrificed so much for me. But I don't know what to think now that I know what you did at the expense of your other children."

Popsie cleared his throat. "Meg, I know it looks bad, but it's not what you think."

Meg leaned forward, her body quivering from the inside out. Her voice grew louder with every phrase. "Can I tell you what I think? It looks like you had a favorite son. You gave him something Ruby also wanted and this probably pushed her over the edge after a lifetime of taking second place behind her big brother. So she set Joey up and sent him to prison under false pretenses to lash out at both of you. When you learned about what she had done, not only did you not turn her in while Joey sat in prison, but after he accidentally died in prison, you still refused to turn her in. Instead, you gave her exactly what she wanted, exactly what she didn't deserve, exactly what rightfully belonged to Joey. Snow Cap."

"That's not it."

Her face flooded with heat, and she barely paused over Popsie's interruption. "Well, I have more. I think you feel guilty. And now you want me to fix everything before you die." The last words hung in the air like Florida humidity in August, inescapable, intolerable, relentlessly spreading misery with equality for all. Any relief Meg gained from unleashing these thoughts on Popsie gave way to extreme remorse, and placed a new sharp pain in her gut, probably the beginnings of an ulcer.

Giant slabs of rain sploshed the window in a sudden deluge, slowing traffic on I-85 to a crawl. Through murky sheets of rain gusting in wide curtains across the road, greenish-gray sky drooped low and pressed closer.

Popsie's response followed a long pause. "Meg, I understand why you think what you do. But there is one thing." He hesitated. "There is one thing I want to explain."

The limousine jolted to a stop. Cars hemmed them in on every side. Rain pelted the car, the volume so loud, she strained to hear Popsie's softening voice.

"You read your father's will."

"He left his ownership of Snow Cap to me."

He took a deep breath. "You know what Ruby did to him when Snow Cap became his."

Hail rattled the car. Golf-ball-size ice pelted the roof, drowning out every other sound. "Wait, Popsie. I can't hear." Meg hurried to turn up the volume on the phone.

But Popsie continued on, and she caught only a part of what he said. " . . . Ruby . . . maintain . . . Cap . . . only you . . . claim . . . true . . .ership . . . hidden . . . irthday . . ."

Meg struggled to assimilate the words. Popsie broke into

another fit of coughing and she heard the phone strike something. His voice almost moaned. "Maaarrs . . ."

Extended rustling and a few clunks filled Meg's ear from Popsie's end. "Popsie? Popsie! Hello? Are you there? Popsie?" Hailstones clattered all around her, bouncing off the car and cluttering the highway, which looked more like a parking lot at the moment.

She pressed a finger to close her open ear and pressed the phone closer. Another voice almost yelled from Popsie's end. "He's not well. He can't talk." Meg strained to hear more, but the call was lost.

Meg dropped her keys on the hall table out of habit. The stillness of the townhouse echoed in emptiness with no crazy dog running to greet her, tongue hanging out, licking her ankles. Why did he ever start doing the ankle thing?

She ambled through the main floor touching her things, running fingers across the countertops, seeking something to cling to—something to tether her heart—to keep her from pitching directionless, in the overwhelming sea of emotion. Unable to raise Popsie, or his nurse, on the phone, she battled her imagination and all the harrowing possibilities, which may have played out on the other end of the line.

She scanned the apartment for anything belonging to Cody.

Surely he would have started moving some of his things in this week, but her mail on the counter revealed the only evidence of his presence in this house: three neat piles. He liked to sort it: junk mail, bills, and other stuff.

As she rounded the kitchen island, her foot grazed Anchor's water bowl on the floor. A tiny hope lit at the idea Anchor could be waiting at the back door to be let in. Crazy. But the thought drove her down the short back stairway ending at a door leading out to the patio. But no, just bare concrete and neglected plants. Silly to even think it. Empty as the house, shadows and rain drenched the private, fenced-in patio. The potted hibiscus drooped. Maybe this rain would revive it.

Meg sighed and swiveled back toward the stairway.

She ascended the stairs to the main floor. Hopping onto a kitchen stool, she picked up the mail starting with the "other" pile. At the sound of a click in the lock, her hands flipped the mail, scattering it across the counter. Cody burst through the door, head down, a bundle of mail under his arm and a bouquet of daisies in his hand. Rain droplets flew from his floppy blond hair as he shook it out while wiping his feet. He bounded up the three steps from the entry-way and propelled himself toward the kitchen.

When he finally detected her presence, he reeled back in shock. "Whoa! Hey! What're you doing here?"

The spell of watching him unaware broke. "Surprise!"

"I can't believe you're back! He held out the flowers. I wanted them to be waiting for you, whenever you came."

He knew how to touch her heart at the exact perfect moment. "Thanks." He leaned close but trying not to hope too much, she had to ask about Anchor. "Any news?"

Cody's shoulders sagged and he leaned back on his heels. His gaze fell to the floor and he shook his head. "I've been looking all day. I feel terrible."

Meg rose and transferred the proffered flowers and mail to the counter. She choked out her words, almost meaning them. "It's okay."

He looked over her head as she moved into his arms. "Missed you."

He held her close. "Missed you too. I'm sorry about Anchor. Maybe tomorrow."

Meg swallowed hard. "Yeah."

Cody leaned back to view her face. "Did something happen? I thought you wouldn't be home 'til at least tomorrow."

Meg placed the top of her head against his chest. "Something definitely happened. I left because, well, they . . . one of them chased me away." She looked into his face and blinked back tears stemming from the mention of all that overwhelmed her.

Cody ushered her to the living area and sat her down beside him on the couch. His eyes searched her face and his comfortable drawl wrapped around her heart. "If you ran away from something, it must be terrible. Why don't you tell me everything."

Meg clutched his hand, hoping the sincerity in his voice reached down deep. "I promise I'll tell you everything, but I really don't even want to think about it right now. Can we talk about Saturday instead?"

His eyes shifted to the coffee table beside them, and flicked elsewhere around the room. "Yeah. We need to talk about that." He cleared his throat and then extricated his hand from hers to cross his arms across his chest. "I busted my tail, spent hours on the phone trying to plan everything for Saturday, ordering stuff and . . . well, I can't pull it off. Not the wedding of your dreams. Not even a quarter of what we want is possible in such a short time. In June. Why does everybody get married in June?"

She threw her hands up. "Cody, I told you it doesn't have to be perfect."

He grabbed her hand out of the air and focused his face close to hers. "Meg, I think it's too fast. Look at our conversations over the last couple days. We hardly said one kind word and you've seemed so distant."

Thunder slammed the back of Meg's eyes. Cody was her

safe spot. Her unmoving rock. "Where is this coming from? Does your mother think it's too fast? I thought she liked me. It was your idea to move up the date for Popsie. If it's not this Saturday, then he won't be at my wedding!" Her voice broke at the end.

"Our wedding." Cody tilted his head, a question all over his face.

Blotchy red and yellow passed before Meg's eyes, as if instead of feeling the pain of the moment, she could see it, seeping into her consciousness along with all the other agony of the day.

"Did you even hear what I just said?"

Meg's face burned. She focused her gaze on her hands. "I'm sorry. Would you please repeat it?"

Using a single finger, Cody lifted her chin until their eyes met. "That's exactly what I'm talking about. Your head is in another place. The weeks leading up to our wedding should be full of fun and family and long talks about our future. Between losing your father and whatever happened in Michigan, I'm not sure you can handle a wedding, much less a honeymoon and a new family."

She shook her head back and forth. Black spots drifted across her line of sight as if she had stared at the sun for a moment, but these spots threatened her mind as well as her vision.

The pain she felt inside conjured up the sunburned summer of 1994. Aptly named, she remembered the spring day she fell asleep on the fly bridge and awoke two hours later, flaming red. Her skin became extra sensitive for the rest of the summer. The slightest time in the sun fried her skin again. But since she lived on a boat, surrounded by water which reflected every ounce of sunlight, escaping the sun proved difficult and she burned the same skin over and over, requiring more time for repair. The emotions bubbling inside her carried the same flayed-open quality as her overexposed skin. "Tell me what you're saying."

He took her hands in his and looked her in the eye. "I think we need to postpone the wedding. You need to spend some time with Popsie and process this whole Van . . . der . . . whatever thing. Popsie gets that."

Meg reeled. "Did Popsie put you up to this? What did he say to you? I can't believe this!" She jumped up and paced in front of the fireplace. She felt tension crawl up her spine and spread across her shoulders like a vise clamping down. "Does he have to invade every sector of my life before he feels comfortable dying? You're the one sure thing I have left in my life, Cody. You can't just quit on me now."

Cody's head backed up as if ducking a swipe. He looked at her like she was crazy. "Gimme a little credit! I'm not quitting. I never said I didn't want to marry you."

"Well, do you?"

"Yes. I do. I want to marry you. But I think we need some time to process all this stuff, and plan our future carefully instead of throwing together a helter-skelter, last-minute wedding to accommodate one particular guest."

Her hand flew to her chest. Cody's words salved and stung her heart at the same time. Without thinking, she pleaded, "He's my father!" She grew quiet. "Grandfather." Maybe Cody had a point. But something rankled in the back of her mind. "You did talk to him about this, didn't you?"

Cody leaned back on the couch and put his feet up on the coffee table.

Meg winced at his distance, but refused to back down from her question.

He crossed his arms in front of his chest again. "Yeah. He started it—I hardly said anything."

She flew to his side. As she sat facing him, her arm went up to the back of the sofa. "I knew it. Did he tell you I wouldn't be able to handle things? Or does he still think I'm too young to marry?"

He sighed and started playing with the fringe edge of a throw pillow. His eyes were trained on his fingers. "He's worried you want to marry me more for my big family and maybe less because you love me." His voice finished very quiet and his eyes did not venture a look her way.

Hard rain splattered against the window in gusts, the sound resembled rocks on metal. Like lightning splits the nighttime sky, Meg sensed herself split down the center. Irrevocably. Cody looked like he was struggling to hold it together. How could Popsie accuse her of this? How could Cody believe it? What had she done to deserve it? A flash of guilt struck. She did crave a family. But why would they question her motives? Did Cody even mean it when he said he still wanted to marry her? If he doubted her, what chance did they stand in the future? Her aching heart bruised with every question.

Meg stared at Cody, still refusing to meet her eyes. A slow burn deep inside worked itself into what she hoped would not appear to be a full-blown conniption. She grasped for control, fingernails digging into her palms. "Is that what you think? I'm marrying you to get myself a big family? I can't possibly be so pathetic you would actually believe that."

Cody's hands stopped fidgeting with the pillow. He tossed it to the side, leaned forward so his arms rested on his knees, and interlaced his fingers. "I'm not saying I believe it. I'm saying we should take some time to give our relationship and our future together some thought."

Meg launched to her feet and let go the last bit of her

control. "I thought that's what we did when you asked me to marry you. Until a few minutes ago, I thought marrying you on Saturday would help me deal with all this other junk in my life right now. Obviously, I didn't think enough. Maybe you better leave me alone with all my thoughts tonight. In fact, since I'm clearly not thinking very well, I think maybe you better leave me alone for the rest of my life. I wouldn't want to saddle you with a thoughtless woman who's using you for your relatives."

He rose to his feet, hurt in his eyes. "C'mon, Megs. This isn't you."

The edges of her vision seemed to blur. "This is me, in shock that my own fiancée believes I'm using him. This is me, completely ticked off that my fiancée thinks it's a good idea to dump a girl at the worst moment of her life."

"Meg. I'm not dumping you. I'm trying to marry you."

"You're not trying hard enough." She crossed the room, twisted the ring off her finger and slipped it into his shirt pocket. "You should go."

His hand covered the pocket as his face twisted in pain. "I don't want to go."

She raised a shaky finger and pointed toward the door. "Go."

His gaze searched her face. She tightened her lips, determined to give nothing away.

He grabbed his coat and disappeared into the rain with the remaining bits of adhesive holding Meg together.

The effects of travel descended on Meg moments after the door closed behind Cody. Her muscles ached and moving her limbs required great effort and concentration. A giant empty space opened inside her. Her gaze swept across the living room, past the front door and then crawled up naked walls, fixating on the broad, barren ceiling.

How could one person manage to utterly destroy her own personal life with so little effort in such a short time? But Popsie started it. He never interfered like this. The document proving his sanity surfaced in her mind. What if he had lost his edge? Or what if Cody made it all up to get out of his commitment?

She leaned against the wall and slid down until she sat on the floor, knees up, head back. Her lungs filled with a giant breath and as she released it bit by bit, her body shuddered with silent sobs.

The vacuous townhouse reverberated with emerging sounds of grief. She stared at a spot on the ceiling. Maybe a tornado would come and smash the roof in or the house could be struck by lightning. A random crisis would drag her focus away from the pain reproducing inside her. To feel small and insignificant would bring relief, but instead, the pain seemed to expand inside her like a giant hot-air balloon.

Meg ran up the stairs past the master bedroom on the second floor and up to the third floor. Sliding the lock open, she yanked on the handle of the sliding glass door in the loft, which opened onto a rooftop balcony. She plunged into the deluge and leaned against the railing at the edge. Arms thrust up, hands in fists, she yelled with all the breath left in her. Like a lone wolf on a hill, she called out to the rain.

Shaking hands gripped the railing. As the cool wet metal sent a chill up her arm, a scary thought accosted her. This very type of situation might cause a person to consider tossing himself over a railing like this. She shoved herself away from the edge with such a force, she threw her backside against the glass door. As if in slow motion, she ricocheted off the door and watched the floorboards of the porch reach out and smack her in the face.

She lay prone for a moment and then curled up on her side like a little girl snuggles into a soft bed when her daddy tucks her in at night. Popsie's days of tucking her in lay far behind. Those tender moments coupled with countless others forged the glue which permanently affixed their hearts to one another. His love for her fueled her life, but now she was running on fumes.

The rain slapped her face. Water pooled in the folds of her shirt. Cody. Would he come back? Surely not. What had she done? Popsie chose this week of all weeks, to meddle in her life. Looking back on their meeting last Thursday, she viewed the events as if he were a poker player across the table from her, flipping the cards in his hand over in such a way as to capture the greatest drama, one by one. Now, with his last card on the table, he waited to see if his "all-in" hand took the kitty or went bust.

His impending death magnified everything with a layer of undulating emotions. Which brought their last conversation back to mind. What had Popsie tried to tell her? Worry for his health amidst the coughing fit, erased every word he spoke to her, except for two: "only you." But what did he mean? What did "only she" have to do with Ruby?

Appraising the shambles of her life all around her, Meg sat up and noticed the birds had left a mess across the floor only part of which had been washed away by the rain. Popsie's will lurked at the back of her mind like a scruffy guy in the back of a bar. Afraid to go there, she kept her distance.

Meg pushed herself up, rising to her full height with as much effort as an old woman. Hair hung in dripping strings across her face. She shook her head to flip it back, but it remained plastered down, as immovable as cartoon hair. The sliding door stood open, as she had left it. Rain soaked the rug. She waded inside, slid the door closed, and held her hands in front of her, watching water drip into the giant puddle at her feet. What man would marry a mess like this?

Before she could think to do it, she stripped down to her skivvies and tiptoed at top speed down the stairs to her bedroom for something warm and dry. All her coziest clothes lay smushed in the suitcase another floor down, so donning a robe, she descended to retrieve her Carolina hoodie.

As soon as the suitcase popped open, Meg saw a file she had shoved into the bag while packing. Loopy handwriting covered the legal-sized, gold envelope. Pink ink complete with hearts dotting the "i's" and exclamation points, spelled out a message.

"Dear Meg,

Thanks so much for helping us!

We can't believe our cousin is a lawyer!

You are the best!

Call us!

J&J

231-555-6693 (our cell)

A spontaneous smile stretched across Meg's tear-stained face. Those girls exuded undying hope and ridiculous confidence in the people around them. On the surface, this projected a ditsy, clueless image. But the more time she spent with them, the more Meg saw an overwhelming willingness to believe the best about every person in their lives. A sniffle laden with sarcasm escaped her when she considered the thought that they probably thought more highly of her than any other living person did right at this moment. Their simplistic approach to relationships seemed naïve, but the lack of conflict in their lives was undeniable. Even now, when the rest of the family suspected the worst of her, she knew the twins would not.

Meg weighed the envelope in her hands. It contained bank statements and written notes from the twins. Her promise to check into their drained checking account pricked her conscience. A project lay before her. A problem she could tackle. Given that her lawyering days would probably be tainted and possibly undermined forever after Ruby finished with her, might as well see what she could do now.

Meg grabbed her sweatshirt and padded upstairs, envelope tucked under her arm. She glanced at her watch: almost midnight. Even if it meant working through the night, she would unravel the twins' troubles. It was the least she could do. But when she reached the second floor, a familiar sound split the silence and she froze. A scratching at the front door.

Chapter Nineteen

Before she opened her eyes, Meg knew from the light saturation in the room, she had slept past eight o'clock. French blue silk drapes billowed from the windows, blocking the view, but not the light. As she rolled over, the sound of crumpling paper roused her—she drifted off on top of her work. Worried about how everything would seem in the light of day, Meg sat up and gathered the papers strewn across the undisturbed blue damask bedding which covered the sleek, platform bed.

Sleep had eluded her for hours. After she ascertained the leak plaguing the twins' bank account, anger and revenge churned inside her, growing every moment as she rehashed the details in her head, guessing at the pieces she still could not connect.

A wet nose appeared at the side of the bed and a long tail wagged crazily, thumping the side table with a dependable drumbeat. Anchor, as if he never left, faithfully performed his morning ritual. He waited with patient eyes as she dragged herself from the comfortable bed and groped around on the floor with her feet in search of slippers.

She lowered her face to meet Anchor's and receive her morning kiss. Her heart twisted as she realized it was probably the only kind of morning kiss she could expect from now on. "Okay, time to go out."

Anchor licked the side of her ankle and followed her past his doggie bed, down the stairs, and toward the front door. He grabbed his leash off the bench in the foyer and held it until Meg came to clip it to his collar. On early mornings, Meg surrendered her sense of decency and walked the dog in her pajamas. Navy silk, today. Maybe everyone else had slept in like her for Memorial Day.

But as soon as she stepped outside, a neighbor called to her from two doors down. "Good morning, Megan."

So much for anonymity. "Hi, Mrs. Blackwelder."

"I see you're back in town."

"Yes, just flew in last night."

Mrs. Blackwelder picked up a watering can and pretended to water the flowers on her front porch, but no water fell from the overturned can. Had she been waiting for Meg to come out? "Now, I don't mean to pry, but there's been a young man stopping by here."

Anchor pulled on the leash, leading Meg to a patch of grass on the boulevard halfway between their two stoops. "Oh, that's just Cody. He's my . . ." her voice wavered, "Friend. I asked

him to take in my mail and care for Anchor while I was gone."
The word "friend" lingered on her tongue like horseradish waits
for something else to chase the bitterness away.

Mrs. Blackwelder scooped a giant white cat into her arms.
"I see you found the little bugger. That poor man canvassed the
entire complex looking for him. I never saw a sorrier face. He
looked pathetic when he rang my bell to ask if I'd seen the dog.
Seemed fairly nice, but you never know these days. I closed the
door on him and set the alarm just in case."

Meg's eyes closed and the pit of her stomach roiled. She
shifted from one foot to the other and scanned the row of town
homes in both directions. No one else in sight. If she didn't
make a hasty exit from this conversation, the morning would
disappear into the canyon of "Inane conversation with Mrs.
Blackwelder."

Meg allowed Anchor to jerk the leash to give the
impression she would have to follow the brute. Shrugging off a
pang of guilt mixed with pity, Meg waved back at her over a
shoulder. "Thanks for keeping an eye out. Have a great
holiday!"

Without casting a glance back, Meg knew Mrs.
Blackwelder's face would be buried in the soft white fur of Mr.
Percy, her best friend, her closest confidant, her raison d'etre.
The thought sent a shiver down Meg's spine as she vaulted up

the front steps beside her . . . best friend. At least he wasn't a cat.

The ringing phone lured her up the short flight of stairs at a trot. Cody already? Her heart thrilled at the idea he might not have given up on her. Then again, she'd never treated him that way before. And he thought she didn't want him any more.

Did she still want him? Would he ever take her back?

Better listen to his message first. The machine picked up the call, and Meg heard a low, confident voice with a thick southern drawl speaking about a large donation toward Orphan Advocates. Her shoulders fell as she realized the voice did not belong to Cody, but with a flutter of surprise, she snatched up the phone to return the call.

After a short conversation, she hung up the phone and fell into a chair, staring straight ahead. Her mouth hung wide open. Out of the blue, Trevor Colt, stock car driver and winner of last year's Sprint Cup called her. On purpose. Because he likes her charity. Unbelievable! She shook her head to clear it and checked the time. He asked to meet with her in an hour—better get a move on.

The doorbell interrupted Meg's thoughts. What now? Cody? Her heartbeat quickened, but she guarded her hopes right away. It might just be lonely Mrs. Blackwelder. Curiosity aroused, she pulled the door open.

Twin voices sang to her. "Surprise!"

Speechless, Meg opened her arms to hug her cousins. Over their shoulders, the blue Malibu sat cock-a-mamie, one wheel up on the curb. After a moment, she managed to sputter a few words. "What in the world? How did y'all . . .?"

Anchor sat upright, tail wagging, waiting patiently to meet the newcomers. The twins oohed and ahhed in baby voices, petting him and proclaiming their love for him. "We always wanted a dog, but Mom would never let us."

"This is Anchor. I can tell he's in love already." Unlike her. But maybe she still was. The bigger question lay with Cody. Could he possibly still be in love with her?

Laughing, they stepped inside and closed the door. "Love your place, Meg."

Janell looped her arm through Meg's and drew her up the stairs to the kitchen. "It's so modern. And clean."

"Yeah. It's almost shiny."

And empty. Meg pulled out a high-backed kitchen stool and sank into it. "What are you two doing here? Are you in trouble?"

Their eyes met, and knowing smiles popped into place. Jane leaned on the island counter, facing Meg as she sat at the bar. "We ran away from home."

Janell pulled out the bar chair next to Meg and plopped into it. "Yup! We up and left. And we might be in a little trouble, if we ever go home."

Marveling, Meg leaned her chin on her hand. "Why? Why now? And why did you come all the way down here? I mean, I'm glad to see you."

Jane repeatedly turned the water in the sink on and off. . "Oh, don't worry. We aren't planning to move in on you or anything."

"We just thought that since you had our bank papers and everything, you could help us get our money back and then we can decide where we want to end up."

Meg sat up straighter. "I know your account is empty right now, so how did you pay for gas to get down here? And food?"

"Well, that's the dicey part. We borrowed some money from mom's safe."

"Girls!" With their family already suspicious of her, the twins' appearance on her doorstep with stolen money in tow would not instill any further good will.

Janell patted her shoulder. "It's not that bad. We've known the safe combination for years. We planned to use it only in case of emergency and then this emergency cropped up."

Puzzling about their situation, Meg tilted her head and

looked back and forth between them. "You must have driven all night."

"We did."

"Yeah, but we took turns, so it wasn't that bad."

Visions of crazy, in-transit switches while driving full-tilt down the highway in the dark at two o'clock in the morning, scampered across Meg's thoughts. "And you didn't have any trouble with the . . . ah . . . directions?"

Jane smile. "I know, right? We usually get lost. But we grabbed a couple other things from mom's car. A radar detector and her GPS."

"We found those other papers in the safe too, sealed in an old envelope. Turns out they're just company documents or something."

Meg's eyes flicked to the clock on the microwave. "Shoot! I'm late." She scanned the room trying to decide what to do. "I have a meeting. Do you need to get some sleep?"

"Oh, we're fine." Janell stood and poked around the kitchen touching things. "Want us to come along?"

Meg hurried upstairs. "I have to get ready quick. Help yourselves to anything in the fridge." A twinge of hunger gripped her stomach. Had she even opened the refrigerator since her arrival? There might be nothing there. Knowing Cody, he probably bought a few yogurts and some bagels, just in case.

Guilt and sadness snagged her heart, but she pushed it aside to deal with her current situation.

Ten minutes later, Meg thudded down the stairs, taking the last few steps on her backside. "Ow!"

"Oh, Meg."

"What'dja do?"

Meg pulled herself up by the banister, a hand rubbing her lower back. "These shoes are so slippery. I don't know why I still wear them." She shook her head and straightened up to her full height. "I need to look professional today."

Janell approached and massaged Meg's shoulders. "I think you need to relax a little bit. You seem stressed."

The diagnosis of the century. "You can say that again. Look, I'm really glad y'all are here, but I'm sorry. I have to go to this meeting. It's up at the lake and I should've left twenty minutes ago."

Jane sauntered over toward Meg. "Let us drive you. We have the radar detector, we can drive crazy fast."

They could drive crazy, for sure. "I'll drive myself, but thanks for the offer." Both pairs of big blue eyes stared hopefully at her. Jane held her handbag in the air, ready to sling it over her shoulder as soon as Meg invited them along. In the interest of time, she relented. "C'mon along. But you'll have to wait in the car. He only invited me."

They bounced downstairs to the lower level, out the back door, through the fenced in patio and into the alley parking lot to Meg's Toyota Rav4. Her favorite car, even when she traveled she tried to rent one just like it. They piled in and Meg regretted the fact that she'd be unable to school them in the finer points of driving. She planned to break every traffic law necessary to land them on the Peninsula at Lake Norman in less than twenty minutes.

Approximately twenty-two minutes later, Meg swung the car onto a quiet street and pulled into a circular drive. A stucco house trimmed out with stone in brown tones towered over them, dwarfing a matching six-car detached garage sporting its own driveway.

The twins leaned out the windows, and stared past the treetops at the pointed gables and pretty window boxes splashing the enormous house with bright red and white blooms. "Wow."

"Who lives here?"

"Can we go in with you?"

"Are we on a lake? I smell lake."

"Yeah, look through those trees."

"Wow."

Meg grabbed her briefcase from behind the passenger seat. "Trevor Colt lives here. He graciously offered me twenty minutes to pitch my non-profit as his charity of choice. I have eighteen minutes left. Please wait for me here."

She burst out the door and started a high-heel run, which turned into a quick-paced trot. She smoothed her pencil skirt, straightened the power-purple jacket and flipped her hair over a shoulder. One meeting that fell out of the sky an hour ago, now stood to make or break the culmination of her dream and more hours of hard work than she could count. If Ruby followed through on her threat to tarnish Orphan Advocates' reputation, and her own, then nothing short of a celebrity endorsement could hope to preserve the organization and save it from sabotage.

The pain of fingernails digging into her palm jerked her attention back to the present. Meg forced her hands to relax enough to keep from drawing blood. What do you say to a stock car driver? Why should he choose her charity?

Taking a deep breath, she rang the bell. Over her shoulder she heard chaotic cheerleading. "Good luck!"

"Hope it's great!"

"You look beautiful."

"You can do it!"

"What's she trying to do again?"

"I don't know, something for kids."

Stealing a glance at the twins, she captured thumbs-up and

fist pumping between giant toothy grins. She motioned for them to stop and snapped her head back to the door when she heard a step on the other side.

To stop her sweaty hands from shaking, she grabbed the strap of her shoulder bag with both hands. As the door swung open, she came face to face with a celebrity. Her eyes popped opened wide and she struggled to hide her surprise as she took in his height—almost exactly the same as her own.

Here goes nothing. "Hi, I'm Megan Marks."

"I propose a toast to Orphan Advocates." Janell lifted a Diet Coke and held it up over the veggie pizza in the center of the raised bar in Meg's kitchen.

Jane hoisted her Diet Coke and bumped the other can. "I second that toast."

Meg tapped in her water bottle and smiled. "Y'all are too much."

"Congratulations on the racing guy deal."

Meg smiled. "Trevor Colt. What a great story this day will be."

Jane sipped her soda. "I can't believe he was adopted!"

Janell googled her eyes. "I can't believe he's so cute!"

"I can't believe he heard about Orphan Advocates and called me."

Janell gripped her drink, hugging it to her chest. She leaned forward over the table. "I can't believe he gave you so much money!"

Jane sat up straight and held her can up again. "And another toast to our fabulous lawyer!"

Janell cried, "Yes! You found our money."

"And we can still go to Alaska."

Meg lowered her water bottle and picked at the pizza in front of her. Avoiding the blue eyes pointed in her direction, she took a sip of water and continued to focus on the pizza. "I may have found out who took the money, but we haven't found the money yet."

Janell frowned. "You said it all went into that account."

Nodding, Meg swallowed some pizza. "Yes. But we don't have access to that account right now, so we don't know if it's still there or not. She may have spent it all."

Both sets of blue eyes stared at her, the reality of the situation seeped into their consciousness. Losing money to a thief can be a harrowing experience, leaving the victim feeling vulnerable and exposed. Losing a dream to a thief who knew about your dream and stole it maliciously in order to keep you under her control would be painful on a completely different level. How could a mother steal from her own children?

Meg tried to keep pity from showing through her eyes.

"And we don't know if she'll agree to give it back, or if we'll have to file suit, or perhaps pursue a sort of reconciliation through mediation."

Jane picked most of the vegetables off her pizza. "I don't want to think about it anymore. Can we just enjoy this dinner and deal with Mom later?"

Meg placed her hand over Jane's. "I'm so sorry. I never thought this is where the trail would lead."

She nodded and blinked back some tears as she looked toward her sister. Janell grabbed her other hand. She started to speak and Jane chimed in at the end. "We're in it together, like everything else, and we'll come through it together, like everything else."

Meg looked around the kitchen, afraid to intrude on such a private, personal moment. Finally, she directed her attention to her plate and silently contemplated the olives and green peppers on the pizza. Not enough mushrooms. Maybe she should have ordered some meat.

When she looked up, two pathetic faces looked into hers, waiting for her to look up. Before she could stop herself, she blurted a question. "Why did you really run away?"

They looked at one another and after a moment, nodded. Jane spoke first. "Mom complained about you and Janell tried to explain that you meant no harm. Then Mom went ballistic."

"She yelled, she screamed, she even threw stuff at us. We couldn't figure out why she was so mad."

"Her eyes got all bulgy and hateful."

"Jane, she doesn't hate us."

"Janell. She makes fun of us and she tells us what to do—all the time. That's the extent of our entire relationship."

The two girls looked at each other, like two wavering mirror images. With any other two people, Meg would have felt isolated and out of place. But somehow, the twins managed to paint her right into their world. "Don't tell me I caused a rift in your family."

"Oh, no. We were born under a rift."

Jane chuckled. "Really. Martha told us we should come warn you about Mom. She's planning to do stuff to you so you can't be a lawyer anymore."

"So you had a fight with your mom and then drove all night to warn me about her?"

Janell's head bobbed. "Pretty much."

"You could have called me."

Jane shifted in her seat, and fidgeted with her fingernails. As she took a breath to speak, her sister interrupted. "Don't."

Jane pressed her lips together and looked at Janell. "Sorry, I have to." She swung her gaze to Meg. "You're the best thing that ever happened to us. You're like a dream . . ."

Janell rolled her eyes. "Jane."

Jane continued. "Look, we just really like you. You inspired us in the first five minutes we knew you. Plus, you treat us like we're real people instead of the . . . Doublemint twins. And we trust you. So we wanted to see if you would still help us with the money thing, but we really just want to be cousins. Or friends. Or something."

Meg met her hopeful gaze. As she endeavored to swallow the lump in her throat, from the corner of her eye, she watched Janell's embarrassment spreading red across her face and chest. Meg had been struck like a perfect chord at the end of a song. Her resistance dissolved, allowing tears to spill down her cheeks. The only words she could speak sounded like more of a croak. "Boy, do I need you two."

The twins hurried around the table to embrace her. When Jane tripped and her elbow landed in Meg's pizza, laughter cascaded all around them, and they gave themselves up to it until all three sat on the floor, propped up against the wall, gasping for breath between giggles.

"No interruptions." Meg closed the office door on her cousins' smiling faces. Taking a deep breath, she circled her desk chair like a swordsman circles his opponent before jumping into the fight. The task before her remained the same. But today, she would begin to complete it, thanks to the twins and all they brought with them in the blue Malibu.

Snatches from her last phone conversation with Popsie replayed in her head throughout the day. She'd left enough messages to raise the flag of concern. He must be waiting to call when they docked for the night. Meanwhile, she needed to know where to book her flight. Her plan to prepare the will in the next few days for signing on Thursday sounded ambitious, but one day with the twins had crystallized everything in her mind. She knew what had to be done.

She opened the file and spread everything across the desk before her. For the first time in a week, she felt she could finally get a grip. Cody's hurt expression sliced through her, inflicting fresh pain. His words echoed in her mind. I don't want to go. A lump grew in her throat; regret soured her stomach. Boy, did she ever burn that bridge. Calling him now might just hurt him even more. With no hope on the Cody horizon, she placed her laptop in the center of the desk and pursued the task before her. If she couldn't patch up the mess she'd made of her relationship with Cody, maybe she could salvage a few other relationships.

The phone rang, interrupting her thoughts. It wouldn't be Cody. Not now.

Through the door, she heard muffled voices. "Want us to get that?"

They were still standing outside the door? Oh, brother. Meg checked caller ID: Popsie.

"No. I've got it. You can get the next one." Swiveling the chair around, she dragged a file box over with her feet and propped them atop. She answered the call, couching the phone between her shoulder and ear. "Popsie."

A faraway, diminished voice responded. "Meggers."

"Are you okay? You sound far away." And small.

"I had a pretty rough day."

"Are you cruising right now?"

"Just coming in to port. Key Largo. My last day at Ocean Reef."

"I'm sorry for my . . ."

He cut her off mid-sentence. "No apologies. I deserve any harsh word you have for me."

"I want you to know I just sat down to write the will. I think I know what I have to do. You know, you have some amazing grandchildren."

Popsie cleared his throat and paused as if trying to push back emotions. "I love every one of them." Coughs overtook him. As soon as he could speak, his words came slow and deliberate. "Key West. Tomorrow. I think you better come. Tomorrow."

Meg's head pounded. "W-what are you saying?"

"I need to sign . . . tomorrow."

"Popsie, are you . . ."

A new voice came on the line. "Hello?"

"Hello. Is he okay?"

"Hi. I'm Marcie, the hospice nurse."

"Oh, good. Is he okay?"

"I can't let him get all worked up again like last night. So, did you hear what he said? He'd really like you to come tomorrow."

"Yes." Images of all the papers she needed to prepare seemed to fly in her face from every direction. Tomorrow was so soon. She teetered on the rooftop between worry she wouldn't make it in time and grief lurking around the corner— far too close. "I'm not sure how, but I'll see you in Key West tomorrow—at the marina."

"That's great. He'll be so pleased."

Unsure how to ask the next question, Meg blundered forward. "So . . . is this it? Does he think tomorrow . . .?"

"It's hard to predict exactly when. But I'd say he's on the clock."

On the clock. The words stabbed her conscience, throwing guilt with a side of regret onto her plate. What happened to stocking up on 'Popsie time?' Wishes filled her head. Wishes for more time, wishes for more conversation, and a wish for perfect and permanent recall of every sweet moment she had shared with him. If Popsie's time was almost out, then Meg wouldn't waste a minute. "Thank you, Marcie."

The wireless phone slid into her lap when she hung up. To Popsie and the twins and her dad, she whispered aloud. "Thank you."

A moment later, Meg sprang from her seat and paced the room, hands on her head. The ache in her heart pushed her into panic mode. Her mind wrestled with logistics. Anticipation set a rhythm she expected to escalate through a mammoth all-nighter. She spun around and leapt into her chair, fingers danced across the keyboard at a feverish pace. What if she didn't make it? What if he couldn't sign the will? Now that she truly wanted to do this for Popsie, her window of opportunity narrowed. She needed more time.

Chapter Twenty

The Key West harbormaster directed Meg toward a reserved slip on the edge of the marina. Toting newly-inked papers in her shoulder bag, she patrolled the docks, watching for Gilda's red bimini to enter the harbor.

A constant breeze tossed Meg's long hair just enough to keep it out of her face. She breathed in the salty gusts, filling her lungs to capacity and trying to relax her stiff muscles on exhale. The fresh air cleansed her aching eyes, stinging from lack of sleep and hours of staring at her laptop.

Water lapped at huge pylons under the docks. This day held all the auspices of a momentous occasion. And she stood here on the dock alone. Every moment she let her mind slide off the will and Popsie, it replayed her conversation with Cody. Her lower lip had been scraped raw from her top teeth chewing through her uncertainty. Regret. But today needed to be about Popsie and his final plans. She refused to blame Popsie now for her troubles with Cody. Blame could not repair the damage she had executed. Best to keep her chin up and pump all the quality she could manage into her last hours with her favorite man on earth. One of her two favorite men on earth.

Bright orange sunlight reflected off the dancing water as the sun slipped lower in the sky. The entire will ran through her mind over and over. Kenneth, Michael, Amy, Martha . . . Her heartbeat thundered in her ears and walloped in her chest at the very thought of what she'd done. What would Popsie think? Would he agree with what she'd decided?

Her eyes scanned the horizon again and finally, Gilda glided into view. Meg's stomach flopped and her pulse quickened even more. She watched her moment of truth approach, willing the boat to hurry, but dreading her first step aboard.

Meg's childhood home eased toward the empty dock where she waited. Memories cascaded before her mind's eye. For years, she acted as mate. Coming into port always raised a flutter in her chest. A new harbor promised new experiences, new friends, and new challenges.

As the bow entered the slip, a gust of wind and accompanying waves tilted the stern too far to port. Captain Steve threw the engines into reverse, narrowly avoiding contact between the port side of the bow and the huge steel pylon at the back of the slip. Usually they backed into a slip when docking, why bow-first today?

The sun's slanted rays nearly blinded Meg as she watched Captain Steve's second attempt. She backed away from the slip as the harbormaster and a dockhand drew near, ready to help secure the new arrival.

This time Gilda pulled halfway into the space before she bobbed over a rogue wake issued by a thoughtless joy-rider, impatient from waiting for Gilda to clear the aisle behind her. Quick maneuvering on the captain's part avoided a scraped hull.

Meg paced in front of the bow as the dockhands adjusted distances and tied lines off. She leaned over the edge of the dock and found her mind wandering as she stared through clear waters to the miscellany coating the bottom. Meg looked around for something else to delay facing Popsie. Her bag slid to the dock as she dropped to her knee beside a cleat. Her expert hands moved quickly with little thought. When she stood and moved toward the next cleat, she admired the perfect knots she had braided into the navy blue lines flecked with gold.

She pictured Popsie's smiling face as he'd explained to her ten-year-old, impatient self. "We braid them because you don't want people tripping over your lines. It doesn't look good when somebody goes over the side, especially in salt water. Plus, you want to look like you know what you're doing."

Meg straightened and tucked some hair behind an ear as her gaze returned to the red bimini. She dipped her gaze to the pilothouse, the brains of the boat, and then to the gleaming hull, which concealed the brawn of the boat, her twin engines. Gilda rose from the water as regal as a queen who welcomed her people with generosity and warmth. She'd heard others talk about their homes as if they were castles. A queen wasn't that far off.

The same Popsie she ran to as a child awaited her now on board. Meg took a deep breath and blew it out fast. She bent to retrieve her bag, and with a controlled saunter, she advanced down the dock, crossed the boarding ladder, and stepped through the door into the pilothouse.

She passed aft to the salon. A huge hospital bed dominated the room, situated toward the stern. The evening's horizontal rays shone across the water and filled the room with sunset light. That's why they docked this way. A short, plump woman in scrubs moved toward her with open arms. From her previous phone conversation with the hospice nurse, she deduced this must be Marcie. From the corner of her eye Meg noticed zero movement in the bed. Alarm bells rang in her head.

Before Meg could get a good look at Popsie, Marcie accosted her with an enormous bear hug. She let out a muffled, "Oh, honey." Meg's heart slowed as if black ink had been injected directly into her chest. No. It couldn't be too late. She struggled against Marcie's squishy arms.

As Marcie loosened her embrace, Meg backed away from her, horror pulsing through her veins.

Marcie clasped her hands together. A look of distress registered when she focused on Meg's face. "Oh! He's still with us. Sorry if I gave you the wrong idea."

Meg experienced a blank moment before blood gushed back to her brain. Relief oozed into the corners of her inner self, and her hand flew to her chest as she took several deep breaths.

Marcie continued in a hushed tone. "I'm sorry to scare you. I'm just so happy you made it in time. He's had no other visitors. He's such a sweet man and, well, I really wanted him to have somebody who loves him nearby. He's sleeping now. They always need more sleep the closer it gets to the end. I'll bet he wakes up before too long. Would you like to have a seat?"

Meg stretched to her full height, reaching for bravery. "Is he . . . How is he? I mean, I know he's . . . you know. But has he changed?"

"He's the same man. His mind is completely intact. Remarkably so. His body has slowed very quickly, though. He refused painkillers this morning, and I find it hard to believe he's able to sleep. He wanted to be completely coherent for your arrival and the business you've brought for him to conduct."

Meg nodded, imagining her whole body in pain. She chewed her lip as her fears were confirmed before her eyes.

"He'll probably require higher dosage painkillers from here on out. We'll start a morphine drip when you've finished your business. It doesn't mean he'll be leaving us immediately, but in order to make him comfortable, we need to up the medication, and that will affect his mental faculties. So you see why we felt the need to get you down here right away."

Meg stepped around the nurse and neared the bed. Her throat tightened and she swallowed hard to maintain her composure. "So he's in a lot of pain?"

Marcie nodded, her lips pressed together in a tight line. "I'm afraid so. But he's tough as bricks."

Meg almost chuckled out a breath, sending a small dose of relief down her spine. "That's for sure." She looked around for a chair. "Can I sit here until he wakes up?"

Stepping out to the back deck for a moment, Marcie returned with Popsie's director chair in hand. "Of course. He'll be so happy to see you."

Meg drew the chair to the foot of the bed and sank down to watch her father. His skin had faded to gray and his cheekbones seemed to protrude, giving him a sunken look. A peculiar discomfort grew inside her as she watched him sleep. This experience belonged to the parent.

His breaths came long and slow. The sound would have reassured her, except that something felt slightly off. Maybe too much time between breaths. Her eyes scanned him from head to toe. Shocking realization smacked her consciousness. She left him a mere five days before. How could his appearance undergo such a radical change?

At his feet lay her quilt. Handmade by Rachel and Amy. Her grandmother chose the fabrics with care and her aunt poured her love of colors into its design. And they made it especially for Maggie Daisy. Large gaps in her personal history had been colored in over the past couple days. Now something as simple as a glance at a quilt confirmed her true identity and connected her with people who once loved her.

Like a boat that misses its mooring, Meg tried to dampen the sensation she had come close, but drifted too far from her intended place in the world. The current drew her away and she could not muster the strength required to overcome it. Now she floated toward her unknown future, at the whim of the tides, her only remaining mooring line about to be severed.

She shook her head. Focus on Popsie, and how to make the most of his final hours. The pieces of her life would be waiting for her later. The grief ahead loomed like a giant tree in a storm, branches swaying in the wind, waiting for lightning to strike.

Popsie stirred. He opened his eyes, blinked several times and then rubbed them. An enormous smile enlivened his ashen face.

Meg moved to sit on the edge of the bed, grasping Popsie's hand. "Don't worry, I'm not a figment of your imagination. I'm finally here."

He raised his right hand, one finger pointing, as if trying to make his words stick before he spoke. "I didn't know . . . if you would . . . come."

"It took me a little while to understand." Meg stroked his hand, unsure if his frail body could even sustain a hug. "But I get it. And I'm not leaving."

He struggled to push himself up to a sitting position. Marcie jumped in, materializing out of thin air, to prop him up and make him comfortable. "How's that?"

Popsie nodded. "Thanks."

Meg bit her lip and braced herself for the rest—time to complete the business transaction started at Provisions last week.

Guy Marks squeezed the smooth hand of his little girl. He couldn't think of her any other way. Placing his will and his heart into her capable hands was easy. Waiting to see if she would forgive him stirred up an agony of soul to match the agony wreaking havoc on his body.

He blinked and his watery image of Meg shifted. She had returned. She even wrote the will as he asked. He dabbed his eyes with a handkerchief and squeezed her hand again. "Did I sign everything you needed?"

"Yes. We're done. Are you sure it's what you want?"

"You did it just right. I wouldn't change a thing. I'm proud of you."

"It's no big deal." She shifted her gaze to the floor. It must have required great sacrifice on her part. Lines ran across her forehead, and her shoulders locked into an unnatural hunch.

"It's a big deal to me." Popsie released the handkerchief and ran his right hand across his thigh. "I'm sorry."

"Don't worry. It's all forgiven."

Nodding, he fought to speak the words lest he tear up again and fail to say all he intended. "I'm sorry I favored Joey. I'm sorry I underestimated Ruby. I'm sorry I was afraid."

Meg tilted her head and placed her other hand on top of Popsie's. "What were you afraid of?"

"Your mother . . . Grandmother . . . Rachel . . . promised to love her kids the way they needed loving best. And then she died. And I thought all the love in me died with her. It was so hard afterward."

Meg stroked the back of his hand as her eyes searched his face. "But—"

Guy held up a hand to stop her. "But then I lost Joey because of my business decisions. If Rachel were still alive, she would be ashamed of me."

"She would not!"

"Even so, I stumbled around in my grief while I tried to stop the family from falling apart." He fingered Meg's quilt, draped across his legs. "For Rachel. I couldn't send another child off to prison no matter how awful her crime, because it was my fault to begin with."

"Ruby chose to set Joey up."

"Because I gave him controlling interest in the company she dreamed of owning one day."

"She wasn't ready for it." Meg shook her head.

"And I didn't make enough of an effort to set her up for a career in our family business. I groomed Joey for the position and let Ruby and the others fend for themselves."

Full disclosure painted an ugly family portrait. Meg's work on his estate would glaze over the worst parts and send into future generations only the best of the Vanderzees, sprinkled with lessons learned the hard way.

Meg bent low to kiss his cheek. "What's done is done. Let's drop the past regrets and get on with life. We don't have much in quantity left, but we can control the quality."

The warmth of her smile warmed his whole body, and Guy felt his spirit buoy under her hopeful cheer. "You're right." He took a deep breath and let it rattle out of his chest. "We'll have to watch the sunset over the back deck tonight. Tomorrow we cruise out to meet it." The confidence undergirding his words leaked away like air from a balloon. His eyelids grew too heavy to hold open, and because she was near, he let them close.

The day crawled by, yet sunset still came too soon. Popsie insisted they cruise out far enough to avoid seeing land of any kind. Refusing such a request never entered Meg's mind. Every word he spoke shimmered in her memory, singular and spaced out like golden pennies falling into the fountain of her life.

He struggled through late morning into the afternoon. Breath became a chore, and he slept, though fitfully. Meg couldn't bear to sit and watch him breathe, but she feared looking away, lest he fail to find the next breath. She finally pulled out a novel and read it aloud to pass the time. One of their favorites, The Three Musketeers. He drifted off to sleep in the middle of a swordfight.

Marcie checked the morphine drip every hour and moved him around in the bed to ensure his comfort.

Meg shook her head as she watched Marcie's expert hands. "I never thought I'd have to worry about Popsie being unable to move himself."

Marcie smiled a knowing look. "Some people stay in one place all day for years, and this don't bother them a'tall. Other folks move so much their whole lives, once they stop, their bodies don't know what ta do."

"I'm kinda surprised he's slowed down so fast. I mean, I just saw him six days ago."

"Honey, I've learned that people go at their own pace. You can't make 'em go faster, and ya can't make 'em go slower."

Meg chewed her lip.

"One thing I do know, last Friday your . . ." Marcie paused. "He was riding a thin line of adrenaline. Soon's I shuttled that photographer off the boat, I watched him shrink, like he finally gave in. It happens a lot when I show up."

She must mean Cody. Did he take photos after she left for the airport? Probably just checked or cleaned his gear. Friday seemed like months ago. Meg's gaze lingered on Popsie's gray face. From the looks of things, he wouldn't have made the wedding anyway, even if it was still set for Saturday. So many plans, so many hopes, all washed away in a few days' time.

Sunset began with a few high thin clouds radiating shiny gold and pink. The sun burned orange-red, shooting its last light of the day directly across the ocean toward Gilda. Nothing stood between the source of light beaming across earth and the dimming glow of a father and his girl on a boat in the middle of the ocean. Eternity shot across the water and paused.

After the sun sank below the horizon, the sky lit up with

hot pink flames low in the sky, reflecting a double image off the water. Orange swaths of light mixed into pale yellow and gilded the underside of every cloud within reach. Above, clear lavender sky faded into periwinkle blue, which eventually gave way to the oncoming deep blue of night and a bright star at the top of evening's dome. Warm moisture hung in the air enfolding them like a blanket. Meg's hand squeezed Popsie's and she waited for his usual, gentle squeeze in reply.

Water lapped against the hull, and the boat rose and fell with gentle ocean swells. The engines silenced. Not even an overhead bird dared destroy the moment with its voice. Meanwhile, the spectacular colors painted across the expanse above them continued to change, deepening, blending, finishing.

With something clearly more substantive than a tremor, Popsie's weathered hand said goodbye.

Funerals in Key West carried with them a heavy sense of absurdity. The very buildings on every street reflected light in bright, clownish hues. Palm trees swayed in tropical breezes and loud island music blared from every bar and restaurant. Meg noticed hibiscus, and other tropical flowers adorning every doorway, porch, and yard as she travelled through the streets in the back of a yellow taxi. No funeral flowers in sight. Yet people died in Key West, like any other place.

Popsie's directives echoed in her ears: "Cremation right away. Scatter me at sea." While he'd been clear beyond questioning, Meg balked at his bluntness. Her eyes had searched out the Bible on a corner table. A steeple slide-show of all the churches they visited—because all they did was visit—played in her mind as she wondered if any one of the pastors would remember Popsie and be willing to say a few words.

But then he'd told her that Herb would come for the service. He awaited her on Gilda. Herb, "the human reverb." At least that's what Popsie called him. His booming voice cut through almost any noise, and sounded like flowing, dark chocolate: pure, deep, and rich. When Meg first met him, she transformed into a chatterbox, rarely leaving his side the entire time he stayed with them on Gilda. Endless chatter on her part, aimed at one thing: get Herb to say "Meg" as many times as possible. His voice warmed her, like sunlight on an upturned face.

As the taxi pulled Meg through the streets of Key West toward the harbor, corners on top of the octagonal box in her lap poked at the palm of her right hand. She and Herb would cruise to a beautiful place, say a few words, and scatter the ashes. And then it would be over.

Despite an extra shot of vanilla, her coffee over the newspaper late this morning took on unexpected bitterness when she opened to the obituaries. As if she hadn't expected it to be there.

Salty Michigan businessman watches his last sunset in Key West waters. If local sea captains never heard of Duke Vanderzee, they surely knew his alter ego, Guy Marks. An accomplished sailor, Mr. Marks lived on his classic 1978 Burger, cruising around the islands in winter, and farther north on the eastern seaboard during summer. He founded a ski resort in Michigan in 1970, retired from it in 1987, and day-traded from the boat for an additional seven years until hanging up his white collar once and for all, trading it in for a Tilley and deck shoes. Every harbor master on the Eastern Shore of Florida perked up when they heard the perfect Charleston drawl requesting overnight dockage for Gilda. Equal parts friend and mystery to all, Duke Vanderzee, aka Guy Marks, will be remembered most for his tip of the hat on the way out of harbor, saluting the sea as he went out to meet her. Mr. Vanderzee was preceded in death by his wife of 38 years and an adult son. He is survived by four children and twelve grandchildren.

The taste of metal covered Meg's taste buds and she winced at the truth captured by a strange writer from a five-minute interview over the phone. Popsie chose his obituary writer. He chose his funeral arrangements, though sparse. And he chose the day he would go. Or maybe he just knew.

Meg shifted under the urn. It weighed no more than a bow-line, but she languished beneath as if it were hewn from granite. Tempted to view the box as an albatross of sorts, she clung to the memory of the sunset. Etched in her brain for now, how long would it linger? What if she forgot?

The taxi stopped with a lurch. Meg's gaze flicked to the dock, where a small crowd of people milled about, looking lost. Meg rolled her eyes and huffed out a deep breath. Not what she needed. Gawkers incessantly passed by to drool over the recently arrived luxury liners, dreaming of a someday they never really expected to arrive.

After paying the driver, Meg hugged the urn to her chest and opened the car door. Head down, she planned to shoulder her way past the jealous mob and signal Captain Steve to leave immediately.

"Meg!"

Her head snapped up. She saw the dark outline of hair framing a pale face. Two matching bobs lined up on either side. Meg's jaw dropped open at the sight of Amy. Aunt Amy. "Wha . . .?"

"Hey! There she is!"

"Oh, Meg."

"Hi, Meg!"

"Thank goodness we made it in time!"

"Look, she's carrying him with her."

Mouth flapping, Meg stared at the entire clan, minus Ruby and Morty. Her leaden arms ached from the weight of the ashes, though they were light as air. "How? Why? I mean, I didn't know . . ." The whole Vanderzee family gathered before her to say goodbye. But they hated her. Didn't they? And they hadn't seemed overly fond of Popsie, either. But he was gone now. Her heart sank at the thought of his family circling like vultures before his ashes had grown cold. Of course.

Exhaustion mixed with shock, wobbled her knees. She swayed and Uncle Ken steadied her elbow from behind. "Whoa there, Nellie. Can I help you with your . . . box?"

Clutching the urn closer to her chest, Meg pivoted away from him. "I've got it." A little too late, she added, "Thanks, though."

Addressing the group, Meg motioned toward Gilda. Her manners battled her natural inclination. Friendly. Be friendly. She stuffed her every conflicted feeling into a closet somewhere deep inside. She would have to deal with them at a later time. She gritted her teeth and addressed the family. "Thanks for coming, everyone. Would you like to come aboard for our little ceremony?"

Leading the way, Meg marched past the aunts, uncles, and

cousins, and turned left off the main dock beside Gilda. They
hung back a bit, maybe afraid to catch a glimpse of their father's
life apart from them. She banished the satisfaction seeping into
her brain at the idea of a battle on home turf. Her pride
threatened to gloat, but Popsie's voice inside her head steadied
her. "Meggers, always listen first, then decide what you'll do. If
you go around jumping to conclusions all day you're likely to
end up in the wrong place at the wrong time with the wrong
people leading you in the wrong direction."

Meg crossed the boarding ladder, slid the door to the
pilothouse open, and placed Popsie's remains on the high seat
behind the captain. With a heavy sigh, she turned to the captain.
"Steve, it looks like our small affair just got bigger. Would you
mind asking Skip to pull out some extra deck chairs?"

"Already done, Megs. And Sheila's got enough provisions
for an army."

Meg closed her eyes, palpably relieved by the capable
hands seeing to every detail before she could even think it.
"Thanks. You're the best."

She watched his gaze shoot over her shoulder and turned to
see the Vanderzees easing their way down the dock. Steve's
voice betrayed his own shock. "Are they all related to him?"

Meg smiled. "Yup. Kids, spouses, and grandkids." As she
watched them make their timid way toward the ladder, she

arched her eyebrows. "And a friend."

Herb popped his head up from the stairs to the main cabin. His deep voice boomed her name. "Megs!"

"Herbie Derbie!" She moved to hug her father's dear friend and the closest thing to a spiritual mentor they had known. Sensing the approaching crowd behind her, she drew back, her hands clinging to his upper arms. "I'm so sorry. I thought this funeral would be just you and me. But . . ." She looked over her shoulder at the same moment Uncle Ken walked through the door.

"She's a beaut." Ken's hungry eyes crawled over the mahogany console and gleaming instrument panel. They landed and lingered on the Furuno NavNet with radar overlay, the latest and greatest in navigational equipment and Popsie's most recent upgrade.

Ken's obvious jealousy for the boat grated on Meg. The will didn't even include Gilda, so he could just chill out. Meg paused and tilted her head. All at once, she sensed a whelming wave headed toward her and she shivered like a wet dog in a cold wind. The weight of Herb's steady hand on her shoulder strengthened her. The moment he lifted his hand portended a crumpled Meg on the floor. But his hand remained. "Uncle Ken, meet Herb. He's our . . ."

Herb cut in, saving her from a lengthy explanation. "I'm a

long-time friend. And I happen to be a pastor as well."

Most of the family took their time boarding, and filed forward to the bow. A few walked aft and settled in on the back deck. And then she saw him again. Mr. Brinker and his briefcase. Like an avalanche video running backwards, everything started to fall into place, transforming the landscape.

Meg leaned against the high bench behind the wheel. "Captain Steve, let's take her out as soon as everyone's on board."

"Aye, Miss Meg." His gaze flicked to the men gathered on the aft deck. He cleared his throat. "I mean, Ms. Marks."

She nodded, appreciative of the added formality. In her childhood home, her heart beat steady, knowing full well where she headed and from whence she had come. Popsie's hand still rested heavy on the day's events and because she knew it would soon be only a memory, she basked in the warmth of his final, provisionary plans and waited to see what he had done.

Herb's melodious voice ricocheted off the water, somehow multiplying rather than dissipating in the open ocean air. His dark skin shone in the sunlight, creases scattered from the corners of his eyes and rounded cheeks pulled the corners of his mouth into a perpetual smile.

The Vanderzee clan, enraptured by a man they never knew,

listened to words spoken about their father, whom they had not recently known, in a place utterly foreign to all but one.

Their greed threatened to cheapen Meg's grief and disappointment weighed down every limb in her body. Nausea churned her stomach at the idea of the Vanderzees commandeering Popsie's memorial service. They barged in on the official memorial. She feared her memory of this day would forever taste sour.

Meg squirmed in her deck chair, closest to Herb, who stood at the prow of Gilda, facing astern. She peeked over her shoulder at Amy's girls, and caught sight of Michael, earbuds in place. From the corner of her eye, Mr. Brinker shifted on the edge of the bow bench, which spanned the beam of the boat. Her heart stood beside Herb, but her mind raced through all the possible explanations for his presence here. Yes, Popsie considered Mr. Brinker a friend. But he was also a lawyer.

Still breathless from the roller coaster of the past week, Meg's mind swam with the secrets from her past, raising questions about the future. Distractions rolled her over continuously, leaving very little brain power for reflection on the details before her, not the least of which included the size of the Vanderzee fortune.

Herb's voice rang out as if he were making a big finish. ". . . goodness and mercy will follow me all the days of my life and I will dwell in the house of the Lord forever."

"Amen." She heard Ken's voice above the others. Their voices sounded from behind her, very somber. Almost penitent.

They all moved to stand, as Meg moved forward with the urn. Herb helped her with the top, and together they scattered Popsie.

Meg regained her seat, slightly numb. But Herb's booming voice melted her from the inside out as he belted out the opening strains of Amazing Grace in an impossible acapella baritone.

". . . a wretch like me."

The niggling, nagging question in the back of Meg's mind suddenly burst into crisp detail before her eyes.

"I once was lost, but now am found . . ."

Popsie owned many things not included in the will she had prepared.

" . . . Was blind but now I see."

Like a strobe light flashing behind her eyes, Meg perceived that Popsie's other will must lie tucked inside Mr. Brinker's briefcase.

Chapter Twenty-One

Wind filtered Meg's loose hair as Gilda cut through the turquoise waters around Key West. She stood at the prow, wishing away the crowd of Vanderzees that filled every corner of her home. Or what used to be her home. A stray tendril stuck to her tear-wet cheek. Popsie's absence filled the air around her like a cloud of dust. Impossible to capture, impossible to ignore.

Mr. Brinker had disappeared belowdecks shortly after the service. Uncle Ken and Aunt Jennifer huddled just behind Meg. Aunt Amy, Amanda, and Andrea hugged her one after the other. The rest of her cousins filed past Meg with somber condolences. These were the people she should have consoled in a normal world—Popsie's first family. She expected Mr. Brinker would approach her when they reached harbor. Everyone would disembark and, then what would happen?

A spinning sensation threatened to tilt Meg off her axis of stability. As she longed for Cody's capable arms, the pit of her stomach threatened to erupt. Popsie's death had destroyed all sense of control, and she felt her grip on things loosening. On a whim, she whirled around and launched herself toward the wheelhouse.

"Stop the boat." Meg grabbed Captain Steve's arm, out of breath.

He scrutinized her face, maybe trying to see if she appeared sane. He spoke with deliberate words. "You want me to stop. Here?"

Attempting the bravest, most not-crazy expression she could muster, Meg straightened her back and looked him in the eye. "I'd like to stop for a few minutes so I can talk to everybody at once."

Steve's hand moved to the engine controls while his gaze scanned the horizon. "Let me scoot out of the channel first, and I'll stop her. Do you need me to set the anchor or will it be a short stop?"

Meg bit the corner of her lip and folded her arms across her chest. A pelican flew beside the boat, as if waiting to witness Meg's next bold move. "Better set the anchor. It's gonna take awhile." She gave one single nod and pivoted, reeling out the door.

With every muscle tensed, Meg fidgeted. Michael slouched, foot tapping to music only he could hear. Girl cousins whispered behind polished nails. One by one they gathered from various corners of the boat. Though she longed to vomit her every thought toward them, she set her jaw and mentally sewed her lips shut, storing up emotion in order to wallop them with her first words.

Standing exactly where Herb stood not an hour earlier, she faced her relatives, Herb, and . . . where was Mr. Brinker? Amy shifted her weight from foot to foot, standing along the rail. Several cousins sprawled over the cabin top on the lounge cushions. Were they all here now? With intentional staccato tones, she launched into her speech. "Duke Van. . ."

Uncle Kenneth's bare feet slapped the deck as he exited the pilothouse and strode forward with both hands waving. "Hold on. Before you start, I need to say something. Trust me, you won't mind if you'll just hear me out."

The corner of his mouth twitched upwards. His interruption caused a flip inside her. Fatigue from keeping her anger at bay and the struggle to hold herself together gave way and all of the fight she had carefully stored up inside, drained away in a moment. Shoulders sagging, she waved as if to say, "Whatever, I'm too spent to care." Meg slouched aside, surrendering her speech before she could even deliver it.

Ken's voice projected a slight rasp when he spoke. "He was our father, but not much of one the last twenty years."

Meg drooped against the rail and allowed the sound of waves lapping against the hull to soothe the darkness inside. She peeked at the ocean between the deck and rail, clear water revealing a sandy bottom not more than fifteen feet deep.

Ken's booming voice summoned her attention. "I guess it looks like we came to the funeral in order to see what he left us. Or more accurately, I guess, what you left us." Ken gestured toward Meg.

Her lips pressed together to stop the quivering. Meg shifted forward, stood tall with hands clasped behind her back.

"But that's not it at all. I for one, don't deserve a dern thing from him. I know you probably wrote us all out of the will because of what we did to you. I remember something in his letter about wanting to give the most to those of us who are most deserving and most likely to honor his memory. Well, we messed that up pretty good when you were at the cottage with us."

Meg rocked forward and back from the balls of her feet to her heels.

"You probably noticed Ruby's not here. To say the least, she's ticked at the lot of us." Laughter murmured across the bow before he continued. Meg almost cracked a smile as a cartoon rendering of Ruby flashed in her mind, steam pouring from her ears. "She poisoned us against you to hide her own guilt." Ken clenched his hands into fists. "We get that now."

Amy stepped forward, nodding. "We believed Joey betrayed us for a long time. Ruby duped us, but . . ." Her eyes searched the sky for an explanation.

Ken jumped in. "We took the bait. And then she told us you were about to continue the great rip-off, and her lies . . ." He shook his head and ran a hand over his dark crew cut.

Amy finished his thought. "Her lies felt familiar and you seemed so . . . new."

Jeffrey unfolded himself from a deck chair and shambled toward Meg. He pulled his baseball cap from his head, and twisted it in his hands. "We came down here to say goodbye to Daddy. But we already said goodbye to him years ago. We really came for you. To say we're sorry."

Meg felt her jaw go slack. She could not detect an ounce of Jeffrey's previous indifference and underlying bitterness in his words.

Ken placed an arm around Meg's shoulders and waited for her to meet his eyes. "You're family and what we dished out, you didn't deserve. Pop didn't raise us like that. Can you forgive us?"

The words, "You're family," rang like a bell inside Meg. As they reverberated through her soul, Meg fell back against the rail and clutched it with all the strength in her fingers. Go slow. Make sure he actually said it. Her gaze flitted from Amy's dark bob to Jeffrey's beard, from twin ponytails, to Michael's earbuds strung around his neck, not in use. It finally landed on

Uncle Kenneth's face and zeroed in on his sparkling blue eyes with wrinkles at the corners. He stared back at her with a warmth that reinforced his words. A breath held far too long escaped her mouth, bringing with it tentative relief.

Meg took a step forward but stopped short, unable to comprehend her thoughts, let alone speak them. All day, she had steeled herself, pushing by sheer force of will, to endure the events of the day. But now, every barrier she had erected around her heart threatened to melt away in a single moment of hope.

"We don't want anything from Dad. We figured you didn't give us anything anyway, and we are all fine with that. Amy? You wanna finish this?" He stepped back, his island shirt, complete with huge palm fronds, flapped in the light breeze. "She's got something she wants to give ya from all of us."

Amy glided across the teak deck in a navy blue shift, with every hair in place. She folded her hands and held them at the waist. "We're not sure you'll want this gift, and it's a little bit unconventional. But we would be so pleased if you would accept Daddy's room at the cottage as your own."

Meg's head twisted to look at Amy full-on, eyes wide in surprise. Amy's lips pressed together, but broke into a smile. "It's been empty all these years, even though it has the best view in the house. None of us felt right about taking it over ourselves, but we all agree it should belong to you. That is, if you think you might find it in your heart to spend some time in Michigan with us."

Meg's hungry eyes crawled across every face before her. This roller-coaster experience of acquiring a huge family defied every dream scenario she had practiced in her mind over the last twenty years. A tiny stab of disappointment pricked her heart at the lack of Cody in this incredible picture before her. Twin pony-tails bobbed up and down, blurring enormous smiles. Uncle Jeffrey proffered a nod. Kenneth walked toward her, arms open. "We're not really worth it, but do you think you could forgive us?"

A fishing boat motored past them at a distance and sea gulls argued in flight off the port side. Meg held back for only half a second before she gave in to his giant bear hug.

"OK. The speech I almost unleashed on you before Uncle Ken interrupted me is not entirely necessary anymore." Meg cracked a sheepish smile from the captain's chair Skip fetched for her. She scanned the family surrounding her and felt her heart leap when she made eye contact with Ken. "But aside from the speech, I wanted to tell you what I did with Popsie's will."

A murmur rustled through the group and many shifted in their seats on various cushions and deck chairs. Surprise dropped a few jaws and popped eyes open wider, and Aunt

Jennifer sat up straight as a poker, as Popsie would have said. The twins beamed their smiles her way, encouraging Meg to continue.

"First of all, the eleven grandchildren will receive $500,000 each." Exclamations shot across the bow like the cries of seagulls cackling as they passed overhead.

"What did she say?"

"We're going on a cruise to Alaska!"

"Dude."

"Sweet!"

"I can't believe it!"

"No way."

"Half a million? Where'd he get that kind of cash?"

"Alright! Corvette."

"Don't even think about it. You're saving for college." Uncle Kenneth stood with his arms crossed and a stern expression.

Meg cleared her throat. "Excuse me." She tilted her head toward Kenneth. "I was actually just planning to address that concern." She raised her voice. "In addition to the direct gifts for each grandchild, we have set up a trust fund with the intention of covering all education costs past, present, and future for each grandchild."

Meg watched as an almost visible weight seemed to lift off Jeffrey's shoulders. A shimmer appeared in his eye and he turned from the group to look at the wide ocean. Jennifer and Amy chattered back and forth and Amy's husband froze, chin in hand, eyes glassed over.

The joy and gratitude on the faces before her opened up a tight knot in Meg's heart. She longed for Popsie to share this moment with her. Regret on his behalf crept threw her mind. He should have reconciled with them before . . . Refusing to allow regret to discolor the moment, Meg nodded to Skip, standing at the back of the group. He ducked into the cabin, but returned with a velvet bundle, which he handed to Meg.

The weight of the soft bundle in her hands impressed on Meg's heart the value of the gifts hidden inside. Enrobed in velvet lay Rachel's jewelry. Each piece lovingly purchased by Popsie, worn faithfully by Rachel, and handled with reverence by Meg as a child.

Meg remembered clipping the ruby earrings onto her lobes and wincing in pain as she pinched them off. The emerald and diamond tennis bracelet often graced the neck of various dolls and stuffed animals. But her favorite piece had to be the wedding ring. Yellow gold supported a center diamond, but smaller diamonds and gold leaves surrounded it, giving the effect of a diamond flower. Although very different from the beautiful ring Cody gave her, this ring evoked an ache in the center of her being. Her hasty words had ruined her chance of ever wearing a wedding ring on her own finger.

Amy's gaze locked on the bundle, as tears filled her eyes. Meg smiled and nodded to her. "He kept Rachel's jewelry because he couldn't bear to let it go. But Amy, it all goes to you." The very thought of Ruby wearing Rachel's things had turned Meg's stomach, but based on her track record, Ruby was more interested in Popsie's business holdings than anything else.

A gust of warm wind tossed Amy's dark hair as she stood, giving the illusion she was flying, and to solidify the point, a pelican dove straight down into the water behind her and launched back into the sky with a fish in his mouth. Tears spilled down Amy's cheeks, and a smile lit her face.

All heads turned as Skip emerged from the cabin again, this time carrying two large picture frames wrapped in brown paper. He set them down beside Meg, propping them against the deck chair.

Meg did a double take. "What? There's only supposed to be one, Skip."

His shook his head and his shoulders went up in the universal sign for "Don't ask me." Without a word, he slouched back toward the cabin, leaving Meg alone to figure it out.

She explained that the next item on the list was an original oil painting entitled "Sunset Sail" by LeRoy Neiman.

"He has a Neiman?" Uncle Ken gasped.

Meg bent over to unwrap the first frame, to ensure it was the correct painting, the one that had hung over the salon couch for so many years. The wrapping fell away, and the painting's bright colors bloomed against the brilliant turquoise of the sea.

"Kenneth, he would have wanted you to have it." She added some smirk to her voice. "There was a boat after all."

Kenneth stepped toward Meg and bowed his head. Under his breath he mumbled "Thanks," and snuffled, wiping his eye with the heel of his hand.

Meg sneaked a stray glance at the remaining paper-wrapped frame. Odd. Questions fluttered through her mind, but it would have to wait. Shifting her attention back to the task at hand, she stuck her chin out and prepared for the 'piece de resistance.' "Two things remain, and they are listed with conditions. The first is a piece of property in Gaylord, MI and the second item is 29% ownership in Snow Cap."

A murmur rumbled across the bow as Meg cleared her throat to continue. "The will provides that the property will be deeded over to Morty Marston, on the condition that Ruby Vanderzee-Marston gives her 20% share of Snow Cap into the Vanderzee Family LLC, apologizes for the crimes she committed against the family, and agrees to quit her job at Snow

Cap."

An uproar sounded at the exact moment a rogue wave dipped the boat. Chairs slid and papers flew. Amy hugged the jewelry to her chest while her daughters grabbed hands. Aunt Jennifer latched onto Uncle Ken's steady arm. She tucked a stray tendril of hair behind her ear. Her words came out soft, but somehow they silenced everyone. "What if she doesn't agree?"

"Excellent question." Meg pointed a finger. "In the event that Ruby Vanderzee-Marston refuses to hand over her ownership share of Snow Cap, the estate of Duke Vanderzee will release to the FBI, proof of her embezzlement and the framing of Joey Vanderzee for said crime.

Extreme hush punctuated the moment. Meg strained to discern whether she had gone too far. Admitting Ruby had committed the crimes was one thing. Prosecuting her for those crimes added up to quite another.

Meg held her hands out before her. "Let me finish everyone. I want you to completely understand what this will mean. An LLC has been formed with Kenneth, Jeffrey, and Amy as limited equal partners. If Ruby agrees to this—and we all know this is a big "if"—then the LLC will own 49% interest in the resort. As Ruby made you aware last week, I stand to inherit the remaining 51% interest on my 28th birthday, which falls next month."

The crowd sobered again and stood silent before her. "I'd like to transfer my interest in the company to the LLC and join you as an equal partner. In addition, so as not to punish Ruby's children, I would like to suggest a trust be set up as another equal partner in the LLC with Martha acting as trustee."

Jane bounced in her chair. "Martha! That's great!"

Janell elbowed Martha and gave her a thumbs-up.

"What does that mean?" Martha sputtered her words and looked at Meg with wide, questioning eyes.

"It means that you and your sisters will receive an equal share of the profits from Snow Cap instead of your mother. This will provide you with income into the future, and pass what would have been your mother's inheritance directly to you."

Martha leaned back against a cushion on the bench, both hands resting on top of her head. "Can I work at Snow Cap?

Meg chuckled. "I will recommend that Sophie stays on in the new role of Snow Cap CEO. I hope that anyone in this family who wants to work at the resort will do so. Each partner will receive an equal share of the profit, assume an equal share of the risk and the business Popsie . . . er . . . Duke built will stay in the family, and the family will benefit equally."

"Except my mom." Jane spoke in a quiet voice magnified by the flat ocean around them.

Aunt Amy's voice wavered. "She gets the property."

Meg cleared her throat. "Morty gets it. But she benefits from it."

The twins' eyes wandered, full of questions, from aunt to uncle to uncle.

Uncle Kenneth stepped forward. "The property. Is that the place that used to be an auto parts store?"

The twin ponytails snapped to attention. "It's Dad's deli land?"

Meg nodded.

They burbled their singular thought in two parts. "He's been trying to buy that land, like forever!"

"So Dad gets to move his deli where he always wanted it?"

"Sounds like a heckuvadeal if you ask me." Kenneth brushed his hands together, strode to the rail, and looked out over the bow.

Martha spouted the question, which must have been on everyone's mind. "What if she doesn't take the deal?"

Meg stood. "It's up to her now. Not many felons get away with their crimes. And even fewer garner forgiveness and inheritances for their families from their victims. It's a small price to pay for avoiding criminal prosecution."

Nods all around brought the discussion to a close.

Janell pointed to the remaining wrapped frame, still leaning against a deck chair. "What's that?"

Meg moved to check it out. "I'm not sure, it wasn't on my list. Skip just brought it with the other, I guess. I haven't seen it onboard 'til now, so . . ."

She carefully separated tape from the brown paper and pulled back a corner to peek at the picture. When she saw it, her heart thumped wildly and tears gathered in her eyes from places she thought had run dry.

Meg dropped to kneel and ripped the paper to uncover a large photo on canvas. Dark-stained wood framed the unmistakable profile of Popsie standing at Gilda's bow. He held his white mug suspended before him and in the background sun sparkled on the water. He gazed toward the sea that he loved, looking at the horizon and what lay ahead of him. Only Cody would have captured this shot, he used the same unusual angle as one of his trademarks. And only he understood what the photo would mean to her.

Guilt battled regret in Meg's heart, shredding her emotions. All the grief she'd endured throughout the past few days compounded, as the enormous reality of losing Cody assaulted her senses.

Such a personal gift . . . and then it hit her like a sandbag to the face. It was his wedding gift. She surely could not hide her reaction, now that tears streamed down her face. Meg became aware of the stares upon her back. She leaned the frame toward her and peeked at the back. There she found what she didn't realize she'd been hoping for. An envelope with her name scrawled on the front. In Cody's handwriting.

She grabbed the envelope as the twins appeared at her side, hands on her shoulders. Shoving it into her pocket on the sly, she lifted the frame and allowed the twins to pull the remaining paper away. She carried it to the center of the bow bench and propped it up for all to see.

A moment of absolute stillness punctuated the day. But a lone ripple in the water rocked the boat ever so slightly, breaking the spell.

Uncle Ken shook his head and gestured toward the handrail. "It's like he's standing right there, it's so real."

Aunt Amy wiped tears from her eyes and pressed her lips together as she stared at the image of her father.

Jeffrey looked at his shoes, stealing furtive glances at the photo.

Meg tuned out the murmurs around her. Her head spun swinging between gratitude for such an amazing gift and guilt and regret and despair. The envelope burned in her pocket, but she craved privacy to read it. She stepped back, one hand over her mouth, unable to speak, and held up a finger before making a bee-line away from this crowd.

Finding the aft-deck empty, Meg knelt on the bench cushions, facing astern. As she tore into the envelope, the familiar handwriting brought tears to her eyes. What had she done? Her soul ached, hanging in shreds. Writing the will, Popsie's death, the funeral—she used them all to avoid this moment. The heavy consequences of her words to Cody pulled her downward, as if she were being dragged through murky waters toward a bottomless, empty place.

A sharp step drew up behind her. Meg saw the briefcase before she saw the man. "Ms. Marks."

She whipped the note behind her back and spun around to stand up straight. "Yes. Hello, Mr. Brinker. For awhile there, I thought you might have disappeared."

"I am quite present, Miss." He cleared his throat. "May I have a private word with you?"

Chapter Twenty-Two

Meg's heart fluttered as she rounded the last woodsy curve and pulled into the "Call of the Loon" parking area. "Wow." She spoke aloud, though alone in the car. Rays of early morning sun dazzled across the verdant sylvan setting. What Meg first experienced as a cozy log cabin in the woods with a beautiful garden had been transformed into a magical pastoral setting, bedecked with roses, petunias, zinnias, and countless other flowers planted in the ground, strung across trellises and hanging in pots from every eave, branch, and garden hook.

Rose petals covered every path like a carpet calling her, drawing her into the heavily scented, perfectly trimmed garden, past the lily pad pond and around to the great lawn behind the house, which should by now, be covered with white chairs, separated by a single aisle.

The corner of Meg's mouth tugged upward as she remembered her first visit here over a year ago, dropped off after a harrowing ride in the Malibu—courtesy of Jane and Janell.

As Meg exited the red RAV4, Mrs. Dooley burst through the front door, arms spread wide open. "Oh, my goodness! Miss Meg! Oh, Miss Meg!" She clasped her hands together in front of her heart and let out a great sigh, "Your day is finally here. Can you believe it?"

The woman's enthusiasm never waned. "No, I can't believe it." Meg gestured toward the front garden. "And I can't believe what you've done with the yard! I loved it before, but this is stunning. It's like I'm getting married in a fairy tale." She finished her thought silently: To a man whose actions spoke better of him than any real prince out there.

Mrs. Dooley shrugged off the compliment. "Oh, nature takes care of the flowers, I just trim 'em a little bit."

"Can I see the back?" Meg hooked arms with Mrs. Dooley and started toward the nearest path.

"Sure! Janie and Janell are finishing things up inside." Mrs. Dooley stopped and turned like she suddenly remembered something. Eyes bright, Mrs. Dooley spoke in a low, hopeful voice. "Do you want to see the cake?"

Meg couldn't hold in her laugh. Mrs. Dooley took her cakes very seriously, especially after all the pastry classes she'd labored through in the last year. A tinge of regret still lingered when Meg thought of her harsh attitude toward Mrs. Dooley when they first met. That fateful Memorial Day weekend had thrown Meg's life into chaos, and her sarcastic coping mechanisms showed little mercy for Mrs. Dooley's stereotypical personality. What a difference a year could make. "Of course I want to see the cake. Do I get to see the groom's cake too?"

"Oh no, you don't. He didn't get to see yours and you don't get to see his until later."

"So, he came by? How's he doing? Is he nervous?" Ten hours apart and she couldn't believe she wouldn't see him until she walked down the aisle. Blasted traditions.

"He's giddy. Wouldn't stop talking. Ya got yerself a sweet one."

Altering their course, Mrs. Dooley ushered her up the driveway toward the house. "I know it sounds like I'm bragging, but the wedding cake is a masterpiece. It's the pinnacle of my cake career to date. I think yer gonna like it."

Meg skipped up the steps to this warm home. Inn. Refuge. Wedding venue. Who would have thought that Mrs. Dooley, the busybody, would turn out to be a genius with icing? And flowers. And icing flowers. "I'm sure I'll love it. I'm really touched that you would go to so much trouble for me."

"Miss Meg. You are no trouble at all. You're the one who made everything better, you know. After you came," She nodded her head in the direction of the driveway, which pointed in the general direction of the Vanderzee cottage. "After you came, they all learned how to be happy again. Even I noticed a difference."

Meg pulled the front door open. "Well, I can't take the credit, but they are a different family now, aren't they?"

From down the hall, Meg heard voices. "She's here!"

"Meg!" Her name rang out like a song.

Footsteps thumped the wooden floors and identical girls bursting with chaotic joy bounced into the foyer, hugging and talking and generally filling the house with mirth and hilarity. Meg's heart pulsed with gratitude toward these twins who'd saved her. Distracted her. Made her a part of a family she had assumed would elude her forever. "Hey, y'all. Thanks for helping Mrs. Dooley. This place looks amazing!" She scooped them into an embrace.

"If you like the front, wait'll you see the back." Each twin grabbed an arm and pulled Meg toward the glassed-in porch overlooking the back gardens.

Jane swept an arm across the view. Her white blouse reflected sunshine pouring through the windows. "Ta Da!"

Janell turned to Meg, her facing shining with excitement. "What do you think, Boss?"

Looking Janell in the eye, Meg grew serious. "We're friends first, cousins second. And you two work with me, more than you work for me. You know how hopeless I am in the organization department!"

Janell smile. "OK, Meg. You're right. You are truly hopeless."

Meg play-punched her arm.

Jane pulled on Meg's other arm. "C'mon! What do you think?"

The view from the window encompassed a sloping lawn, hemmed in by mounds of hosta, a riot of pink and purple shaded holly-hocks, and many shades of pink and yellow rose bushes. A dark wooden arch stood at the front of the white chairs set up in rows. Grapevines covered the arch, and countless varieties of white flowers adorned the framework creating an innocent, yet breathtaking effect.

Behind the chairs stood another arbor, the entrance to a formal rose garden. White tea roses smothered the entire structure, providing a hidden shelter beneath it. Potted flowers bordered the ceremonial area, along with two dozen shepherd's hooks, wielding more pots overflowing with brightly colored blooms. She fancied the fragrance in the garden would smell just like a flower shop.

Meg felt the tears running down her cheeks. "It's . . . it's so much more than I ever dared to dream. I can't believe this is happening. To me." Shaking her head, she wiped her face with bare hands, took a deep breath, and huffed it out. "Surely I can handle this."

Mrs. Dooley placed a hand on her shoulder. "Happiness can be tough to absorb, Meg. Don't let it run off yer back like water off a duck. Ya need ta make sure it soaks in." The "o" in soaks came out long and low, along with what Meg fondly called "Dooley R's" which flew out of her mouth with sharp cornerrrs, bringing a smile to Meg's face.

"Thanks, Mrs. D."

Mrs. Dooley waved her off and turned her head at the sound of the phone. "The advice is free, Dearie. Looks like I'll have to show you the cake later."

Turning to the twins, Meg jumped back into planning mode. "Did we get a final headcount?"

"Yes."

"Ninety-nine."

Oh. Not a hundred, then. She looked down at her feet for a moment, and injected her words with all the tenderness at her disposal. "So your mom didn't change her mind?"

Jane's gaze hit the floor. Janell picked at a fingernail. Meg's insides slumped. Though so much had changed over the last year, Ruby still managed to tinge the family with her special brand of bitterness.

The twins busied themselves filling miniature Chinese food-style boxes with truffles. Jane fumbled to tie a ribbon on the next box and Janell popped a truffle into her mouth, avoiding Meg's eyes.

"I'm so sorry."

Janell twirled her ponytail through her fingers. "It's not your fault, Meg."

"Yeah. It's her loss."

Meg shook her head at Ruby's stubbornness, a trait all too familiar to Meg from the previous summer. "How's she doing?"

Perking up a bit, Jane tilted her head. "I think she's okay. She's starting to get the hang of the whole retirement thing. Except she works at the deli on Saturdays, to help with the rush."

"Yeah. And she's been doing all that macramé stuff like crazy. You know, the plastic screen you cover with yarn?"

"It's not called macramé. It's needlepoint."

"Well, it's on plastic."

"Plastic needlepoint."

"Yeah, she makes tissue box covers and coasters."

"Mom and Dad have a LOT of coasters now." They giggled.

Meg tried to picture Ruby sitting by the fire with her needlepoint in hand and failed to conjure the image. Forced to choose between retiring from her job and state prosecution, Ruby's rage had made ripples on the grapevine. While taking the deal, Ruby refused to go gently. She did not take well to other people calling the shots in her life.

Janell sank into a nearby wicker chair. "I know I say this all the time, but trading Mom's stock in Snow Cap for Dad's deli property was pure genius. It kicked her out of Snow Cap, but kept her out of jail."

Jane cocked her hip. "I might have sent her to jail."

"Jane! You would send our mom to jail?"

"Well, maybe not if she acted sorry. She still thinks we messed everything up for her."

The sting of Ruby's power-play against Meg last spring still smarted. "How's business at the deli?"

"Morty's Deli is like, the hottest place in town. Martha said all the skiers swamped the place when they passed through on the weekends last winter. The new location is perfect."

"And you know Martha opened up a satellite deli location at Snow Cap too. I hear she's doing a great job."

"So now Dad has more time to spend with Mom."

"They played in a bowling league last winter. Isn't that funny?"

The idea of Ruby swinging a bowling ball forced a chuckle from Meg. If Ruby and Morty spent time together having fun, it had to be good for both of them. "Sounds like Martha's doing well. I'm so glad. She's coming, right?"

Janell popped out of her chair. "Not only is she coming to the wedding, she's coming with Bryan. Her boyfriend!"

"What? How did I miss that little tidbit?" Meg's love for her groom warmed her heart toward anyone who had not yet tasted the nectar of true love.

"She waited 'til our flight landed to tell us. Can you believe it?"

Happiness bloomed in her gut. "I'm thrilled for her. Is he a good guy?"

They nodded together. Jane looked out the window with dreamy eyes. She spoke her words with a wistful lilt. "He tells her she's beautiful every day."

Meg's heart fluttered. She knew what that felt like. "There will be a man like that for you one day. For both of you. Although, I must say, I hope you find those men in North Carolina, because if you have to move away, my office will undoubtedly become a disheveled mess, like it did this week when you left early to come up here."

"Meg, don't tell me you stopped filing stuff again." Janell crossed her arms like a strict taskmaster.

"Give me a break. I have the two most organized people on the planet keeping my whole life collected. When you both leave at once, it's like quitting smoking cold turkey. Remember your cruise last summer?"

Both ponytails bobbed. Starry eyes probably veiled memories from their "trip of dreams." Since Popsie left them enough cash to take at least one "trip of dreams" every year indefinitely, they would need to start dreaming some more.

"Ya'll're too good at what you do."

Meg turned on her heel and headed toward the door. "Now, who wants to walk down to the garden with me?"

Meg stood under the arbor overgrown with climbing white roses. Their scent suffused the air, and their foliage hid her from sight of the wedding guests, seated and waiting for the music to start.

Heart pounding, she fought to contain the thrill of the moment. He waited for her on the other side of the garden, out of sight for now.

She peeked between thorns and leaves as the string quartet began playing. Aunt Amy, and her whole family sat in the front row. Meg fingered the black opal pendant Amy had given her from Rachel's jewelry. "Something old."

Loosely pinned high on her head, Meg's dark hair hung in curls all around, just the way she had hoped. She twirled a rogue tendril around her finger. Leaning toward the arbor, Meg pushed aside a few stray blooms, and marveled at the number of guests seated on the "bride's side." Her life-long fear it would be empty on her wedding day gave way to relief oozing through her chest at the sight of those who loved her and honored her with their presence and support.

Aunt Jennifer, Michael and Brett sat with straight backs befitting a military family. Brett sported his first official uniform, prepared to deploy in a few weeks. Pride welled up inside her at the sight of them. And Michael wore no ear buds for the occasion.

On the end of a row, beside his children, Jeffrey posed tall in the seat. His profile struck Meg as different. He held his chin up for the first time since she met him. His children had miraculously started receiving his emails after a letter from a certain attorney reached their mother via certified mail last summer.

Meg fingered a spray of tiny beaded silk flowers trailing from the waist of her A-line gown, where the fitted bodice blended into a full tulle skirt. Sunlight and shadow played across the dazzling white fabric as it filtered through the leaves of tall hardwoods above. A quiet breeze cooled her blushing countenance as it swept across her bare shoulders. She looked up at Uncle Ken, her escort. He still fit into his dress white uniform, a tribute to extreme discipline and maybe a little vanity. She threw him a wobbly smile.

He stood in the classic "at ease" position. "Are you ready?"

She looked away. Tears welled up from nowhere.

"He'd be so proud of you."

She nodded, swallowing hard.

"Heck, I'm proud of you. What you did last year . . ."

Meg turned her eyes toward the underside of the arbor above her head. Thorny vines criss-crossed every which way, like the underside of an old tapestry. Popsie's will. Every time she recounted the decisions she made on Popsie's behalf, she felt the heaviness that had weighed on her during the process. But then she felt again the lightness, the extreme freedom she experienced when Mr. Brinker opened his briefcase that day.

Like the release of white doves, her heart soared when she learned what Popsie planned. Of course, she felt surprise that her portion of the will comprised only twenty percent of the entire estate, but what he allowed her to do with the portion he allotted to her, had brought the family together. If her heart were a hot air balloon, the first four sandbags dropped upon learning this simple fact, leaving her lighter than air. The reading of the second will had been like adding a giant pile of icing to an already wonderful cake. Popsie's extreme measures protected her, just like he said.

The string quartet paused and then launched into the processional music. Pachelbel's Canon in D. Jane threw Meg a wink as she started down the aisle. Her pale blue dress flowed with the gentle breeze like crystal clear water.

From Meg's vantage point at the back of the ceremony area, she captured a wide view of the entire back garden. The tranquility of the moment ruptured as a large woman in a peach colored suit crept onto the scene. Unbelievable.

Bent at the waist about twenty degrees, she tottered across the lawn on high-heeled tippy-toes toward the back row. Since the processional had already begun, Jane advanced down the aisle, her back to the scene. But Janell viewed the whole thing while waiting her turn to march. She looked back over her shoulder at Meg and pointed out the obvious with wild gestures. They shared a sparkling smile.

Uncle Ken grunted. "There's something you don't see everyday. My big sister sneaking around in the back yard, dressed like a circus peanut."

Meg took a deep breath and blew it out. "She came."

"You wanted her here? After everything?"

A sensation like fitting the final piece into an enormous puzzle clicked inside Meg. "It's the last thing."

Ken nodded sideways.

Meg chided him. "You have to admit, Duke knew what he was doing."

Ken gazed at the treetops. A small breeze sang through the

leaves. "I thought I knew him. I thought he turned tail and ran away from us."

"But . . ." she prodded.

"He loved us. And he managed to die in the one year without estate taxes."

Meg shook her head with a knowing smile. "I think he did that just for you."

Janell reached the front of the makeshift church. The string quartet grew silent for a moment, and then a new song filled the air.

Ken offered Meg his arm. "Shall we?"

Heart thundering, Meg took a deep breath. Her groom awaited her. This day was the start of a forever relationship. He belonged to her and she would forever belong to him, heart and soul. Through her nerves, a calm at her core spread until it reached her fingertips and almost down to her toes, wiggling naked in the deep soft grass.

With a curt nod and another deep breath, Meg whispered. "Ready."

She slipped her arm through Uncle Kenneth's, and they stepped out of the arbor in full view of the guests. She stood facing her groom, a mere twenty yards, one hundred chairs, and several thousand rose petals strewn on the ground between them.

Bride and groom locked eyes and he winked, sunshine turning his blond curls to gold. He stepped into the middle of the aisle as his hand moved to cover his heart.

The Vanderzee clan and all the other guests rose and turned in her direction, expectancy on every face. Meg fought the urge to look behind her. How could so many people be here? How could the bride's side be full? She swallowed the growing lump in her throat. How could she ever deserve this man? How could she acquire this enormous family—blood relatives, in-laws, and others who cared for her?

She looked to the sky and wondered if Popsie knew. Even before he left them, did he know it would turn out this way? He must have hoped for it. He obviously believed in her capacity for mercy and her need for these people.

As they started forward, Ken stopped her for a moment. "You sure about this?"

She beamed, eyes on the curly blond man who truly knew her and loved her anyway. She loved his heart and after searching her soul she knew she loved him for all the right reasons. What looked like Popsie throwing a wrench into her plans last year, turned out to be exactly what she needed. This day, filled to bursting with joy, proved far better than a rushed wedding initiated under a cloud of grief. "Never been more sure of anything."

Meg took a step toward Cody and felt a gentle tug on her heart like an anchor when it finally takes hold.

Acknowledgements

In the beginning was the Word and the Word was with God and the Word was God. John 1:1.

I am indebted forever to my Savior, the Creator of everything, who instilled in me a love for words and ultimately, a love for The Word.

My amazing critique partners are more than just readers of my words, they are encouragers, prayer partners, and the truest of friends. Christy Truitt, Jennifer Rogers Spinola, Karen Schravemade, and Shelly Dippel, you have helped give this story wings and I can never say enough to thank you for your invaluable support.

Heidi Main for reading early drafts, and Kay Craven for reading the last draft, you are like bookends. Thank you.

I have so many friends and acquaintances who tirelessly asked how the book was coming. These things take so much time to come about, and I'm grateful you kept asking, and believing that I was actually doing something despite the lack of concrete evidence.

Tracy Ruckman, thank you for believing in this story. Your faith in me strengthened my faith in God.

Gary Labadie, your extensive knowledge of all things nautical and boat related made the details of this story shine. Bonnie Labadie, your willingness to stand in the gap while I was travelling to conferences to learn this craft, allowed me to focus on the work, knowing everything at home was handled. You are the perfect parents for me.

Suzanne Labadie, Marc Labadie, Heidi and Mark Fromke, Kara Fromke, Susan Fromke, Vince and Carole Fromke, you all cared enough to ask how it's going, to give advice, and to let me talk ad nauseam about this book. Thanks for listening.

Emily, Claire, and Thomas, you bring me such joy in life. Thank you for supporting this dream of mine. I'm so proud of who you are and I'm giddy as I thank God every day for gracing me with the privilege of walking beside you on the way to accomplishing each of your dreams.

Lastly, my most profound thanks go to the dear man who looked at me one day and said, "I'm living my dream right now. It's time we made yours come true." Without the support, encouragement, and enthusiasm of my husband, this road would have been lonely, scary, and most likely, a dead end. Jon, you are my true love forever and I'm grateful from the depths of my soul that we get to live this dream together.

About the Author

Jennifer Fromke won the ACFW Genesis Award for *A Familiar Shore* in 2010.

When forced to separate from the laptop, she can be found with her nose in a book, one hand around a latte, and the other hand sometimes stirring something on the stove. Soul food for Jennifer includes laughing with her family, teaching Bible studies, and talking about books with anyone.

She grew up in Michigan, and served tours of life experience in Wheaton, Minneapolis, and St. Louis. She writes from North Carolina, where she and her family await their annual escape to their favorite lake "up north" in Michigan.

Visit Jennifer online:
www.JenniferFromke.com

Look for other books

published by

Pix-N-Pens Publishing

www.PixNPens.com

and

WIP

Write Integrity Press

www.WriteIntegrity.com